THE
BLOODWIND

CHARLES L. GRANT

Chapter 1

The end of January, the middle of winter, and the silence they brought to Oxrun Station. There were greys and there were blacks, and there were crusted harsh whites; colors sharp and accentuated that would have been lost in the explosion of spring. Storm clouds gathered less arrogantly here than they did in late summer, wisping instead of marching, creeping to an overcast like a slow congealing web. A wretched wan sun subdued and fading, and dawn little more than a kitchen clock's whirring.

And the cold. There was always the cold. A whip crack against the forehead, a razor along the cheek. Exposed to it too long and there was a pressure at the temples that made your cheeks ache, a rat-like insinuation wherever clothes were not clinging. It hardened the pavement to jolt the ankles, made brittle the trees to slice at the sky; it intensified sounds to the point of distant screaming; it invigorated and wearied, brought clarity and black ice, and settled in the eaves to make a house groan with age.

It burgeoned and surged, and it seeped through the windows without benefit of a wind to swirl over the floor in serpentine draughts.

Pat felt them and shivered, scowling at the intrusion and pleased at the assistance in driving back sleep. She sat slumped on the edge of her high-canopy bed and gripped the back of her neck as if it were necessary to keep her head in place. Her lips were pursed, her breath a soft whistle. For a moment she listened to the faint thud of rock music billowing up from below, could feel through the shag carpeting the rippling vibrations against her bare soles. But only for a moment. When she felt she could move without shattering like glass she grimaced and shuddered, finally willed herself to stand. Swayed until she balanced, and dropped her nightgown to the bed.

"God," she muttered, and pressed a knuckle to her eyes.

A gasping at the fire stars, a deep breath for courage, and she walked gingerly into the bathroom, her tongue trying to wipe the fuzz from her teeth. Again her hand snaked to the back of her neck, and she smiled weakly at her reflection in the ceiling-high mirror, her bare hip pressed lightly against the swirled-marble counter. A shake of her head. A tsking, and a finger aimed in mock admonition for the excesses of the previous evening, and the physical damage sullenly on view. It could have been worse, she thought then, leaning closer and sighing. At least her hair was kept short—a quick brush with fingers or bristles through the almost iridescent black and she looked virtually normal.

Still closer, and she winced. Normal, that is, except for the eyes. They were of a dark and deep blue when the light was clear and she was smiling, hard and obsidian shortly after sunset. The corners were slightly pinched, the lids heavily lashed, and they gave her a pronounced Eurasian cast when she narrowed them in anger.

Now they were bloodshot, light-sensitive and accusing.

All right, she thought with a conciliatory palm upraised; *all right, all right.*

She retreated a few paces from the counter and set her hands on her hips. Not too shabby for thirty-nine and terminally lazy, she decided, tucking her chin to her shoulder and winking at the reflection. A slight bulging around the waist, a small protrusion at the belly, but nothing drastic like the sagging of her breasts or extra lumpy padding around her slender thighs. She suspected she might be able to stand some exercise now and again, and she definitely had to curtail her drinking. Before she knew it there'd be horrid red veins lacing her pug nose, pouches would begin nesting at the crest of her high cheeks, and the once-cherubic jawline would descend slowly to jowls. It was, in fact, precisely the way her mother looked now, and she had no intention of following that course of decay.

Her mother had her father, but Pat knew she herself had no excuse. Not anymore.

Another sigh, mockingly drawn to a whimper of self-pity, and she turned on the shower, twisted back to the mirror and launched into a punishing series of calisthenics that had her skin glistening before five minutes had passed. Her head complained, her stomach lurched, but she would not slow down until she had achieved some sort of penance for last night's insanity. Not that she didn't deserve a night out once in a while, she told herself twenty minutes later as she dressed. She did. She worked hard, damned hard, and these occasional explosions of energy were very nearly the only releases she permitted herself, about the only release one could get in a place like Oxrun Station in the middle of winter.

She laughed, and buttoned the cream-and-fluff blouse, adjusted the loose tie around its open throat. She was doing it again, and she did it every time—a stodgy, defensive rationalization for her party-going simply because she lived in a village where affluence was an aftertaste of breathing the clean air. Where peace was valued and quiet jealously maintained, and wasn't that exactly the reason she had come here in the first place?

She hesitated in front of the vanity mirror, the bed reflected behind her and diminished somehow. On the corner of the dresser was a silver-framed photograph of a young girl no older than eight, squinting at the camera with a fearful smile on her lips.

The thought came unbidden, and unwanted, breaking through a resolve that had held for nearly five years: she would have been sixteen today. She would have been in high school. She would have been able to tell her friends that her mother was an artist and her father lived in California, and her grandparents had this absolutely monstrous penthouse in New York City where they honest to god vegetated among furniture so old you could smell the dust ingrained in the wood. She would have been. But she wasn't.

Pat set her left hand to her forehead, fingers gently rubbing. The sense of loss was not quite so sharp, but neither had it faded; it persisted, like a scar that was every few years rediscovered with unpleasant surprise.

Lauren would have been sixteen. But she wasn't. And Pat was thirty-nine and in a battle for her professional life. And for a moment she felt sick. It was unfair her daughter should return on this day, unfair and unkind and so damned unlike her. She loved the girl still, in dreams and in memory, but she was eight years in her grave and it just wasn't fair.

The nausea passed. And the guilt that was its source. Her frown smoothed, and she touched the photograph with a thumb that traced the child's face. All right, she told the image, but please, Lauren, stay out of my way today, okay? Believe me, I'm going to need all the strength I can muster, and I really don't think I can handle you now.

A laugh, rueful and short, and she headed for the kitchen not quite as eager as she'd primed herself to be.

The apartment was half the second floor of an elegant three-story Victorian on Northland Avenue. Above was a full attic used for storage, across the wide landing a retired couple named Evans. On the first floor was the landlord, Lincoln Goldsmith, who lived so alone it was months before Pat even knew he was there; and directly below her the residence of Kelly Hanson and Abbey Wagner, two women a decade and a half younger than she, who worked over in Harley and lived in the Station because they liked the address, not to mention the fact that it made an impression on job applications. And if it hadn't been for Kelly's preference for blaring music in the morning, she knew she might as well be living alone for all the noise there was. There were days— stormy days and days marked lonesome—when the silence was maddening and she was tempted to scream; there were also times, however, and more often than not, when she blessed every saint she could think of for the luck that had provided her with such a perfect place to live.

The front room was thirty feet square, the ceilings high, with elaborate moldings. The street-side wall was broken by a pair of tall, arched windows flanking narrow French doors opening onto a roofless porch she shared with the Evanses; in the back wall and set opposite each of the windows were doorways leading to a common corridor dimly lighted and small, running the width of the apartment: in the left corner her bedroom and bath, in the center the kitchen, on the right a second and far smaller bedroom she'd converted to a studio. Spacious, almost grand, and she had debated for weeks before deciding to decorate it as simply as she could with furniture of the house's era, not so much because she liked the embroidered upholstery and deep-carved wood, but because it tended to

5

keep the place from growing overwhelming. The floors had been carpeted in solemn browns and golds, the white plaster reduced by judicious hangings of oils and prints Romantic and Impressionist. Floral draperies and cream under curtains tied back on occasion to let in the light, to let in the dark.

And it was quiet. It was safe. Even on mornings when her head felt crammed with wool she imagined herself a ghost drifting through the softly blurred glow, smoothing her edges and lending her mystery. Here, nothing could touch her unless she gave it permission. It was safe. Safe. A world within a world where she was the queen, and the fact that she had no consort didn't stir the guilt her parents still tried to ladle.

A slow shake of her head and she proceeded to make breakfast.

The kitchen, like the bathroom, was a concession to the times—copper and brown, a stainless-steel sink and glittered Formica on the counters. Most of the beige-tiled floor was taken up by a large, round iron table and four ice cream parlor chairs for which she had made green cushions during one autumn's stretch of intense homemaker crafts. The cushions, though comfortable, were far too large, and at least once a week she vowed to give it another try.

She sat facing the rear window, sipping at steaming and dark Earl Grey and nibbling on a piece of lightly buttered raisin toast. She supposed she ought to prepare a more substantial meal for the day she had to face, but there was always the college cafeteria in case she felt faint. She grinned, and wondered how she had been able to survive this long without padding the walls and curling back to the womb. A simple breakfast, nourishment and strength, and she wouldn't make the effort. God help her if that ever spilled over into the way she worked.

Beyond the window she could see a half-dozen oaks filling the back yard. They were a startling black against the overcast's grey, still layered in powdered white after a pre-dawn dusting. A cardinal clung to an ice-coated twig, bouncing in the gentle breeze and eyeing the house as though considering it for a meal. She winked at it, lifted her cup to it, and exaggerated a disappointed frown when it finally flew away, a blur of red disturbingly like blood.

The fingers of her left hand drummed hard on the table.

Her left foot tapped the floor impatiently, arhythmically.

She buttered another slice, poured another cup of tea, and checked the oval clock on the wall for the fifth time in five minutes. It was seventeen past eight, each minute beginning to slip by more rapidly than the last.

"Damn," she said to the window, to the trees. "This is stupid, you know. This is really and truly god-awful stupid."

It was an admission at last that she did not want to go. She did not want to leave. And it wasn't the cold or the drive or the facing of her students; it wasn't her new project or Greg Billings or even the obsequious Ford Danvers. She just did not want to leave the tea and the toast and the memory of the cardinal. What she did want to do was strip off her blouse, her green-and-black tartan skirt, unclasp her gold necklace, kick off her mid-thigh boots, roll up her pantyhose and fall back into bed. And sleep. As long as she could. Maybe until April when the green returned, and the robins, the flowers, the sharp tang of lawns newly mowed. By then, if her luck held and no one came to find her, the meeting this afternoon would be over and they would have forgotten all about her. Dean George Constable would bluster his pleasant way to oblivion (with Ford Danvers slavering in his wake), the Trustees would have all died and been replaced with robots, and she would be able to continue as she always had, this time without opposition.

7

The problem was, she wasn't at all tired. A little skittish from all that partying, but not at all tired.

Frightened. My god, she was frightened.

No, she decided in sudden panicked retreat; she was apprehensive, not frightened. The pressures she had subjected herself to in her struggle for the new department's creation were finally reaching her now that the judgment was at hand. And last night hadn't helped. It hadn't helped a bit.

This time it came as a question: frightened? Well, yes, just a little. Apart from the college and the department and all she was attempting … yes. Unreasonably, illogically, without any foundation beyond a few too many drinks. Just a little. Because for a moment last night the world hadn't played by her rules.

Patrice, her father had said some years before, this nonsense of yours about rules and more rules has got to stop.

Why? It works, doesn't it?

Because sooner or later you are not going to be able to live by your own rules, or force others to follow them.

They do all right.

That's because the ones that don't you drop.

Not my problem, is it?

It is, Patrice. It is. One of these days something's going to happen again, something's going to happen that doesn't play your game and you're not going to be able to drop it or run from it … you know what I mean.

I got through the divorce, Father.

Yes, you did. I give you credit for that, much credit. But your luck won't hold, Patrice. Your luck just is not going to hold.

Her station wagon was small, yet she knew when she left the party it wouldn't warm up before she arrived home. The ride was less than a handful of blocks. She shivered then in the front seat, gloved hands bouncing in spasms against the

8

steering wheel, her slightly befogged mind swearing at the light snowfall that had started just as she'd left the Chancellor Inn. There had been no wind when she'd switched on the ignition, but it had been waiting for her after she'd turned the first corner. That's how it had felt. Waiting, until she'd left the protection of her friends, was on the whitening streets alone. It had struck sharply, suddenly, like a padded fist, and she cried out in shocked surprise. Leaned closer to the wheel and squinted through the windshield.

The snow blurred, streaks instead of flakes. Her eyes began watering in an effort to clear her vision, and her ears filled with a faint, curiously deep rumbling—the sound of a slow-moving locomotive entering the far end of a long black tunnel. The windshield wipers sounded like gunshots, the engine began whining as if stuck in the wrong gear. The wind strengthened, buffeting the station wagon and nearly shoving her into the curb.

There were obscenities now, directed at the drinking she'd done more than the storm. It was confusing her. The lingering taste of the liquor, the snow, the wind— and she felt her breathing quicken and grow shallow, tearing away somewhat at the webs that befuddled her.

Another block, and she was sure someone was following her. Her gaze flickered to the rear-view mirror, but she saw only the white stained red by the taillights. Beyond that there was black. If it was a car its headlamps were out; if it was someone walking behind her in the street he was too distant for seeing. But she was being followed. She would have sworn it. She could feel it. The presence of something other than herself on the road, other than herself and a good deal larger.

Then the flakes had gained a direction, a spinning right to left, and she screamed to herself she'd been caught in a tornado. She'd almost flung open the door to escape, had braked sharply instead and cracked her forehead against her hands fisted around the wheel. Like a slap for hysteria the dull stinging had calmed her, and she'd driven the rest of the way home at a slow walking pace.

The wind died when she reached her own block.

The snowfall eased.

She had sat trembling in the driveway for nearly an hour, convincing herself it was a freak wind-surge underscored by the drinks. Nothing more. No one was there. Nothing was there. Yet she sat trembling in the driveway for nearly an hour and watched the street and the sidewalk, waiting for someone, or something, to pass.

Suddenly her cup rattled harshly in its saucer, and she pulled her hand away to bury it in her lap.

The faucet began dripping; the refrigerator coughed on.

She looked at the window and prayed for a blizzard.

"Pat!" she said then, very nearly yelling, and slammed a palm on the table. The cup and saucer jumped, the butter dish skittered, the plate that held her toast almost flipped over the edge. She turned her hand over and stared dumbly at the reddening skin. A moment, and she decided that as of now she was a teetotaler in the heroic mold of ancient Carrie Nation. It was that, or she would have to believe that Oxrun Station was beset by midwinter tornados and she was the abrupt subject of covert surveillance.

And she wished her nerves were as convinced as her brain.

Chapter 2

A blur of red and a darker shadow behind it. Pat looked to the window and saw the cardinal back on its perch, a blue jay on a thicker branch closer to the trunk. Neither of the birds remained there very long; the cardinal fled first, the jay a moment later. But it was enough to quell the unsettled surging that had begun in her stomach.

A finger to her lips, across her cheek and through her hair, and she reached blindly for her purse and the first cigarette of the day. A few seconds' fumbling and she laughed aloud, relief and abashment giving her a case of gently lingering giggles. The purse, she remembered, was on the butler's table beside the front door, and the thought of getting up, walking all the way out there and all the way back, stayed her for the present. And that, she thought with smug self-satisfaction, was precisely the idea. The longer she delayed that initial coughing spasm, the less time she had to finish her two packs a day. By March she hoped to be whittled down to one. By April, a half. That she might eventually quit altogether was a fantasy she kept deftly at bay—this slow and easy method of cutting down at least managed to entertain no uncommon illusions. And it was certainly more effective than the time she had attempted an abrupt withdrawal, without any preparation but a quickly reached resolution. That had been an unmitigated disaster, not only for herself but for her students as well. Their work had suffered measurably under the onslaught of her fierce critiques,

11

and they had only regained their sanity and their progress when one of them—she'd never learned who, though she suspected either Ollie or Ben—had left a new pack of English Chesterfields on her office desk one morning. The wrapping was undone, a cigarette halfway out, and a lighter stood beside it waiting to be used.

It had been the most succulent tobacco she had ever tasted in her life. And when she had returned to the class not one of them had been smiling.

Dears. They were, most of them, dears. They called her Doc with affection, formed and reformed groups around her latest work, her latest exhibitions (depending on tastes, depending on grades), though her only cavil might be their singularly unenthusiastic support for her campaign. She would have thought the creation of a Fine Arts Department devoted entirely to the visual arts would have made them rapturous—in the manner of students who were getting their own way at last. But not them. Or, rather, not all of them. Ollie, Ben, and Harriet, in particular, had somehow decided that she would be chosen to chair this new entity, which in turn would leave them in the hands of someone else.

Silly. They were dears, but they were silly. On all counts.

A prickling, then, at the back of her neck, and she turned her chair around slowly. There was a thick, dark pine shelf attached to the wall beside the door. On it was a statuette just under a foot high—a grizzly half-risen, its great head cocked to one side, massive paws up to strike, its mouth open to reveal gleaming pin-needle teeth. Its name was Homer, the first satisfactory piece she had completed after arriving in Oxrun. A talisman he was, something to be patted wearily before bedtime, to be caressed cheerfully in the morning. Its doppelganger in flesh she had met at dusk in Montana, eight years ago on a trip she had made to cleanse the divorce from her dreams and her child's funeral from her nightmares.

The creature had stood there watching her from the other side of a stream given color by October's early foliage. She had been too terrified to scream, too weak to run, and the grunts it had issued while it paced the grassy bank nailed her to the ground. Then it had reared in a single swift movement, and she had been positive it could have reached across the narrow band of water and swiped off her head with no trouble at all. But it had only watched her and had tested the cold air and had gestured as if were batting at insects. For a full five minutes before it had dropped to all fours and had lumbered into the woodland. She had not moved. She could hear it grunting for what seemed like hours, hear the thrashing of underbrush, hear its paws thunder the earth.

She thought she had died, and had somehow been reprieved.

Now the grizzly was reduced to a gleaming grey-white marble she had quarried herself, back in the hills that coddled the Station on three of its sides. The gleam came not from polishing; it was a quality of stone she had not seen in any other, and it gave the bear a translucence that at times gave it movement, when the lighting was right and she wasn't quite looking. And in its reduction—with eyes deliberately left blank in the ancient manner—it had become a partner, a friend, and a stubbornly silent confidant.

"All right," she told it. "All right, so I'm stalling. Sue me."

Homer simply stood there, testing the air.

Another check of the clock, eight thirty-five and sweeping— and when the telephone rang she nearly dropped her cup. *God,* she thought as she scraped back the chair, *get hold, woman, get hold.* She plucked the receiver from its wall cradle and sat again, her right hand curling the cord once around her wrist.

13

The voice was decidedly masculine: "Was it as good for you as it was for me?"

She couldn't help it; she laughed. "Good morning, Greg."

"Sorry to call so early, Pat, but I wanted to be sure you were ready for battle. After last night, I'm surprised you can still breathe without a machine."

"I can breathe just fine, thank you very much." Her smile began to drift, one corner turning down. "I'm not so positive about the battle, though." She thought of telling him about the ride home, thought of what he would say and discarded the notion.

"Sounds like a good dose of the nerves, huh?"

She nodded, stuck her tongue out at Homer, then blinked and grunted.

"Well, welcome to the club, Dr. Shavers. But listen, I was thinking, see, and the meeting's not until four-thirty, so why don't you and I have lunch or something? Maybe we can get Stephen and Janice to go with us. I mean, we could plan strategy in case the Trustees have shafted us. Like, we could create a minor diversion, like slitting Danvers' throat. That would really throw Constable off his stride, don't you think?"

"I don't know, Greg. Don't you think that's a little drastic?"

"Who for? Danvers? Hell, he'd never notice until he figured out he couldn't lick the dean's shoes anymore."

She laughed again, gratefully and loudly. She knew it wasn't all that funny, knew that poor Danvers wasn't really as bad as they liked to pretend. But apprehension spurred her (and a cold finger of the wind that had pursued her last night), and it was some time before she was able to control herself long enough to thank her colleague for the release and ring off, still chuckling and just as aware as he that she hadn't answered his invitation. He tried too hard sometimes, Gregory Billings did, but somehow he always managed to sense when she needed being silly, needed a willing target for her occasional undirected bitterness, needed to be alone. And it bothered her quite a lot lately that she was often incapable of reciprocating in kind.

Immediately the receiver left her hand, however, she patted Homer's head and walked to the front door, where her fawn overcoat was waiting in the cane rack against the wall. Though her first studio class did not begin until ten, Greg's call had served to magnify the apartment's silence, and her suddenly unpleasant solitude. She was giving herself too much time to think, to worry, and she had no intention of assuming the role of the instrument of her own defeat. She had worked too long and too hard for this day, had yielded the feast possible number of compromises for it all to be wasted just because she didn't have the nerve to leave her own home.

"Darling," her mother had asked just three weeks ago, at the end of her last visit, "I don't understand what you're trying to prove. Don't you realize you're jeopardizing your position at the college with what you're doing?"

Pat hadn't answered. Mother and Father entrenched in their penthouse museum hadn't even understood why she had chosen to come to the Station; how could she expect them to understand her now?

Once the coat was on and buttoned, she grabbed a tasseled white woolen cap and pulled it down over her ears, down to her eyebrows, flung a six-foot white muffler cavalierly around her neck, and drew leather-palmed gloves over her long fingers. The door closed behind her, and she tested the lock—more often than not she didn't bother to use it. A bad habit, perhaps, but she had never felt other than safe in the Station.

It was done. She was out. There was no turning back.

15

She stood on the front porch and allowed the damp cold to attack her, pulling stiffly at her cheeks and nose, stinging her chin, slipping beneath her skirt to tighten her calves and thighs.

Her blouse turned to ice.

She tucked her purse under one arm and shoved her hands into her pockets.

Like most of Oxrun Station this side of the huge park, Northland Avenue was lined with homes ranging from gingerbread Victorians to stately Dutch Colonials, all of them considerably bulky, all of them maintained in scrupulous repair. The lawns were broad, the trees ancient and massive, the inhabitants with few exceptions well enough off not to worry about the direction the rest of the country was taking. A self-contained street in a self-contained community that carried its wealth like a topcoat well worn.

She inhaled slowly, deeply, the last of the evening's punishment driven to hiding by the chill, the last remnant of her scare made ludicrous by daylight. Behind her the house loomed quietly, the bay windows on either side primly white-curtained and reflecting the pale new sun in each of the square panes. Two blocks to her right the street dead-ended at the fencing of the town's cemetery; two blocks west the traffic on Mainland Road was easing as commuters gave way to those just passing by. Directly across Northland, old man Stillworth was sweeping snow from his walk, puffing white breath like smoke and grumbling loudly at his broom about New England's insane weather. The block's children were already in school, but their spirits remained hovering around abandoned sleds on porch steps, in snowmen guardians behind hedges, in a stray red mitten propped atop an evergreen shrub. The steady clanking of a snowplow several streets over. The frigid call of a bird. The brittle slam of a door.

Nothing had changed during the night, then. It was definitely safe to leave. The ritual she'd inaugurated the day she'd moved in was completed in the space of a few familiar seconds.

She took the steps cautiously, one hand out for balance while the other held her purse. Goldsmith had already cleared the inlaid stone-block walk to the pavement, had already overspread patches of ice with lumps of salt. She shuddered when she estimated the hour he must have risen in order to do it before the others had left for work, and she decided the man should be struck a special medal. Not that he would accept it, even in jest and good humor. He was very much the recluse, keeping to his own rooms most of the day as far as she could determine, shambling out only when there were repairs to be done, grass to be mowed, the back garden to be weeded.

He was indeed amazing—just like her performance the night before.

She had been at the Chancellor Inn with Greg, Stephen DiSelleone and Janice Reaster. It was Janice's twenty-ninth birthday, and the intention had been to have a quiet celebration while Janice—who was a lecturer and art historian—bemoaned her imminent plunge into the infamous thirties. Within an hour after they'd ordered, however, as more of the faculty had wandered in with spouses and dates, the party had blossomed to a boisterous two dozen. DiSelleone took to the piano, Janice to her quavering voice, and what had once been a grand farmhouse trembled for hours.

She had drunk too much, flirted too often, had eased her car from the parking lot just after midnight so incredibly slowly she hadn't believed she was really driving. It hadn't been a long ride—one block north to Steuben, right one block to Northland, and a time-frozen skid as she wrenched the station wagon left.

The snow. And the wind. And someone …

A clumsy U-turn to remind her of her condition, and a near-collision with Stillworth's tin garbage can to send her further into panic.

Amazing she had not slammed into a tree.

Amazing she'd been able to get into the driveway at all, much less manage it so the car was facing back out toward the street.

God takes care of little children and idiots, she thought as she walked, and was halfway up the drive when something about the car struck her as being wrong. It was small, squared, all of a dove grey with a chrome luggage rack on top. And it was clean. Perfectly clean. She looked over her shoulder and saw only the tracks of her boots in the light dusting that covered the blacktop. There were no tire marks, no bird tracks, no indication of any kind that anything mechanical or otherwise had come back here since the end of the flurry. Kelly and Abbey, she realized, must have parked their cars at the curb instead of in the garage, though she did not recall seeing it when she'd come home last night. And Lincoln had evidently decided a good wind would do his work for him before the next fall broke from the clouds.

She shook her head once and sharply, dispelling an image of a giant picking up the station wagon and carrying it safely back here. That was foolish. She had driven it here herself. And it had been snowing; it had been windy, and she had sat here watching it while she'd tried to rein her nerves.

So it must have been the wind that had erased the car's tracks. That only made sense. Nevertheless, the unsettling sensation prodded her into walking around the vehicle slowly, checking the tires, brushing stray flakes from the edges of the window ... and stopped when she saw the dent in the passenger door.

"God ... damn!" She crouched and traced the concavity with a finger. The surface hadn't been cracked, nor were there any signs of whatever it was she'd struck: no pieces of bark, no chips of chrome or paint, just a shallow indentation centered and oval. She straightened and jammed her hands on her hips. "I don't believe it. My god, I don't believe it."

She kicked at the door with the side of her foot and boxed an ear with an open palm. Then she stalked back to the driver's door and yanked it open, slid in with a scowl. It took her several moments before she could insert the key and fire the engine. Another full minute before her hands stopped trembling in rage. It certainly wasn't the first time she'd drunk too much at a party, but she had never before been so befuddled that she'd endangered herself to the point of having an accident without even knowing it.

She thought of the wind, of the grumbling, of the snow.

Her anger turned to Greg—why had he permitted her to drive home in her condition? She didn't recall him emptying his glass so terribly often. So why the hell hadn't he stopped her? Why hadn't he at least gone with her, or forced her to walk home, or filled her with black coffee before letting her out?

She held her breath, her cheeks puffed and her fingers strangling the beveled steering wheel.

Her eyes closed tightly and she directed herself to review the drive home, from the moment she had backed cautiously onto Chancellor Avenue to the moment she had backed into the driveway. And her eyes snapped open as she bit down hard on the inside of her cheek— she could not remember. Somewhere during the drive she had struck something hard enough to damage her car. But she could not remember it. Unless it was ... the garbage can. Instead of narrowly missing it, she must have sideswiped it. She must have. But the memory of the impact was just not there.

19

Her shoulders slumped as a slithering cold not born of the winter or the snow made its way into her stomach and curled there, aching. It was the pressure, of course. Bucking the system and fighting her memories and battling her parents and fending off Greg—it was the pressure, just the pressure that had lashed down her caution and allowed her all that drink.

And the consequence of that was a kind of selective amnesia induced by the liquor, and made firm by guilt. She did not want to remember having the accident because it was stupid and it was embarrassing and it underscored something that might possibly become a problem.

With no desire to remember ... she didn't.

"Yes," she whispered, and grinned her relief. "God, what a fool!"

She shifted to a less rigid, more comfortable position, glanced around the car, and scowled at the small pebbles lying on the black mat on the passenger side. Figures, she thought; for all the work she put into keeping the car clean, her stumbling around the last few days had soured even mat. She thought to open the other door and brush them out, changed her mind and decided to do it later. After she came home and apologized to Stillworth. She would offer to buy him a new garbage can, and he would be furious, as usual, but she would take the fury as part of her punishment. For now she was thankful she hadn't found any blood.

Chapter 3

S hortly after the turn of the twentieth century, Ephraim Hawksted and a handful of his closest associates decided the children of Oxrun Station should not have to be denied a superior post-secondary education simply because they happened to live in a remote section of the state where travel was difficult and expectations high. He was also the guardian of a long-standing grudge born the afternoon he'd been refused entrance to both Harvard and Yale (Princeton, of course, was out of the question, being out of New England). Though he could have attended any one of the smaller and no less prestigious colleges in the Northeast, the gall of the twin giants in forbidding him study soured him to the point that he'd made his fortune without a degree. He regretted it. He felt incomplete. And despite any number of examples of similar men with similar successes, he felt almost embarrassed there was no sheepskin on his wall.

He called in debts, then, favors owed and obligations outstanding, and within twelve months had founded a two-year community college which, for its time and ambition, proved singularly more than adequate for the training of dedicated teachers and shrewd mid-level businessmen.

It wasn't until the end of the Second World War, however, that it became evident to Hawksted that not only was two years insufficient for the contemporary world, but also the students themselves were increasingly reluctant to transfer to other institutions. The mark of Oxrun had taken firm hold of one arm, while the other was in the grip of their unquestionably remarkable education.

On his deathbed the old man suggested two years double to four, and when he finally died in 1953 no one complained publicly when the school's name was changed—especially in light of the trust he had established to maintain the facilities independent of the vagaries of economic and enrollment flux. The only conditions were two: that all the trustees be natives of the Station, and none of them be graduates of Harvard or Yale.

The two-hundred-acre campus was two miles east of the last street on Chancellor Avenue, a stretch of road on the way to the depot bordered by thick woodland on the right and barriers of the Station's estates on the left. Pat paid little more than automatic heed to the blur of brown as she drove. She concentrated instead on the slight damage to her station wagon, on the upcoming meeting, on the work she needed to begin with her classes. Her radio was tuned to a classical-music station, and the passages of strings, the lilt of muted horns, lulled her, calmed her, and when she turned right between a pair of massive stone pillars topped by flaring eagles she was almost ready to face it all without shrieking. Her grip loosened on the wheel, her spine grew less rigid, and as the road canted upward to a gentle incline she rolled down the window to catch the sharp scent of pines that lined the narrow blacktop.

A mile, and Hawksted broke from the forest.

And there was so much ground-snow her eyes began to water before she had time to squint.

The campus' main plant had been constructed on a deep step in the hillside. The central building was a three-sided rectangle whose base was well over a hundred yards long, its quadrangle reaching to the edge of the flatland and sweeping down through white-jacketed hickory and birch, elm and evergreen to the forest proper. It was of large-block brownstone with broad-silled casement windows, towers that split each of, the three sides into thirds and added a fourth story double-peaked and imposing. At the school's founding all the rooms had been used for classes; now they were dorms— front-to-back suites with a large room facing the quad and two bedrooms in back that held two students each. From the central tower east the rooms were occupied by women; west was reserved for Hawksted's men. There was also a belowground level marked by half-windows that never opened and a smothering view of sun-blotting shrubs. This was the home of several professorial offices, and classrooms for courses in business, religion, philosophy and logic.

Aside from the main structure, and connected to it by underground tunnels well-lighted and walnut-paneled, were four additional buildings raised just after the school had begun its four-year program. On the left as Pat approached were two immense brick-and-turreted squares three stores high, one behind the other. The nearer housed English, History, and eleven foreign languages; the one in back belonged to all the laboratory sciences. On the right beyond the western arm was the Student Union behind, the refurbished auditorium and Fine Arts directly in front. Upslope of the Union was a glass-and-marble library so architecturally uninspired it made the rest of the facilities seem almost grand.

A chapel on the hillside overlooking the campus. White stone and Gothic, cloisters and thick oak.

The playing fields to the east, behind a wall of spruce, and used by the high school when Hawksted's teams were visiting. There was also a mammoth gymnasium, cold and generally damp, an unspoken reminder of where the school's sympathies lay.

Pat hesitated as the road finally came to an end. Immediately to her left was a large circular parking lot already jammed. There was another alongside Fine Arts, but to use it would deny her a walk across campus. She thought of the dent and the jibes it would produce from those who'd seen her drinking, and spent the next ten minutes creeping between rows before she found a proper space.

A moment, then, to pat the dashboard for luck, and she was out and walking briskly, up a dozen stone steps to the quad's inner sidewalk.

A pause. She turned and looked back toward the woodland, caught the wink of a windshield far down on Chancellor Avenue. Frowned. Rubbed the back of her neck absently and turned back to face the quad.

And smiled as if she'd just returned from an extended vacation, tucking her handbag against her chest and hugging herself warmly. It was quiet here, but of a far different degree than she felt in her home. A few windows were open and she could hear radios muttering; students were on the walk, laughing, talking, scooping snow from the buried lawn and pelting it at friends. From the chapel she could hear the carillon in one of its morning concerts, the melody almost solemn, the bells sounding medieval. A quiet. A peace. A pleasant jolt to the nerves and a goading of the mind without opening a book or taking a lecture.

In more ways than she found it comfortable to admit it was the perfect hideaway; a liberal arts school and one of the last where knowledge could be pursued for the pure sake of that knowledge, where the outside world was admitted only by invitation. With less than nine hundred students living in or commuting, it had developed a fierce pride in its independence that reached far beyond graduation. The faculty, too, was loyal, though neither blind nor hidebound, and the few individuals in both camps who found the intensity stifling seldom lasted longer than their first winter term.

Suddenly she heard a voice above her shout "Fire!" She continued walking, though a blush reached her cheeks and her chin ducked toward her chest. It was a young man's shout, and a signal that a woman was on the Long Walk, a woman much older than the women who attended. Then another voice grumbled, "Hell, it's only a prof," and Pat lifted her head to laugh at the pricking of her ego.

A beautiful day, she thought, in spite of the beginning, and with a mocking backward wave she passed under the archway in the far right corner.

Stopped in her tracks when the Fine Arts building caught her.

The Student Union was two stories and unadorned; Fine Arts, however, was a triplet of English and Science: dark brick with marble trim, a turret at each high corner, its most distinctive feature a white stone marquee curved around the front and supported by squared pillars. A series of double glass doors opened onto a crescent lobby done in soft reds and golds, centered by a chandelier now unlighted and teardrop. Directly across the black-and-white-checkered floor was the college's auditorium, giving Pat a constant impression of a squat, fat cylinder rammed down the building's throat. It was the home of film festivals, meetings of every description, college and village, the school's vaunted amateur theater, and Ford Danvers' drama classes that seemed to her more often than not to be somewhat clumsy exercises in primal group therapy.

To the left and right of the bulging wine wall were staircases that wound to the second and third floors; and against the far left wall a warren of postboxes behind narrow glass eyes. She checked her own apprehensively, released a quick-held breath when she saw it was empty. No pink slip. No memo. That had to be a good sign.

She grinned self-consciously at herself as she unwrapped her muffler, hurried to the near stairwell and began the climb. Her boots cracked loudly on the metal-tipped stone, the slot-windows at the landing laddering the floor. The woolen cap was swept off and jammed into a pocket. Gloves next, and her topcoat unbuttoned. She shivered in spite of the warmth; she held the brass railing though there was plenty of light. She could hear muffled voices, a distant laugh, something falling. And when she reached the second floor she stopped and listened harder.

She thought she heard her name. She looked back down, frowning, wondering, decided it was nerves.

Coffee, she prescribed, and rushed along the corridor that wound round the auditorium's wall, heavy pine doors inserted there and chain-locked. Around the outside were the lecture halls, offices, and in the back a handful of studios that hadn't been relegated to the uppermost story.

She didn't like the silence. It was too expectant. It seemed to be waiting.

She wished she had brought Homer; if nothing else he would make her seem properly foolish.

Her own office was at the left-hand front corner, frosted glass on the door and her name typed off-center on a three-by-five card taped to the dark frame. She unlocked it, walked in, and before taking off her coat plugged in a coffee pot she kept filled and ready. Then she stripped off her coat and hung it on a wall peg. Thought for a second before slumping into a worn swivel chair behind her glass-topped desk. The wall opposite was shelved to the ceiling, books and papers and sketch pads in profusion; the wall behind was covered with photographs of sculptures she'd taken around the country, a few tiny oils from her own students and Greg's, sketches of projects she intended to begin whenever she had the time, and a blank space in the center where Lauren's picture had been tacked until she'd taken it down last summer.

She sighed wearily, blinked slowly, with a push of her left hand shoved open the window that overlooked the slope. The cold tightened her arm as it drifted over the radiator, vanquished the must that had invaded the room.

She stared at the trees, at the snow, at the distant road. A long time she'd been looking at that view; and a corner of her mouth twitched in a half-smile. Thirteen years, if you count the two sabbaticals, and the half-year she saw nothing but the funeral of her child.

Married at twenty-two, divorced at twenty-seven, bereaved at thirty-one. A hell of a progression.

"Knock, knock."

"Who's there?" she said without turning to the door, refusing to acknowledge the startled jump of her pulse.

"It's not a joke, Pat. I'm just too lazy to lift my precious hand."

Greg was tall without slouching, his hair an unkempt thicket of premature grey that somehow managed to add youth to a face smooth and slightly flushed. Underneath an open, paint-soiled smock he wore a blue-splattered shirt, grey trousers and wide brown belt, and cordovan shoes that should have been discarded the first time a brush had dripped across their laces. He was smiling anxiously, and she waved him in, pointed to the coffee he poured for them both.

"This is rotten," he said, grimacing his first sip. "You ready?" He took the bandy-legged wooden chair she kept by the door.

"Nope." She tasted the coffee, spat and put it down.

"Good. We should do well, don't you think?"

She swiveled round to face him, delighting in the imp that seldom strayed from his eyes. "I had an accident last night."

He frowned. "You didn't say anything when—"

"I didn't know." She told him about the dent, though she still didn't tell him about how she had been followed. No longer convinced of it herself now, she decided she didn't need one of Greg's patient lectures. "I swear to you, two drinks at dinner and no more, ever again."

"Wow," he said softly, and shook his head slowly. "You're all right, though?"

"Sure." Her smile was cock-eyed. "As well as can be expected, given the day." She pulled open the center drawer and took out a pencil, tapped it once on her knee and rolled it between her fingers. "I'll tell you, Greg, I don't mind admitting this is driving me nuts. I mean, the whole tiling is making me absolutely paranoid." She caught herself, and waved away the question that came to Greg's expression. "I just don't understand why Constable has to wait. Why can't we have the meeting now and get it over with, huh?"

"Because he thought you'd shove one of your kids into one of your sculptures, that's why. Like Vincent Price in *The House of Wax*, and all that."

Her throat constricted. "You think they turned us down?"

He shrugged. "I don't know, Pat. I honestly don't know."

She chewed absently on the eraser. "I think he hates me. Ford, that is. Constable doesn't care one way or the other."

"No," Greg said, stretching his legs and crossing them at the ankles. His voice was naturally low, a rough-edged complement to her own deep timbre. "Actually, if the truth be known, you scare him."

"Me?"

"Now, Patrice," he said, cautioning against lying to someone who knew her better. "Come on, come on."

"No, I can't buy it, Greg. What he's afraid of is the expense. Setting us up in a separate department will mean hiring at least two more full-time people, giving you and me at least promotions, and—"

"All right," he conceded, "that's part of it too. But you know damned well that isn't all of it, not by a long shot."

She looked at him thoughtfully. He'd joined the faculty only four years ago, a multi-degreed artist who'd grown weary of the games he'd had to play with the larger galleries. It wasn't sour grapes because of no talent; he just didn't have the stomach for the competition he had to face. At first, Pat had thought him a quitter and had been scornful for retreating into teaching; then she realized there was something else, something that had unnerved him and made him leery of going on. She still didn't know what it was, but she knew he would tell her sooner or later. It was in the way he would look at her when he thought she wasn't watching; in the way … in his way of building a friendship between them so he could begin the unburdening.

She was patient. She could wait.

Meanwhile, a second look showed her hints of exhaustion tightening the folds around his eyes. When she lifted an eyebrow in silent query, he shrugged and drained his cup. "No sleep."

"You were drunk," she accused lightly.

"I was passed out," he admitted with a rueful laugh. "I don't know how the hell I got home, believe me, and I kept waking up every hour or two. The damned tree outside my window kept hitting the pane. I almost went out and cut the thing down."

"That would be just like you," she said. "Get straight to the root of the problem."

He glared. "That's terrible. You oughta be shot." Then he blew her a halfhearted kiss and left, wasn't ten feet down the corridor before a pair of young women fell in beside him, laughing instantly at something he said, gesturing as if they had a mobile canvas retreating before them.

Pat watched until the doorframe cut them off. And wondered how many of those girls Greg had taken into his bed.

"Oh, nasty," she scolded. Her right hand brushed over an end of the collar tie, tugged at it lightly before she closed her eyes tightly, snapped them open. A groan at feigned aches in the small of her back and she stood, stepping around the desk to fetch her books from their shelf. A finger to her chin, scratching. Thinking about Greg, the younger women who constantly surrounded him ...

... and someone was watching her.

She tensed, her shoulders pulling back as if expecting a blow. Slowly, all the while telling herself she was being paranoid again, she turned to face the door. Two young men were standing on the threshold.

Her smile was as relieved as it was warm. "Yes," she told them before they could ask. "I made the call yesterday."

Oliver Fallchurch—blond curls, pudgy, a half-grown beard—clapped his hands once; Ben Williams—lean and dark-haired, his left sleeve pinned up at the elbow— only nodded. Suddenly they were shoved aside and Harriet Trotter nearly spilled into the office. Her face was flushed in embarrassment, her freckles so thickly sprayed they made her otherwise pleasant face seem mottled and scarred.

"Some sonofabitch goosed me," she complained in a high-pitched, too-young voice.

Oliver shrugged disinterest, and Ben lifted the stump of his arm as evidence of innocence.

"The three of you ought to be locked up, you know that," Pat said. The boys stepped aside as she left, flanked her in the corridor with Harriet scrambling behind. "I spoke to the gallery yesterday, as I promised, and everything seems to be going well. Spartan is a good place, fair, and the pictures of your work seem to have pleased them."

"Then the show isn't really set," Oliver said glumly. He wore what Pat had come to think of as his only set of clothes: a blue-and-pearl-button cowboy shirt, jeans too snug for the breadth of his rump, and black boots with pointed toes. "I knew it. I knew it was too good to be true." The accusation was evident: you didn't try hard enough, Doc.

"For god's sake, Ollie, she didn't say that," Ben said.

"Yes, I did," she corrected, averting her gaze from the pain in his face. Someone, she thought then, ought to teach him how to shave; the sight of all those nicks and scabs always made her queasy. "It isn't set, not yet. But I have an appointment with Mr. Curtis in two weeks, so I'll bring him a few of the pieces and let him see them firsthand." When Ben groaned his disgust, she slowed and punched at his arm, not entirely in jest. "Look, I've told you a hundred times, when a gallery like the Spartan shows this kind of interest, it's only a matter of time. To be honest, I'm aiming for June. A pretty fair graduation gift for the three of you, don't you think?"

"Only if someone buys something," Harriet said behind her.

Pat turned, frowning. Normally, the redhead was overenthusiastic, if anything. Today, however, there were shadows under her eyes and a tremor at her lips, and her arms had folded a large notebook against her shirt-straining chest.

"Oh, don't mind her," Oliver said. "She claims a hurricane almost took off her roof last night."

Pat stopped abruptly, and Harriet had to sidestep to avoid a collision. "What?"

"Well, it's true," the girl insisted, her glare defiant as the others moved on. "I couldn't sleep, you know? I went down for something to drink, down in the kitchen, and I heard something

31

outside. I thought it was a cat at the garbage can, so I turned on the light and …" She took a deep breath, suddenly wary. "At least I thought it was a tornado. Not a hurricane, a tornado. It was right there in the middle of the back yard."

"A dream," Pat said, turning quickly and walking.

"I was awake, Doc!"

"Something like a dust devil, then."

"Huh?"

She smiled. "For heaven's sake, Harriet, you've seen them before. It happens all the time. A freak wind current, that's all."

"Yeah," the girl said, obviously unconvinced. She muttered harshly under her breath and strolled ahead, leaving Pat alone in the corridor, sweeping around the back of the auditorium toward her studio. She tried not to think. In spite of philosophers and psychologists there was still such a thing as coincidence in this world, and the dust devil, snow devil, whatever the hell it was, could easily have spun its way into her own path last night before dissipating in the snowfall; Harriet, after all, only lived one block over. It was her own drunkenness that had exaggerated what she'd seen, just as half-sleep and shadows had done it for the girl.

But she wondered if Harriet had heard the throaty grumbling.

Chapter 4

Pat slowed the station wagon when her stomach threatened to disgorge the lunch she'd taken quickly in the Union cafeteria. Her tongue touched at her lips nervously and her eyes began a rapid blinking. She swallowed- She gulped for air. She guided the car to the curb and rested her head against the steering wheel's rim. Alongside her, in the park, she could hear the faint shrills of children skating on the L-shaped pond. And she wept.

A small rowboat in the bay off Bristol.

A smaller child determined to prove her mother really didn't know what a fine sailor she was.

Dark water. Dark wind.

Pat stood at the stone embankment and watched as a young man scrambled into a sailboat, a frail thing, a tiny thing, and breasted the swells. She might have screamed, she might have been shouting, all she could think of was Lauren and the spanking the child would get for frightening her so.

The young man—Paul? Andrew?—cupped his hands around his mouth and called for Lauren. The girl turned, the girl waved, the girl stood in the center of the small rowboat in the dark water and faced the dark wind, hands on her hips proudly. Black hair. Black eyes. Summers with her mother, the school term with her father in San Diego.

She was eight years old when the first wave unbalanced her, eight years old when the second capsized the boat.

She was eight years old when, two hours later, her body washed ashore, and it took almost a full day before Pat understood Lauren wasn't pretending.

Too much. It was really too damned much. What on earth did they expect of her, all those people clamoring for her attention, all those eyes glued on the clock, all those hands touching the stone and trying in vain to turn it to art? And watching. Always watching her every move, hoping that by examining the crook of her hand, the grip on the mallet, the cock of her head, they would know how she did it and be able to do the same. They would know, so they watched. Watching. Every minute of every class until she'd dismissed them early and ran out of the building. Into the Union where she'd taken a table at the loneliest corner. No one sat with her, but she knew they were watching. Whispering. Knowing what she had faced already today, knowing what the dean had in store for her later. They knew, and they watched, and before she had done she could no longer taste whatever spread across her tray.

She had driven less than a mile down Chancellor Avenue toward the village when she realized she was being followed. Yet there was nothing substantial to prove her suspicions. Hers was the only car on the road, there was no one standing just back of the trees, there was no one ahead, waiting in the road.

Following. Closer. Close enough to touch.

As the young boy had been—Paul? Andrew?—when he'd reached out for Lauren and the boat had gone over. He'd panicked, lost control, and the moments wasted before he'd stripped off his clothes and leapt into the bay were the moments it took for Lauren to drown.

Close enough to touch, while Pat had stood gripping the stone wall and screaming until she tasted blood in her mouth.

She swallowed hard and straightened, swiping the tears from her cheeks with the trembling backs of both hands. One.

The other. Diving into her handbag to root out a tissue. Daubing. Blowing her nose. Scanning the road in both directions, trying to discover who it was who followed.

My god, she thought; *my god, my god.*

She coughed, and hiccoughed. She blew her nose again and tossed the tissue out the window. It would be just her luck now to have Fred Borg come by in his patrol car and give her a ticket for littering; or worse, Chief Stockton and his granite voice, granite face, leaning in the window with a laconic Down East lecture.

Then she grabbed hold of the wheel at nine and three and pushed until her elbows had locked. Fool, she told herself then; you're a half-baked fool and you're going to blow it all if you don't stop feeling so sorry for yourself. But it had all come down on her so suddenly, and with such intensity, that she really didn't blame herself for wanting to flee. On the very day the class decided it was going to spy on her, on the day Harriet told her about the tornado, on the day Constable would tell her volumes about her future, on this day Lauren would have been sixteen.

Her wrists began to throb.

And the longer she sat there punishing herself the more she understood she was using the girl's birthday only as an excuse. She was preparing herself for failure, reeling in snippets of blame and tying knots she could point to as stumbling blocks unforeseen. It was natural, it was not extraordinary, and if she didn't get moving she was going to be late for her afternoon seminar.

It was only a matter of minutes, then, before she had parked in front of the house and was up the stairs to her apartment. The idea had been ridiculous from its inception just before noon, but the longer she scoffed at it the more she couldn't shake it loose.

And when she had fled the cafeteria it was the first thing she had thought of to give her flight direction.

Homer snarled on his kitchen perch.

Pat grinned at him and ran a thumb along teeth she had made quite deliberately sharp.

"You," she told him, "are coming with me. If you don't bring me luck, I'll use you to bash Constable's skull."

She jammed the statuette into her handbag and took the stairs down two at a time. Laughing to herself. At herself. Depression and gloom lifting when she burst onto the porch and saw Kelly angrily kicking a flat tire at the rear of her car.

"That's not the way to do it, my dear," Pat called out, unable to keep a grin out of her voice. Kelly was, like her roommate Abbey, prone to hysterics over mechanical failures, gnats, and boy friends who didn't show up precisely on time. The younger woman claimed it was her Latin background, though Pat could not imagine anyone more blond, more fair-skinned, more school girlish than Kelly.

"Oh, Pat!" she wailed, racing to the steps with her mittened hands clasped to her chest. "Pat, if I don't get back to the bank on time today I'm going to lose my job."

"So change the tire. Surely you know how to do that."

"The spare's gone flat."

Pat searched for sympathy, could find only the tolerance of a mother toward a scatterbrained child. She shook her head slowly and descended to the walk, slipped an arm around the woman's waist and turned her back toward the street. "Listen," she said, lowering her head, "if you swear to me on whatever it is you hold sacred that you'll have someone from King's get a tow truck over here to take care of whatever needs taking care of, I'll let you drive me back to—"

36

"Oh my god," Kelly said in relief, and hugged Pat tightly, the beret-capped head barely reaching her shoulder, "you've saved my life."

"Just be careful," Pat told her sternly as she took the passenger seat and handed Kelly the keys. "This thing may be new, but it's got personality. It doesn't like maltreatment."

Kelly, however, was beyond listening. She jerked the bench seat up as far as it would go, virtually rested her chin on the rim of the wheel as she charged away from the curb. Pat closed her eyes and mumbled a brief prayer, opened them when they pulled into King's a few minutes later and listened as Kelly charmed the mechanic on duty into heading over to Northland instantly, if not sooner. Then they were out on Chancellor and speeding east toward the school.

"I haven't seen Abbey in a while," Pat said, trying to give her mind something else to think about besides the driving. "Is she all right?"

"Oh, you know how it is," Kelly said, a practiced twist of her right hand flipping her air-fine hair back over her shoulder. "She thinks she's in love with this guy from Hartford. Insurance, yet, if you can believe it. She spent the weekend with him up at Stowe, and now she's trying to decide if she's going to marry him."

"She certainly works fast."

"She thinks that about every man she meets, almost," Kelly said sourly. "And every time it happens I have to bail her out. It gets pretty tiring after a while, you know what I mean? I mean, she's like a kid, for god's sake."

Pat's nod was carefully neutral, remembering as she did the intense infatuation the woman had with Greg Billings only last summer. Greg had taken her out a few times, and each evening Kelly (or so she claimed) had been kept up until dawn with a blow-by-blow description of every move Greg had made, every word he had said. Pat, too, had grown weary of the affair by the time it had ended, and angry with herself for even hinting at the notion she might be jealous.

"So how are the Musketeers?" Kelly asked.

Pat grabbed the edge of the seat when the station wagon hit a small patch of ice and its tail swerved alarmingly.

"Coming along," she answered when her voice returned.

"Nice people."

"Sure are. A little frustrating, though."

Kelly laughed. "I can imagine. Y'know that cowboy one, Oliver? I think he has the hots for Abbey."

"Like hell."

Kelly looked at her, surprised. "Hey, no kidding! Whenever you're not around that pickup of his is always at the curb. In fact, he even tried to take her to work a few times."

A pause. "Well, did he?"

"I don't know," she said, shrugging. "I'm not her jailer, you know."

Another moment's silence, another patch of ice.

"Handles nice," Kelly said approvingly.

"Yes."

"Guess she was drunk or something."

"What? Who?"

Kelly glanced over, back to the road. "Oh, sorry. Thinking out loud, I guess. About that accident last night."

Pat squirmed into the corner, as much to look at Kelly more easily as to avoid watching the road speeding dangerously at her. "What accident?"

"Honestly, Pat," Kelly said with a tolerant grin. "Don't you ever listen to the radio up there? For heaven's sake, how do you know what's going on in the world?" She shook her head slowly. "Well, last night, out on Mainland, some girl wrapped herself around a telephone pole." Her voice lowered in a parody of mystery. "In a little car just like this, in fact. At least, that's what I gathered from the report I heard. Right smacko into a pole, killed her right away. The way I figure it, she was over to Harley and fell asleep or something, see. The guy on the radio said it happened just after midnight." She gave an exaggerated shudder. "It was dumb, you know. I mean, who goes out drinking on a Wednesday night, anyway? In the middle of the week. Stupid. Poor kid."

Pat looked away, distantly sorry for the accident victim and feeling her own mortality much closer to home. She sniffed, felt herself relax somewhat as Kelly slowed to take the college entrance.

"Kelly, did you … that is, I was going to stop by this morning on the way out to work, but I guess you and Abbey had already gone. I, uh, wanted to apologize for last night. I mean, for the noise I must have made coming home."

"Noise?" Kelly frowned, wrinkling her nose as if a distasteful odor had suddenly invaded the car. "I didn't hear a thing, Pat, not a thing. I was dead to the world, if you want to know the truth. I didn't hear you at all." She glanced sideways, her face grey-shadowed by the trees that closed overhead. "Pat. Oh, Pat, you got tanked up again, right?"

"Slightly."

"Great. Open mouth and insert foot. Hey, if I'd known I would have said—"

"It's okay, Kelly, it's okay. Meant or not, I deserve it."

The overcast deepened, and she knew the next snowfall would not be a mere dusting.

"Y'know," Kelly said, "you oughta try smoking now and then instead of hitting the hard stuff. Relaxes the hell out of you … and it's a lot safer than alcohol."

Pat said nothing. She had heard this same argument from her several times, and though marijuana was not as alien to her as Kelly seemed to believe, she'd never been able to enjoy the highs she'd heard so lovingly described. It had taken her only a handful of times to learn that the equivalent of a single joint only put her to sleep, and that, she'd decided, she could do just as well on her own.

Kelly took the narrow service road around the buildings much slower than she'd driven out from town, commenting on the age of the students as if she were decades older, being slightly too uninterested in the looks of the men and the marital status of the few instructors they noted. Pat kept her comments to herself, smiling instead and wondering if she were more green-eyed than concerned about her roommate's easy conquests of men. Abbey, though Kelly's age, had always seemed to her to be far older, far more in control of her life. But maybe, she thought, that was an outward compensation for her handicap—Abbey Wagner was deaf.

She had no time to speculate further. Kelly suddenly slammed on the brakes behind Fine Arts and began a flurry of promises to guard the station wagon with nine lives, if not more, to leave a tankful of gas when she and Abbey returned from work that evening, and an eternal vow never to leave her own car vulnerable again.

Pat laughed and nodded through it all, slid out and slammed the door. Immediately, she hurried through the side entrance, not wanting to see how Kelly would reverse the compact vehicle and leave the campus. *I may have to ride in it,* she thought, *but I don't have to watch it.*

On the other hand, Kelly's infectious high humor had served to dispel all the remnants of her gloom. A silent thanks, then, as she reached the second floor, and her cheery "good afternoon" to her one-thirty class surprised even her with its firm optimistic ring.

The Bloodwind

The studio/classroom was large and well lighted, arranged through several hectic semesters of trial and error to comfortably accommodate a full dozen students, their workbenches and materials, and a space of her own behind a tall rattan screen she'd purchased down on Centre Street three years before.

The class was gone.

Oliver and her friends had sensed her need for solitude and had left without their usual extra hour or so of talk, of gossip, of worrying over how their latest projects would be completed. They said nothing about an accident, and Pat assumed the woman involved had not been from the Station. Forgot it as soon as Oliver wished her solemn good luck, Harriet rose up quickly to kiss her cheek, and Ben gave her one of his rare genuine smiles. The word was out. Though she had said nothing to them herself for fear of jinxing the outcome, it would have been a poor excuse for a campus if her efforts had gone unnoticed, and unremarked, and the day of judgment passed over without some sort of reaction.

A lovely group, she thought as she wiped her hands on a well-used damp rag; a great bunch of people.

She stood in front of a sculpture she'd been working on for several weeks, the stone taken from the same area where she'd found the piece for Homer. It was just under forty inches high, the base ten inches wider, an intricate series of looping curves and abrupt angles almost but not quite ready to be polished. She laid a finger on her right cheek, a thumb to her lower lip, and she studied it. Her head tilted in concentration. For those who asked she said it was untitled as yet; for herself, however, it was Greg at his desk—or rather, it was his shape, his form, barely recognizable as human to the untrained eye, a dizzying snap into focus once the subject was revealed. It had taken her too long—with too long to go for the span of her life—to study

41

the Moores and the Segals, the O'Keeffes and the Pollacks, before she had developed a synthesis she felt comfortable with, that suited her, that allowed her to slice away what she thought was the mundane to what she hoped was the artistic.

For the most part it worked.

She had already shown in Boston and New York, and much to her parents' distress and amazement had sold virtually every one of the pieces she could bear to part with. But it was hard. It was close to physically painful. These leavings of marble and stone, those castings in bronze, had often become such intense parts of her life that there were times when she wondered why she bothered with them at all. To see them admired on pedestals, under spotlights, was one thing—they were children on stage, children on screen, children adults turned to watch as they raced down the street; to have them taken away forever, however, was a rending of a soul already much battered.

Greg had known exactly what she'd been trying to say when she hadn't been able to stop crying after the sale of a piece only last November.

"You think I don't feel that way about my canvases?" he'd asked. "But why bother doing it at all, Pat, if we're going to be the only ones to see them? It's like … well, it's like Emily Dickinson. All that scribbling on wrappings and newspapers, and nobody knew how tremendous she was until after she'd died. My dear," and his voice deepened, his hands darting professorial to his lapels, "artists starving in garrets went out with the nineteenth century. I may never get rich, but I'll be damned if I'm going to starve. And who the hell am I to say this one can't enjoy … well, can't enjoy my children as much as I? If they don't leave the nest they're going to get moldy."

Maybe, she thought as she dropped a clean cloth over the bench and cleaned up her tools, placing them in racks affixed to the wall. Maybe. But it doesn't make it any easier, does it. She hefted a large wooden mallet thoughtfully, then set it on the floor just as a sharp noise filled the room like a shriek. She froze, looked at the mallet, shook herself in a scolding and stepped around the screen.

Greg stood on the threshold, smock off and patched suit jacket on. His tie was askew, as was his smile. The noise had been his fingernail drawn down the blackboard where Pat made her class sketches.

"You aren't ready," he said in mild admonition.

She glanced at the tall windows. The sun had already slipped below the trees, the storm clouds' grey now turned to gunmetal. The dim light was cold. The sky seemed to be less than a hand's breadth above the highest branches.

"It's beautiful, isn't it," he said quietly.

She nodded. It was.

"So," he said with a clap of his hands, "which role do we play, Doc? The lions or the Christians? If you want my opinion, I hate raw meat."

She shook a fist at him, hurried to the row of sinks by the door and washed her face and hands in cold water. A brush snagging through her hair, her own smock to its hooks, and she picked up her handbag, turning her back momentarily so he couldn't see the pat she gave to Homer's head. Then she took hold of his arm and led him away, one hand trailing behind to switch off the lights.

The corridor was deserted. The lights inlaid in the walls and covered by white glass had been dimmed. A red light over the fire exit glared cyclopean.

The conference room was in the corner down the hall from her office, but when they reached it he surprised her by moving on toward the front, past her office, past his own room as well.

"Round and round," he said when she looked quizzically at him. "For luck we'll pretend it's a carousel, okay?" He gestured toward the curved wall of the auditorium. "A peeling lion there," he said, pointing. "A llama, an ostrich, a bench for two, one for four." They were on the east side, darker, all the rooms empty, a chill that seemed writhing in the recesses of the ceiling. "Here a chick, there a chick, and over there a purple galumph."

"A galumph? What in hell is a galumph?"

"A galumph," he announced, "is a sacred African animal much like the spotted leopard. The primary difference, however, is that it doesn't have spots, and it isn't a cat, and it would rather eat junk than anything like food." He stopped and stepped in front of her, his hands on her shoulders. "Much like Ford Danvers, wouldn't you say?"

She giggled. She felt like an idiot marching around the corridor, but she giggled as he took her elbow and led her at last to the conference-room door.

The light crept into the hall, and as she approached the threshold she looked up at him and stopped suddenly. He went ahead and turned around, his face drifting abruptly to black.

"What?" he asked.

She didn't know. Not positively. But she touched a finger to his tie, nudging it into place. "There's something wrong, Greg. What is it?"

"Not now," he whispered loudly. "Good lord, Pat, they're listening in there."

"They're not it, are they?" And suddenly, without any proof, with nothing more than a flickering pain that had escaped his control and flared across his face, she knew. "There was an accident on Mainland last night. You ..."

"Yeah," he said. "I knew her." Then he grinned and laid a palm to her cheek. "However, it is not to worry. Right now I intend to find out if I have a job tomorrow. If I don't, my dear, I'm putting a cot in your office."

He left her then, and entered the room. A murmur of voices, and his laugh leavened the air.

There was a brief moment when she thought him remarkably brave to carry on like that, another when she astonished herself by thinking him horridly callous. But her last thought as she followed was a wondering about the dead girl, and what she had to do with Greg Billings.

Chapter 5

She almost panicked. Standing alone in the corridor, listening to Greg chatting with the others as if nothing momentous were about to be discussed, she almost lost her nerve. Her arms folded across her stomach and she hugged herself, anticipating a bout of nausea that did not come, wondering if her face were flushed, her lips trembling, her posture more like a supplicant than one who has courage. It was irrational, this sudden attack, and it came close to shaming her. She had always prided herself on being a woman who had never flinched, who had taken the slings of a man's world and caught them in her bare hand, flung them back with a smile not of contempt but of competence. And now she was behaving as though the room ahead contained the gas chamber, not a table and chairs and a handful of gossiping colleagues.

And then, just as Greg called out to her, she knew what she was doing. Again. Anticipating failure so that her possible conquest might be all the sweeter.

She scowled at herself, recomposed her features into what she hoped was confidence, and entered, adding a deliberate swing to her mid-calf skirt as she cut right toward her chair that made her smile.

It was going to be all right, she told herself nervously. Not to worry. It's only your life, after all, and she jammed her tongue between her teeth to keep from giggling.

The room was the smallest on the floor, barely large enough for a light pine oval table and the dozen chairs that surrounded it. On the plaster walls were prints and oils of the college's previous chief administrators, a sailing vessel in Bristol harbor, and the school as it had been at its founding, in 1904. Her place was midway to the chairman's seat. Greg was beside her on her left, on her right Stephen DiSelleone, a chain-smoking young Sicilian whose subjects were music theory and piano. Opposite her Janice Reaster, a dark blonde whose figure was fuller than Pat thought anatomically possible without artificial aid, and whose deep brown eyes never once left Stephen's. There were six others, most of them as meek as anyone Pat had known, and just as liable to slip her a razor as congratulate her on whatever had been her last achievement. They were Ford Danvers' people, but only as long as Danvers occupied the mountaintop.

Smoke curled to the lighting in the ceiling. Chatter was quiet now that she had taken her seat, gazes flicking from the wall prints to the table to her and away. Pat smiled at them all, nodded when Greg touched her arm in support, and wished suddenly and violently she had not left her purse in her office. She wanted a cigarette. She wanted it badly. And more so when Danvers came into the room and sat in the chair nearest the door.

He was a head shorter than she, slender and thin-lipped. His hair was gleaming black and slicked close to his scalp; a handlebar mustache that never quite managed the flair. He was given to tailored tweed suits and silk ties, a waistcoat when the weather was chilly, and an imperious manner that was never quite gracious. He looked at her and smiled, a shark's smile unconvincing, and she felt her pulse quicken. His eyes were puffed, and he kept moistening his lips. It was the first sign she'd had that she might have actually won.

Again the craving for the cigarette, but before she could get one from Stephen, George Constable strode in, bloated and tweeded and smelling of witch hazel. A bulldog's face, complete with jutting chin and swaying jowls, and brown eyes so cold they reminded her of the dead. He said nothing to Danvers, merely nodded at the greetings murmured his way and took his seat at the head of the table.

Pat's throat suddenly dried. This was it. A small segment of her dream either created or relegated, and she wished without warning she didn't have to be here to hear it.

And it was a wish that reversed itself drastically ninety minutes later. Constable had insisted, shortly after Danvers called the meeting to order, that me department go through its regular monthly affairs before, as he put it with a smile to Pat, "we break out the news." She had wanted to scream, but she smiled grimly back. She wanted to kick under the table everyone who spoke, and to strangle Danvers, who obviously knew the results of the Trustees' deliberations and was determined to drag out the small items as long as possible: scholarships granted and denied for lowerclassmen, supplies, showings in the building's lobby for Greg's and Pat's seniors, more supplies, an announcement from the president about the June graduation, a notice from Chief Stockton concerning the increase in village vandalism directly linked to students living on campus.

She wanted to scream.

And astonished herself by agreeing when Constable, at six o'clock, suggested they break for a quick meal in the Union cafeteria before getting on.

Both Greg and Janice had been ready to dissent, but were stopped by a frown that left them both visibly puzzled. She could not explain, however, that she needed some time to banish the tension that had been spilling acid into her stomach. And after three years of fighting, another hour wouldn't make any difference. She wanted now to be completely ready in case she had to start the fight again.

The Bloodwind

She waited, then, until the others had left the room, grinning encouragement at her friends while she traced meaningless designs in the table's high-polished top. The drone of voices and the slap of soles faded before she rose, were gone by the time she had reached her office and had closed the door behind her. She did not turn on the light. Instead, she took her seat behind the desk and pulled Homer from her handbag. It was night-dark, chilly, and she felt a curious drowsiness pulling at her eyes after less than five minutes. But she did not fight it. She only congratulated herself on not taking the cigarette, and laid her head on folded forearms, intending to run through a series of conversations she would have with the Dean should it all go wrong.

An arm of the wind slowly closed the casement window.

The white globes of the campus lights shimmered in the dark like stars trapped beneath black ice.

Homer, on the desk, almost seemed to glow.

Pat slept. Lightly. A portion of her mind listening for sounds in the hall, her mouth slightly open, her eyelids fluttering.

She slept while Homer watched, and there were images: a storm-roiled bay and a child helpless on a raft; a demon crimson and brown rising slowly from a steaming sea; her parents shaking their heads as she tried to explain through a white silk gag why she was divorcing the man they claimed to love; a demon crimson and orange slavering over a woman chained to a block of granite; Greg smiling; George Constable smiling; her station wagon sailing over the edge of a cliff, Abbey inside wide-mouthed and screaming; a demon thudding down a deserted dirt road, taller than the trees, wider than the valley, yet leaving no footprints and not making a sound; a classroom, her classroom, filled with blind and mute students; Greg smiling; Janice smiling; the demon in all colors smashing up through the floorboards of her office and reaching—

She sat up, gasping, slamming the chair back against the wall. The wind was keening, the panes quivering, the radiator clanking as it fought against the cold. She pulled at her face to waken her while she scrambled for her handbag and shoved Homer inside. Then she reached over and locked the window, shuddered for a moment as she looked over the slope to the black forest wall. Down on Chancellor Avenue a streetlamp winked. An eye, she thought; a white eye watching.

She turned, then, and hurried back to the conference room, taking her seat just as the dean rapped his knuckles on the table, sounding the call to order.

Danvers was the only one not in his place.

Constable cleared his throat and tugged at the wattles stiff below his neck. He sat and opened a file in front of him, stabbing at a series of papers with a diamond-ringed finger. He glanced up at the empty chair, at his watch, at the chair. There was no expression on his face, but Pat sensed a frown.

"I expect Mr. Danvers is ... shall we say indisposed in the restroom?"

A stifling of dutiful laughter.

"However, due to a meeting in an hour or so I must attend with the Town Council, I think he'll forgive me if I proceed without him." He smiled, a bulldog's smile, and touched the diamond finger to the greying at his temple. "I also don't believe it fair that we should keep Dr. Shavers waiting any longer. She had worked extraordinarily hard on this project, and I believe I'm speaking for the Trustees when I say how much we appreciate all that she's done."

Her hands were clasped on the table, knuckles white, thumbs jumping. As best she could without showing it, she bit down on the inside of her lower lip, shifted her feet until her soles were flat on the floor.

Greg shifted in his chair; she did not look at him.

Janice winked at her; she barely managed a ghost of a smile.

The others were little more than mannequins positioned as background. For all she knew as her gaze scanned the room, they weren't even breathing.

The wind again, pummeling the outer wall, shaking the single corner window in its stone frame.

The dean glanced at her then, and she fought to keep a smile at bay. There was no clue in his posture, none in his bland expression, and she wished to hell he would either pull the damned trigger or put the damned gun back in its holster.

"Dr. Shavers."

She started.

Constable pointed at the folder. "I have been instructed to read this to you, and to the others. I trust you will bear with me and my rather untrained voice."

She could do nothing but nod, nothing but pray she could restrain herself from strangling him.

"This afternoon the Board of Trustees, Hawksted College, Oxrun Station, Connecticut, met in camera," Constable read after a flurry of shaking out a parchment-like sheet of paper, "regarding the proposition that the Fine Arts Department—current chairman, Dr. Ford Danvers—relinquish its administrative authority over those in the, uh, the arts."

He glanced up suddenly, looking directly at Pat. "I apologize for the confusion of language, Dr. Shavers, but I'm afraid even this small-town bureaucracy hasn't had the time to create a new phrase that also made no sense."

She blinked, refusing to look at the others even though they were staring. George Constable never, but never, attempted an off-the-cuff joke with them. Never. It wasn't done. It wasn't his style. And she could not help but think the attempt was a sign. She paid no attention to the goose flesh suddenly on her arms.

Constable rattled the paper, cleared his throat with a slight stretching of his neck. "Be that as it may ... the Trustees have decided unanimously on the following, to be announced to the immediately concerned faculty in private session, to the faculty and student body as a whole at the earliest possible convenience.

"That the president shall be directed to appoint Dr. Patrice Lauren Shavers to the position of Full Professor effective immediately. That Dr. Gregory Allan Billings be appointed to the position of Full Professor effective immediately. That Janice Reaster be appointed Associate Professor effective immediately."

Janice squealed; Greg grunted and grabbed for Pat's leg to give it a squeeze that almost made her wince. And Pat, still biting her lip, could only close her eyes.

"That," Constable continued, oblivious to the growing commotion, "three new departments be created commencing with the fall term: Theater Arts, Music, and the Fine Arts. Dr. Danvers will chair the first, Dr. DiSelleone the second, and Dr. Shavers the third. It is further directed that the implementation of this directive be done with the understanding ..."

Pat did not hear the rest. In spite of her resolution not to show weakness, not to break down and bawl if she had won, there was an abrupt surge of moisture at her eyes and a burning behind them, and it took several clumsy stabs with her fingers before she was able to see clearly again. Could see Greg beaming as if he'd just been chosen to show at the Met, Janice weeping openly into a lavender handkerchief, the others astonished enough to begin whispering and reaching across the table to shake her and Greg's hands before the dean had completed the Trustees' resolution. Whispering, shaking hands, and glancing fearfully at Danvers' still vacant seat. Then talking. Loudly. Chairs shifted and the table nudged. The room growing suddenly brighter, almost too bright to bear.

She felt her cheeks aching, her jaw the same, but she kept enough presence of mind to accept Constable's offered hand and thank him without babbling. The dean nodded once and slowly swept his papers back into the folder. He was neither the most diplomatic of men nor the most beloved on campus, but he was sufficiently sensitive to know when he had become superfluous, and when the control he had over the meeting was no longer in his hands.

He rose, then, after a perfunctory adjournment no one listened to, smiled grandly as if the entire affair had been his idea, and had taken two steps around the table when the door slammed open, smashing into the wall and jarring one of the framed prints loose. It fell to the floor, the glass shattering on impact.

A shocked silence; only the dying wind.

Pat was on her feet; Greg half-risen.

Danvers, his houndstooth jacket open, his blue silk tie yanked away from his collar, glared directly at her. His lips were quivering, and a prominent tic half-closed his right eye. It was Pat's first confused impression the man had been drinking.

"Dr. Danvers!" Constable said, his voice cracking in admonition.

Danvers ignored him. He lurched over the threshold and grabbed hold of the back of his chair.

"Danvers, explain yourself at once!"

He swayed, looked to the dean as if he didn't see him, looked back to Pat and jabbed a finger at her. "Thought you'd lost, didn't you?" he demanded, his customary whine laced now with venom. "Thought you'd bloody lost, am I right, Shavers?"

Pat shook her head in bewilderment, looking first to Constable, then to Greg. "Ford, I don't understand you. I ... what are you—"

The man's face was deep red with rage, and he cut her off with a vicious chop at the air, his other hand leaving the chair and reaching back for the doorframe. "You know damned well what I mean."

"I don't, Ford," she said, suddenly afraid, aware that Stephen and Greg were moving slowly toward him around the outside of the room. "I haven't the slightest—"

"You thought you'd lost, so you ..." He looked around helplessly, enraged momentum slowing him, but not calming. "Well, you won't get away with it, Shavers, not by half."

"Get away with what?" Constable said. "What are you accusing this woman of, Danvers?"

"You'll see, you'll see," Danvers sputtered and backed into the corridor. "Just come outside, the lot of you. Just come outside and see what the precious little lady has done to her betters."

"Greg?" She reached for him and he took her hand.

"Now!" Danvers demanded. "Right now, so you can talk to the police."

Chapter 6

It was the silence more than the cold that caused tremors to skitter along Pat's arms, that snapped her head in small jerks from one face to another, that made her wish someone would scream.

They had followed Danvers timorously, half afraid he would turn on them with some sort of weapon, yet too curious to remain behind in the safety of the building. They'd taken the stairs to the lobby—moon bright and glittering and snaked across with shadows—and out the side door to the parking lot. There wasn't enough room for all of them on the narrow stoop, so several had stepped down to the pavement, several more to the wide concrete apron that surrounded the blacktop.

And no one spoke.

The frantic whispering was choked off, Constable's irritated grunts smothered, and Danvers had suddenly reined in his imprecations and accusations, his arm-flailing melodramatics that called down retribution from the gods of his nightmares. They stood in small groups and kept their own counsel, pale images of themselves under the gooseneck lampposts that rose from each corner of the lot. The snow a foot deep on the ground seemed imbedded with mica, the stars distant and harsh. There was muffled sound from the Union, but no one listened. They watched, instead, as two patrol cars flared their roof lights and turned faces purple, the snow bloodstained, the air far colder than it ought to have been.

The parking lot was small, holding at most two dozen cars nose-in around its perimeter. Now it was virtually empty, and on the far side, alone and in half-shadow, was Danvers' vehicle. An old one, simply black, far beyond its prime though all of them knew it had been lovingly treated. Now it had changed, and as soon as Pat saw what had been done she pressed a fist to her mouth and turned her face to Greg's arm as though denying the sight, denying the presence she felt lurking in the trees.

There was very little left that had not been destroyed. Windshield and windows had been smashed inward, shards and powdered glass glittering on the seat covers; the hood and trunk had been battered and crumpled, the doors dented so deeply the paint had cracked and flaked off to the ground; the grille was twisted from the center outward, headlamps and taillights shattered to dust, and the hubcaps had been wrenched off and folded in half, tossed into the snow bank brown with slush. All the tires were flat, though there was no sign of slashing. The only sound a faint dripping from the radiator's ruins.

DiSelleone spoke first: "Jesus ... Christ." It was less than a prayer, more a horrified whisper.

Danvers had moved to the center of the lot, arms limp at his sides, his oversized head lowered in defeat. A broad-shouldered patrolman—Pat recognized him as Fred Borg—had left the warmth of his vehicle and was talking with the professor quietly. A small crowd of students, drawn by the spinning lights, had started to gather on the pavement, in the snow, but they too were silent, were staring, their faces only segments of shadows as they watched and they waited.

Pat had lost all track of the time. She only knew she was outside without a coat, without her gloves, and her hands were beginning to tremble violently at her waist. Yet she made no move to return inside. Like the others, she waited, listening to speculations and avoiding the few glances that stole her way and retreated. Then Danvers turned slowly, heavily, Borg at his side, and they walked to the patrol car, where they were joined by Dean Constable.

And again a long wait, punctuated by coughing, a sneeze, a nervous giggle. Then Borg reached into his front seat and pulled something out. Pat stifled a gasp and grabbed for Greg's arm. It was a large wooden mallet. Her mallet. And embedded in its face were sparkling eyes of glass.

Danvers looked straight at her, and Borg walked over to talk.

They waited in the second-floor corridor while Borg sat with Danvers and the dean in the conference room. One by one they were summoned in for their statements, entering quickly and leaving the same way because no one could say anything except that Pat had not eaten with them during the recess.

She took the chair at the foot of the table. Borg, his cap pushed back on his head, his pencil almost invisible in the grip of his right hand, sat beside her, nodding, half-apologizing in the tone of his questions.

"I was in my office," she said, staring at her hands clasped on the table. "I'd dozed off. I wasn't hungry. Good god, Fred, you don't think—"

"Don't be silly, no," he said quietly, glancing over to Danvers, who was sitting in the far corner and ignoring the ministrations of three of his cronies. "It'd take you all day to do something like that, and the way I see it, there was only about thirty, forty minutes for it to get done. Nope. I don't see it."

Her spine grew less rigid. "What do you see, Fred?"

"I see a gang of them, that's what I see. Five or six, maybe, I don't know. There is the mallet, though. It is yours, right?"

Her initials had been carved into the underside of the head. She had no choice; she nodded. "But the studio wasn't locked. Anyone could have gone in and picked it up."

"Yep." He scribbled something in his notepad, looked again at Danvers. "He don't like you very much, Dr. Shavers."

"I know. He hasn't liked me since the first day I walked in here."

"Easy to see why he blamed you, though." He flipped a page over. "Cutting his department in three. I can see it."

She said nothing.

"Sleeping, huh?"

"Damnit, Fred ..."

"Yeah, I know. And I suppose you didn't hear anything?"

"No. I was ... I was having nightmares." The smile was weak. "Nerves. I didn't hear about the new department until after the break was over."

"Congratulations."

"Thank you."

"You can go now. Stockton wants any more from you, he'll call."

She was the last, she was numb, but she wanted to talk to Danvers, to say something to him if she could. He looked so deflated, so beaten in the corner, that she couldn't hold his accusation against him. Greg, however, deterred her with a touch to her arm, handed her coat and hat and white cashmere muffler. He was right, and she knew it as she followed him downstairs. Danvers would hear nothing now but the sound of his own grief, the beat of his own bewilderment. Nevertheless, she hated leaving him there with sycophants and phonies.

And she hated it twenty minutes later when she and Greg, Stephen and Janice, took their places in a Mariner Cove booth.

The Cove—the left half a restaurant catering mostly to families, the right half a lounge catering to quiet drinkers—sat

58

back from Chancellor Avenue to face the length of Centre Street, the community's business avenue. The streetlamps were harsh without foliage to mute them, shop lights either dark or etched into cold plate glass as the hour crawled toward nine. There was little traffic now, and what pedestrians strayed outside moved swiftly, hunched as if goaded by a stiff storm wind. The police station was on the corner diagonal, the Town Hall two lots to the Cove's left.

And for the Cove, red brick and white trim in imitation of Monticello, it was a slow night, a January night, when the bartender in red velvet and the waitresses in nautical black wanted nothing more than to go home and warm their feet by a fire.

Pat sympathized, thinking as she stared at her gin-and-tonic that the way she felt now she'd never be warm again.

They were in a booth as far from the entrance as they could find. The bar was in the center, encircled by round tables and captain's chairs padded with black leather; the walls were a deep wine textured to the touch, the booths themselves partially obscured by draperies of fish netting. Mahogany, ebony, squared posts and carriage lamps, on each of the tables fat candles in red chimneys. The restaurant had closed down an hour ago, and there was nothing left now but the clinking of glass and ice, the soft footfalls of a waitress, a whisper or two, no music at all.

Greg sat beside her on the outside, Stephen and Janice opposite. They had downed their first drinks without bothering for taste, had ordered a second round and were sipping them slowly.

"I don't believe it," Pat said finally, shaking her head.

"You saw what you saw," Stephen said. His black hair was cropped close to his skull, his eyes deep-set, his cheeks hollow.

Most of his female students were in love with him, most of them jealous of the way he looked at Janice and smiled.

"No, I don't mean that," she said. "I mean, why me? My god, he must have known already what had been decided, for crying out loud. I can tell that now from the way he acted at the beginning. But why … why blame me?"

Stephen considered, then sketched a circle in the air around his temple. Janice poked him hard. "Don't be silly, Steve. It isn't fair to him."

He frowned. "Isn't fair to him? To Danvers? Jesus." And he looked to Greg for support against illogic and women. "Look, Pat, the man doesn't like you, pure and simple. You beat him out of his precious little fiefdom, with"—he grinned immodestly—"another chunk gone he probably didn't expect. Plus, you're a woman. You're taller than he is by a head—and stop smiling, it's true. You know he's a refugee from the nineteenth century. God, his forebears practically settled this place in the year zero."

"All right," she said reluctantly. "I can see all that, but I don't have to like it, okay?" Stephen nodded, Janice shrugged. "But what I still want to know is —who? Who would do a thing like that?"

"Oh, come on," Greg said, just short of impatiently, as if the culprit was too obvious to mention. "Who else could it be, huh? Ford may be one of the best in his field—and let's give him that, the poor dope—but he's certainly not going to win the Mr. Chips Award. He's been tough on us, but he's wicked with his so-called actors and actresses, and I'm really surprised they haven't had a crack at him before."

"Tell me about it," Stephen said, pushing back into the corner of the booth. "In spite of my extreme beauty, believe it or not there are kids who don't much like me, either."

"I believe it," Janice muttered, and took an elbow lightly in her ribs.

"And Pat, too," the musician continued.

"Who? Me?" She smiled, but didn't feel it.

"Sure," said Greg, staring at a point over Janice's head. "You should hear ..." He stopped and shrugged.

"Hear what?" she said, curiosity overcoming a growing distaste for the subject. "Come on, you started to say something. What is it?"

"Well ... your Three Musketeers aren't exactly camping on your doorstep these past couple of months, are they?"

She blinked her astonishment. He couldn't be talking about Oliver and the others, but the expression on his face told her he was. "No," she said in swift denial. "No."

"The show," Greg reminded her gently.

"But I've told them a hundred times how long it takes to arrange something like that!"

"Pat, you and I understand these things. But think back for a minute. Try to remember what it was like when you first started, when you were so sure you'd take the world by storm every gallery owner in New York would be falling all over themselves trying to sign you on. And let's face it, m'dear, Fallchurch and Harriet especially aren't the most stable people in the world. And they're kids! My god, we all keep forgetting that. I do it, too. We see these eager young students with all that talent, we talk to them, we learn about them, and we forget they haven't a clue about what the world's like. Kids, no matter how old they are, no matter how much they've traveled on Mommy and Daddy's money."

She wanted to refuse the truth in what he said, and told herself she should have known it all along. He was right. It happened at least once a year, but this time she'd been so anxious to get the three started she'd been blinded by her own enthusiasm. Her shoulders sagged slightly, and Greg laid a hand on her arm for a moment, just long enough before she stirred and saw the embarrassment in Stephen's eyes.

"All right," she said. "Boy, am I stupid."

"No more than the rest of us, Pat," Stephen said with an encouraging smile. "We just don't like to be reminded that we really do have feet of clay. And I think sometimes we forget how much we can hurt these kids without meaning to. We're human, and they don't like it. Especially when they hang their dreams on our shoulders without our permission."

"Okay, okay," she said, palms up. "But really—if we can get off my troubles and back to Danvers—really, smashing up a car like that? That's incredible. I can see vicious pranks, but what they did there was downright destruction! There would have had to have been an army of them. And why was my mallet left behind? It's like they were deliberately trying to implicate me."

"No," Greg said instantly. "Most likely, they had someone watching. He saw Danvers coming and they split. One of them dropped it, that's all. You start thinking like that, Pat, you're going to end up in a Hitchcock movie or something."

She half-smiled an admission the thought had crossed her mind, then lifted her glass to finish her drink while Greg beckoned to the waitress to bring another round. When she'd finished, however, she frowned. Janice was staring at her intently, and one hand automatically went to her hair, her throat, for something out of place.

Then: "Yes? What? Have I got a piece of lemon on my tooth or something?"

Janice blinked rapidly, startled, and a quick flush spread over her cheeks. "God, Pat, I'm sorry. I was just thinking."

"Uh-oh," Stephen muttered.

Pat glared at him, turned back to Janice. "About what? Did I do something wrong?"

"No, no," Janice said, lowering her gaze to the rim of her glass. "Nothing like that, Pat. I was just thinking about tonight, that's all."

A pause, and Pat encouraged her with a smile.

"Well ... your office overlooks the parking lot, doesn't it?"

"No," she said, "not really. I don't have a window on that side. Just one that ... why?"

"But the conference room does," Janice said. "I know that. That's right."

"So?" Greg said. "What does that have to do with anything?"

"So why didn't any of us hear what was going on? Or anyone in the Union, for that matter. I mean, you don't smash a car like that without making a hell of a racket, right? Right."

"My window was open," Pat whispered, thinking.

"And you didn't hear a thing the whole time?"

"I was sleeping. I fell asleep."

"And you didn't hear anything."

Pat realized suddenly that the woman was frightened, her eyes shifting from side to side in search of an answer, narrowing angrily when Stephen laughed shortly.

"Well, damnit, don't you think it's spooky?"

Greg lifted his hands in confusion. "Spooky? Jan, what the hell are you talking about?"

Janice sighed loudly, her exasperation bringing a sheen of moisture to her eyes. "I mean, Greg, that it seems awfully damned funny that with all those people around, with Pat right there in her office with the window open, nobody heard anything. A whole car was slammed into the ground and nobody heard a goddamned thing!"

Chapter 7

It was the most obvious question, and not one of them had thought to ask it, and then had no time to respond when Greg suddenly exploded into a paroxysm of laughter that had him coughing and sputtering until Pat, unsure whether to be furious or amused, slapped his back several times. By the time he'd subsided, yanking a handkerchief from his hip pocket to wipe the tears from his eyes, she noticed the waitress standing by the table, her expression puzzled though her lips worked at a nervous grin. Clever you, she thought when he winked at her. Word of Danvers' misfortune would be all over town by morning, and all they needed now was a waitress carrying tales to as many customers and friends as she could get hold of.

"Nice," Stephen said dryly, seconding her unspoken compliment.

Greg made a show of exaggerated modesty, then reached across the table and put a finger to Janice's wrist. "The wind," he said.

Janice leaned away from him, as if distance would bring the words into sharper focus.

"The wind," he repeated. "If you recall, it came up right after we left for dinner. It's apparent even to us non-scientist types that it carried most of the sound away, and we just plain did not hear the rest."

"Yes, I suppose ..."

"See?" he said. "No problem, once you put a superior mind to the task. Besides, it's not our job to worry about it. That little puzzle belongs to Abe Stockton and his band of merry men. They'll find out soon enough who the culprits are, and I'm taking odds right now it was someone like …" He hesitated, and Pat tensed. "Like Ollie or Ben."

"Hey," Pat protested, twisting around to face him more squarely. "Now that's a little much, don't you think, Greg?"

Greg was startled by her reaction, but he set his jaw to jutting in defense. "Well, maybe not, but you have to admit, Pat, they're hardly the darlings of dear old Hawksted. And lest you forget, I know them fairly well myself. And I just happen to know they're madly in lust with Sue Haslet, who just happened to have been Danvers' premier actress." He stopped, then, and grabbed for his water glass. He didn't lift it, however; he turned it slowly between his palms. "She was already in one Long Wharf production, and Ford was pushing her hard, very hard, to try her luck in New York over spring vacation. He didn't seem to care if she graduated or not. She was a nervous wreck. I wouldn't blame Ollie if he and his friends …"

As his voice trailed into silence, Pat looked to Stephen for an explanation, saw instead Janice wringing her hands just below the level of the table. It took her several moments to realize that Susan Haslet must have been the woman killed in the crash the night before. And she could see then how Fallchurch might blame Danvers for it. So torn between the lure of Broadway and the tangible result of four years of studying, she might well have lost her concentration for a moment, might have been drinking too much, might have done any number of things that finally, fatally, led her onto Mainland Road.

"Greg … ?"

He shrugged. "Well, she needed someone neutral to talk to, you see."

Another silence somewhat awkward and extended until Stephen, lighting a cigarette whose paper was as brown as its tobacco, drolly slipped into a story concerning one of his own students, a recognized miscreant whose millions were, it was alleged, the only reason he was still permitted on campus. By the time he had finished, Greg was ready with a story of his own, and Janice was clenching and splaying her fingers eagerly, waiting for a chance to cut into the round.

Pat listened with a dreamy smile for a few minutes, then withdrew into a glum series of speculations centered around Greg and his relationship with Susan haslet. He was, she had come to learn, an intensely emotional man, quick to laugh, quick to weep, liable to slide into moods that were, at best, puzzlingly incomprehensible. That she might actually be jealous stung her for a brief second, pleased her for a longer one, until an image of Ford Danvers surfaced suddenly and unbidden. She scowled to herself. It definitely wasn't fair. On what should have been the sweetest, most exhilarating night of her life, she wondered if it had all been worth it. The man was more than likely going to make the rest of the term as miserable as he could for her, and the look of anguished confusion he'd given her as she'd left the conference room would be enough to keep her awake for the rest of the winter if she wasn't careful. She had noted no threat there, only the shadow of a beaten man, and the salt of the hideously demolished automobile had obviously added substantially to his pain.

Hollow, she thought, with a trace of self-pity. Why not, just once in my life, can't I do something right for myself and not feel so damned guilty about it? Not that she would race right to his office in the morning and hand it all back to him; but she was positive it was going to take a long while before she really felt like celebrating.

"They're all bastards, no doubt about it," Janice said, loudly enough to bring Pat back to the lounge. "Cute, hunks, some of them horny as hell, but essentially they're all class-A bastards.

They don't want anything from me but what I can give them, as long as I give it to them so they don't have to work, or think."

"So why do you teach?" Stephen said.

Another familiar field that invited replowing.

She retreated once again, this time hoping the politics of running an embryo department in an established school wouldn't prove too much for her to handle. Though she believed she'd proved herself handily by getting this far without losing her position, accepting the Fine Arts chair only meant more responsibility, not only for herself but for those working under her, the students who picked it for a major, the reputation of the college ... through all those months of maintaining that the department did in fact need creation, she realized she had not really considered the aftermath.

Unfortunately, dear, she reminded the doubts and the niggling dark fears, there's not much you can do about it now, is there?

"Hey, Pat, what's the matter?" Greg whispered then, leaning so close his chin almost rested on her shoulder. "Is it something I said?"

"No," she said quickly. "It's ... the car. If you only knew how Kelly drives ..." And as soon as she'd spoken she chastised herself for not having thought about Kelly and the station wagon since that afternoon. It made her feel almost guilty, as if lack of concern somehow constituted vehicular abandonment.

"Never mind," he said. "We'll send out a search party if it isn't back yet."

She gave him a brief smile, not bothering to reveal the lie, and immediately she did he launched into a series of torturous, lengthy puns that soon had DiSelleone working to top him. And unlike Greg's head-thrust underscoring of the punch lines, Stephen's pianist fingers wove the air into designs she could almost see if she peered hard enough through the dim lighting.

It was easy to understand why Janice was taken by him, why she seldom moved more than an inch from his side in spite of the fact that he made a cautious show of not noticing. He was mesmerizing, and witty, and the four of them were not long in laughing freely, desperately reaching for the pun long before it could be delivered.

Then, just as Pat thought the stitch in her side would send her into tears, Greg excused himself, returning a few minutes later with an ice bucket speared with a bottle of champagne. He poured for them all, lifted his tall glass and winked. "Lest we permit the poor dope Danvers to spoil this forever," he said, his crooked smile wide, "I suggest we remember for the moment that we've all been promoted. That Stephen and Patrice here are destined to assume Constable's place on the academic pantheon through a bloodbath of politics five years from now, while Janice-love and I will be outfitting our togas and sharpening our knives. To us, my friends. God love us, and spare our dear children."

And it ended that way, the quiet, satisfying celebration Pat feared had been lost, a settling of moods and tempers that lasted until Greg parked in front of the house and kissed her gently on the cheek.

"You are a marvel," he told her. "I swear, I would have given up the first time Ford said no."

"You don't know me very well, then," she said, hoping it sounded more a joke than she felt.

"No," he said somberly. "No, I guess I don't."

———

The heater was billowing too-warm air around her legs, and the combination of gin and champagne laced a fuzziness through

68

her thinking she could not control. And she suspected it was making her tongue looser than it might otherwise have been.

"Greg, that Susan Haslet …"

He pulled away and folded his gloved hands into his lap, staring at the center of the steering wheel and nodding to himself slowly. The windshield fogged over. In the dashboard's unnatural glow his eyes vanished, his mouth broadened to a thick, gleaming slash.

"She was a good kid," he said quietly. "A little pushy, but I suppose that comes with an actor's ego. I wanted to protect her from Ford's shoving as much as I could, to let her grow her own way, but toward the end she wasn't listening. Ben and Oliver came to me once, a couple of weeks ago, and told me to leave her alone. It was like something out of a Cagney movie. The cowboy and the one-armed bandit."

The abrupt eruption of bitterness in his voice took her aback, but his reaction was understandable. She wouldn't have been surprised if he too had somehow managed to find a way to blame Ford for her death. He turned to her, then, and she had to check herself hard not to back away from the hunger in his eyes.

"Greg …"

He looked back to the windshield and hunched his shoulders as if against the cold.

"No, it isn't like that," she said, though she made no move to touch him.

"I know," he said. "It's funny, in a way. All those creeps, all those slimy little men and blue-haired women who were after me while I was in New York. They never let me alone, you know, never let me do my own work. Art was something that matched the furniture, matched the walls." A laugh, short and acid.

"You survived," she said, perplexed at the direction he'd taken.

"Sort of," he said. "But you, you're different. You overcame. A divorce, Lauren's death, your parents thinking you should be a good little girl and do good little girl things. You overcame, Pat. Like today." Then he did look at her, his smile tentative. "I am given to clichés, Pat, but we're birds of a feather, you and I. And if you ever need help …" And he said nothing more. He reached across her lap and opened the door, at the same time brushing his lips against her temple. She gripped his hand and squeezed it, slid out before she did something foolish like invite him upstairs.

And when the faded VW chugged down the street and turned the corner, she decided it was too soon to leave the night yet. A walk; and she moved up the corner and turned left, heading for Mainland Road. There was a thin ice feeling to the air, no stars that she could see. Cars parked at the curbing were lifeless and uninviting. A few of the homes still had their porch lights burning, and windows were glowing brittlely. She inhaled slowly and deeply, her hands thrust to the bottoms of her pockets. The breeze she made as she walked sifted under her skirt, and the tingling at her thighs made her grin. After a single long block she felt a dull stinging at her ears and adjusted her woolen cap more snugly around them.

Her stride became more brisk, more military.

She had done it. Today she had done it. And it was a hell of a fine feeling.

At the end of the second block she reached Mainland, a two-lane highway aiming north and south as it passed the Station. No houses faced it, only a tall, dense screen of evergreens that swallowed most of the light beyond. A block to her right—like all the blocks in Oxrun nearly twice as long as those in other towns—Williamston Pike spilled into the road, its flashing amber traffic light the only sign there was a community here. Across from her was a dense black wall of embankment and wild shrubbery, a few straggling trees, beyond that the dead expanse of a long-abandoned farm.

She stepped in front of the corner stop sign and leaned back against it, arms folded loosely over her chest. She supposed it would have been nice to let Greg up, to sleep with him, to wake in the morning with her head on his shoulder, but she hoped he understood this wasn't the time, that the night of her victory she wanted to spend alone. Savoring. Wondering. Perhaps indulging in some unwarranted melancholy. Without question he was one of the few men she knew who didn't press for an advantage. He wasn't masochistic, but neither did he ignore the signals when there was something she needed he could not provide. Otherwise, he made no secret of his desire to protect her. When he could. When she permitted.

And it occurred to her suddenly, painfully, that perhaps it was he who needed her tonight. Because of Susan Haslet.

A lone car sped past her, and she followed it until it had vanished over the rise just beyond Oxrun's north end. When her gaze drifted slowly back, however, she frowned and rubbed a finger under her eyes, trying to rid her vision of the taillights' afterglow. Then she shook her head. There was nothing over there; it was only her eyes readjusting.

Her nose began to run, and she wiped it with a sleeve. First thing tomorrow, she decided, she'd see Ford. She had no idea what to say, but it was important he didn't believe she was gloating. Especially after what had happened tonight.

A tickling at her cheek and she shook her head once. It was snowing out of the black. Large spiraling flakes that swiftly coated the crust of previous falls, greyed the blacktop, clung like white burrs to the front of her coat. One landed on her nose and she brushed it off reluctantly, grinning as she pushed away from the sign to head for home.

A sound, then; a great weight snapping a thick branch in two.

She shaded her eyes to peer across the highway, but the dark was unrelieved save for the blurring snow, no light beyond to give whatever moved an outline. But whatever it was, it seemed to be pacing. Slowly. A few yards left, a few yards right. Hesitant, as though debating crossing the road. Another branch cracked, a rifle shot in the silence she hadn't realized had fallen. Her tongue poked between her lips, withdrew, poked again. She moved to the edge of the curb. And saw nothing.

Only the snow, sifting more thickly now in and out of the street lamps' spill.

A shape, and she almost leaped back to the pavement. It was there. She was positive she'd been able to discern a shape, though of what she didn't know. But it was tall, it was broad, and it had moved in its pacing to the embankment's edge.

Greg, she thought. Oliver and Ben.

Or Danvers, troubled and angry.

She turned around quickly, determined not to run. High Street stretched toward the center of town, awash in snow, scrabbled over by branches defining a diminishing tunnel. The blacktop and sidewalks were covered and slippery, her boots soundless as she hurried, her breath plumed over one shoulder.

This is ridiculous, she thought; all I have to do is stop and yell, and whoever it is will either run away or expose the gag. It's silly. It's stupid.

There was a lump in her stomach that turned grave cold.

The stitch in her side that laughter had caused returned and spread, made her hand clench tightly at her waist while hedges rose and the snow whispered softly.

One block gone. One more to Northland. And she couldn't help feeling that the shape was still watching.

Her shoulders hunched in reflex, her arms folded again so her hands could grip her sides.

On many occasions while she'd lived in New York she had walked the streets at night and had felt gazes following her from alleys and doorways. That was to be expected, and she'd turned it to a game the rules of which she forgot when she heard something crashing through the shrubs.

Watching. Moving. The same feeling she'd had that afternoon when she'd fled the school to fetch Homer. Immediately, she plunged her left hand into her handbag and gripped the statuette, wincing when one of its teeth pierced her glove and finger.

Watching; but she would not look over her shoulder. She told herself it was the champagne, it was the gin, it was the way Greg had looked at her before she'd left his car. There was nothing out there, nothing in the field so huge it terrified simply by being. It couldn't be. What it must be is a deer down from the hills, or even something smaller whose traveling sounds were magnified by the night and the snow and the alcohol in her veins.

The wind struck her at Northland.

At the corner she turned right, ready to break into a run as she dared a look behind. But a sudden explosion of wind blinded her, stole her breath, whirled her off-balance, off the curb into the street. Her hands flailed, her woolen cap spun from her hair. She cried out—or thought she did—and fell to one knee. Gasping against the roaring in her ears, covering them with her palms until her lungs filled again. Then she staggered to her feet. Looked around wildly and could not find her house. The snow spun right to left in front of her, behind her, trapping her in an ice-bar cage that held until she lurched

73

forward and tripped over the curb. A tree slammed against her shoulder, spinning her back to the street.

Watching.

She felt it watching.

Towering somewhere above her, leering at her, studying, but not moving at all when her fear galvanized and she ran blindly, arms outstretched and mouth open to breathe. The snow slapped her cheeks, her forehead, tangled in her hair and slipped down her collar. There was nothing soft about it now, nothing peaceful, nothing pure; it rode the fierce screaming wind and tried its best to drown her.

The streetlamps were gone, their lights useless, dark.

Again she reached the curb, this time slowing to avoid collision and sobbing when she found herself in front of her home.

Watching; she felt it watching.

The wind punched at her side and shoved her into the hedge. Twigs dug at her hands, her wrists, but she ignored the needle pain and ran up the walk to the steps, to the door—it was locked.

"God, oh god," she whispered, struggling through her handbag for the key chain she carried. Not finding it, and feeling the shape watching, and wincing at the stings of the snow on her face, and finally dumping the bag's contents onto the porch and scrambling to her knees, one hand on the stone bear, the other frantically shoving aside compact and lipsticks, cigarettes and debris from the bottom of the bag that except for some small stone shards was blown away along the porch. The keys, then, just as she thought she'd lost them.

The wind shrieked, the shape watched, and once the door was open she leapt over the threshold and slammed it hard behind her. Backed away toward the stairs, Homer held high to her shoulder in case she had to throw it.

The Bloodwind

A single bulb in the high ceiling gave more shadow than light, but it was sufficient for her to see the snow sweep onto the porch as if thrown by giant hands. It spattered against the glass panels on either side of the frame and made the curtains tremble; it slipped a small contingent under the door; it turned to ice; it turned to hail; and just as her heel thumped against the bottom stair the wind died, and there was silence.

Chapter 8

She sat, hard, and the tartan skirt pulled up to her knees, her hands dropping into her lap white-knuckled around Homer. Her heart raced; she could feel it in her chest. Her jaw was tight, her head slightly quivering. She looked away from the door, and back … to the translucent panes that flanked the frame, to the flocked white curtains on the door itself. Beyond was a dark flickering, the snow falling heavily. No wind, no shape, and after a few moments of trying not to move she pushed herself to her feet and walked slowly across the foyer, Homer waiting silently on the step she had left.

A hand on the brass doorknob.

Another parting the curtains.

Snow. Nothing but snow. White in the streetlamps, grey in the shadows. A lump in the center of the street—it was her cap, and she had no urge to fetch it.

A tear glinted in the corner of one eye, coursed down her cheek before she could catch it.

Wood creaked and a hinge protested, and before she could turn around a hand touched her elbow. She almost cried out, bit her lip fiercely and tasted blood instead.

"You okay?"

Kelly stood hesitantly beside her, eyes narrowed with concern, hands holding closed a shimmering Chinese robe. Her hair was in curlers, her face puffed from sleep, and back in the apartment Abbey stood waiting. Pat smiled shakily, did not protest when Kelly led her out of the foyer and into her home.

Into a place of chrome and vinyl and travel posters on the walls. Abbey immediately led her to the sofa and sat beside her, a taller and much thinner version of her roommate.

She lifted her hands and spoke in sign language: What happened to you?

Pat stalled by unbuttoning her coat, pulling her muffler from her throat and folding it neatly on the gold-and-glass cocktail table set too close to her knees. Abbey poked her arm, her sharp chin raised, her nearly black eyebrows lifted in question.

"I had a scare," she said finally, not turning away but listening to Kelly bustling in the kitchen.

Abbey's hands moved again.

Pat grinned sheepishly. "No, I wasn't mugged." She remembered, and hid a shudder. "I got a promotion today, you see, and—"

Abbey applauded, her lips parted in silent laughter. The two women had known of Pat's battles and had candidly told her they didn't think she would make it. Too many men in a position to thwart her.

Kelly returned with a tray laden with coffee cups, a box of tollhouse cookies, and floral tissues they used in place of proper napkins. "I'll be damned," she said, settling easily into a beanbag chair on the other side of the table. "You did it, huh?"

Pat nodded, and Abbey grabbed her shoulders and kissed her.

"Incredible." Kelly handed her a cup; instant coffee and the water barely warm. "But my god, what happened to you out there? That art guy get fresh or something?"

Pat leaned back, as much to relax as to allow Abbey to see her lips. "No. It was the wind. You ... you heard the wind?" When they nodded she almost ran to the window. If they had heard it—Abbey more correctly sensing the house trembling—

then it had happened. This time she couldn't blame it on her drinking. She felt them staring, lowered her gaze to the cup and sipped once, twice, shook her head slowly. "I guess I celebrated too much or something. I went for a walk over to Mainland and thought I saw something in the fields. It spooked me."

What was it? Abbey asked, her expression patiently doubtful.

"I don't know, I didn't see it. I just ..." She cleared her throat. Now she was feeling foolish. "I ran. If anybody'd come along then, I would have belted him with Homer."

"Tension," Kelly said firmly. "I know about that stuff. It all builds up, it gets released, and you react. Some people fall asleep, some people get giddy, but you have hallucinations. It's normal. Really."

Whether it was normal or not, Pat thought for the moment what the woman said made sense. She had drunk the champagne, she had had that awkward moment with Greg, and a sudden spat of gusts in a snowstorm wasn't unusual. Add Danvers' car, her abrupt memory of Lauren ...

"You're incredible," she said.

Kelly shrugged. "It's nothing. I didn't take all those psych courses just to fill up some notebooks, you know. It's also common sense. Abbey, do you remember the time I was interviewed for that job over in Hartford, with Travelers? It was managerial, and I had a week's notice." She grinned wryly. "I was a wreck. I lost fifteen pounds and had to buy all new clothes just to go talk to the guy." She glanced down ruefully at her still-pudgy figure. "I should be so lucky again."

Abbey touched her knee. *She was late coming back, and I got worried about her so I went to look for her. You know how she is.*

"Hey," Kelly said. "Watch it."

Her roommate ignored her. She was standing there on the riverbank, talking to herself about swimming upstream all the way to New Hampshire. Her eyes brightened, and she winked broadly. She got the job, you see, and that's how she was going to celebrate. I was a wreck, and she was going to swim to New goddamn Hampshire.

Pat laughed and looked to Kelly. "But you work in a bank, now, Kel."

"Yeah, tell me about it. The guy made so many passes I thought I was trying out for the Patriots. I quit in less than two months. Small world, though. Would you believe it was Abbey who hired me for the job I have now?"

I'm not perfect, Abbey signed. *I do make a mistake now and again.*

Once more the laughter, freer now and less strained. Pat filled them in on the details of the meeting, omitting the car incident and the expression on Danvers' face.

I'll bet Greg was happy.

Pat smiled. "I think so. I hope so. At least he seemed to be, and I didn't feel he was jealous or anything."

He's a good man.

"Oh, he's okay," Kelly said. "God, Abbey, if you're not careful you're going to start lighting candles to him next."

Pat looked away for a moment, not wanting to see the embarrassment in Abbey's face. But Kelly noted the sudden silence and rolled her eyes toward the ceiling.

"Jesus, I put my foot in it again, right?"

Abbey nodded vigorously, humorously, and Pat grinned to tell her no offense was taken nor feelings bruised.

"Ah, shit. Well … hell, the coffee's cold," Kelly muttered. "Nuts. Hey, Pat … ?"

She sensed the abrupt approach of another favor about to be asked, but it didn't matter. Talking and laughing had made her feel much better.

"Would you mind … that is, I think I did a really terrible thing."

"You wrecked the car."

"No, I did not. But I figured that as long as that cute guy at King's had our junk heap, he might as well do a job on it. It's been months, you know. He said it would probably be ready by dinnertime tomorrow. Tomorrow's Friday, right? Yeah, tomorrow. You think we could borrow yours again? Abbey hates to ride the bus."

Abbey pouted, but nodded contritely, and when Pat agreed as she rose to leave she could have sworn she felt a severe wash of relief. It puzzled her, but she said nothing. At the moment she was suddenly too tired to think about the car; it was going to be hard enough just getting up the stairs. She made her exit quickly, then, snatched up Homer where she'd left him, and let herself into her own apartment without bothering to switch on the lights.

Her clothes trailed behind her. Her legs slowly filled with lead, and her fingers were barely able to unfasten her blouse. By the time she peeled back the coverlet she was already half asleep vowing once again moderation in her drinking, and wondering as her head lowered onto the pillow what sort of creature it was she'd imagined had been stalking her.

Her eyes closed, her lips parted.

Greg, she decided. All very symbolic. Or Homer given life and protecting her, guarding her, shepherding her until she had returned home, to safety.

She nodded in her sleep.

That made sense. That made perfect sense. Greg the shepherd and Homer the sheep-grizzly. Of course. Why hadn't she thought of it before? All her protectors lined up in a row, and why the hell couldn't she admit that she needed protecting now and then?

The Bloodwind

The demon rose from the blue-black sea and slowly turned its head toward her. Fish eyes. Scales. Ears that flared to the back of its head, pointed and scalloped. Arms thick as tree trunks, hands more claws than fingers. It rose from the blue-black sea and it began to wade toward her. She was sitting on a bed, a canopy bed done in greens and distant corn silk, sitting on the bed and floating toward a shoreline that jutted out of the surf to cliffs a hundred feet high and covered with gulls. Black gulls, white gulls, and in the center of the colony a crimson gull that shimmered as it rose from its nest and turned into a demon that soared over her head toward the fish-eyed, scaly demon driving with piston thighs toward her. She could not turn around. There was a hush of wind as the crimson demon swept over her, a clash of flesh and bone and claws and teeth as the two demons collided just above the water. But she could not turn around. She could not tell which of the demons was after her heart and which of the demons was after her blood. She could only hear them fighting, only hear them screaming their rage, while the bed rocked with the turbulence of their battle and the blue-black water washed over the edge of the mattress and soaked her nightgown until it was transparent.

Her pillow floated away. Homer was resting on it, pushed down in its center, its front paws high, its nose testing the air.

The bedspread floated away.

The quilt.

She saw her furry slippers bobbing in the waves.

She saw the cliffs nearing, and saw the gulls slowly turning pink, turning red, turning crimson, lifting from their nests to fill the air with a sailor's warning sunrise. Her flesh darkened. The temperature rose. The water boiled. Whitecaps flared and the cliffs began to melt and behind the demons were thrashing closer and closer until she could feel the wind-shock of their blows, of their screams, could barely feel the claw that pierced

81

the back of her neck and penetrated her spine and slowly, slowly, so slowly she dared not nod separated her head from her torso.

Then Oliver Fallchurch rode by on a raft, his cowboy hat stained with sea spray, his fringed gloves blackened, while Ben knelt between Harriet's legs and drove into her while she shrieked Greg's name.

"Draw," Oliver said, reaching for his holster.

Pat began to laugh.

"Draw, you two-timing sonofabitch," he shouted as the raft drifted out of range. "Draw, goddamnit!"

His hat fell off and his gloves turned to lace and Harriet's orgasm knocked Ben into the blue-black sea where he grew his arm back and turned into a demon that rose from the water. Fish-eyed. Scaled. Piston thighs driving toward her.

She laughed. She screamed. She drove herself upright and saw the muted light filtering through the curtains to lie in a cloud across her bed.

It took her five minutes to stop trembling, and five more before she dared slip her legs over the side and try to stand. She made no attempt at interpretation, even if the demons somehow vaguely resembled Danvers. Rather, she stumbled into the bathroom and turned on the shower, stepped in quickly and closed her eyes until the dream fell to fragments which were washed down the drain. Toweled dry and brushed her hair. Wrapped a terry-cloth robe around her and tied the sash snugly while she walked into the kitchen and set the kettle on the stove. Not tea this morning. Coffee, black, as much of it as she could drink until she was positive she was awake and wasn't still in her bed, riding the sea, listening to the demons that now, as she thought about it, sounded frighteningly like the wind.

She looked outside, cup in hand. A good deal of snow must have fallen during the night: the rose bushes had lost all trace of their burlap capes, there was little bark to be seen on the trees, and when she leaned close to the pane she could hear a shovel working in the driveway.

Good man, Linc, she thought with a sour grin, then turned to the clock and gasped when she saw it was fifteen past nine.

A race, then, to finish her breakfast, to sweep on her makeup, to dress and get halfway to the door before she remembered that Kelly and Abbey were taking her car today. She cursed her generosity and ran back to the kitchen, dialed their number and cursed again, loudly, when nobody answered.

"Great," she said to the room. "Just great."

Neither Greg nor Janice was at home, either, and she almost despaired until she remembered Harriet. One block over on Fox Road. The telephone book was in the cabinet under the sink, and she wasted a few moments looking under the H's until she caught herself, forced herself to sit down and regain some control.

It was more than the dream that had unnerved her. And it was more than the wind that had driven her to her knees. Somewhere, back where she tried to imagine herself the best possible teacher, she could not quite believe that Greg had been right, that Harriet and the two boys were that angry with her simply because she hadn't gotten them their show as quickly as they'd hoped. Had he been talking about anyone else she would have had no trouble; Oliver, however, despite his excesses and his carefully tended temperament, surely had to be more realistic than that. And even if he wasn't, there was no way she could imagine dour Ben holding a grudge. Not against her. My god, not against her.

A shuddering inhalation, and she dialed Harriet's number. Six rings later she answered.

"So," Pat said, after explaining her predicament, "you think maybe I could hitch a ride with you?"

There was a hesitation, a murmuring in the background. Then: "Sure, Doc." Brightly, almost too loudly. "Give me a couple of minutes, okay? I got to get my stuff together. Gee, you really shouldn't lend your car like that, you know? My pop always screams when I do something like that. Like I was lending it to Bonnie and Clyde, you know?"

Pat told her she understood, then mentioned the weather and the snow and what they would be doing in class today until finally, several minutes after she'd begun, Harriet cut her off politely.

"Doc, we're never going to get there, you know, if I don't start now. Though I guess it won't make any difference if I'm late, will it? I mean, you're my first class and since you're coming with me, I guess it doesn't make any difference at all."

"You're right," Pat said, and rang off, leaned back in the chair and put a palm to her forehead. Shifted it to her throat, to the table, and watched the veins rise slowly on the back. It always happened when she was tense, or when she'd avoided something she'd feared might be unpleasant. Like asking Harriet if she'd known where the boys had been last night, or if it was true they were all so disappointed with her that they were slipping away.

She hadn't asked because she hadn't wanted to hear what the girl would say.

And in that moment she felt a rush of indignation against Greg, for planting a seed that refused to be dislodged no matter how hard she tried.

"Hell!"

She took her time fetching coat and gloves and muffler, spent a useless ten minutes searching the apartment for her cap before she remembered—the last time she'd seen it, it had been lying in the middle of the street.

The wind. It had been the wind.

She opened the door slowly, her breathing sporadic, her tongue working at her lips as she took the stairs in a virtual crawl. The banister was wood-cold. The foyer tracked with melting snow brown around the edges. On the mail table by the door was a shoe box with a tented sheet of typing paper resting on top. She glanced at it as she reached for the doorknob, saw her name scrawled across it. A look to Goldsmith's door, to Kelly's, and she picked it up.

The note was short: Found this on the walk before we left. You must have lost it last night. Is it yours?

Abbey had signed it, and Pat smiled at the woman's thoughtfulness, finding her cap and bringing it in. She was, indeed, a rare creature, and despite all Kelly's grousing, Pat hoped she would find the man she was looking for before long. Whoever he was, he was never going to know just how lucky he would be.

She lifted the lid and reached in, snatched her hand back as her eyes focused on what lay inside.

It was a glove. Brown leather, and fringed at the cuff.

Chapter 9

The discovery was something akin to a physical blow. Expecting to find her cap in the box, she found instead Oliver's glove, usually seen poking out of one of his hip pockets. She almost dropped it. Changed her mind and stood by the door, looking at but not seeing the frame-high glass panel so marked with facets you couldn't look through it without your eyes watering. Her arm dropped slowly and the glove dangled toward the floor. Oliver, she thought; how long had he been out there last night? And what had he seen?

She passed a hand over her forehead, made a fist and rubbed at her left eye. This was silly. It was obvious he had been at Harriet's to whatever hour and had walked by here, perhaps on the chance of seeing a light on in her apartment. He might have wanted to apologize for his less than generous moods lately. Or maybe he was just nosy. Whichever it had been, the hedge had probably snagged the glove from his pocket and he hadn't noticed.

A slow, brief constriction in her chest made her hold her breath. And who, she asked silently, is being less than generous now?

The nightmare. The wind. She knew as she opened the door she was in no condition to face her classes today, despite the triumphant news she'd received at the meeting. She glanced over her shoulder at the stairs, thinking she might be able to get back up in time to call Harriet. A horn stopped her, and she was down the steps and rapping on the passenger window of a much-traveled sedan. Harriet leaned over and rolled it down.

"I'm not going," Pat said apologetically. "I'm sorry, Harriet, but something's come up and I'll not be in today. You can spread the word if you want, and I'll call the dean. If you have a chance, would you mind tacking a sign to my office door? I'll be in on Monday, for sure."

Harriet's face pinched in concern. "Doc, you okay?"

"Nothing I can't handle, Harriet. And I'm sorry again for dragging you over here."

Harriet looked toward the street. A snow plow had been by at least once, but the snowfall had been too great, the temperature still too low—there was a thin and browning sheath over the blacktop, already beginning to glisten where ice patches had formed. She looked back. "It's all right," she said, though her tone was unable to mask the reproach. "Maybe, if you feel better later, you can call Mr. Curtis and see about ... you know."

"Yes. Maybe I'll do that."

She stepped away from the curb, kicking back through the hillock of plowed snow until she was on the sidewalk. She watched as Harriet drove away, rear tires spinning for a moment in apparent indication the girl was angry and wanted desperately to speed. Then, with a white-breathed sigh, she hurried back upstairs and called Constable. Neither he nor Danvers was in his office, but she left a message with both secretaries and assured them vigorously she would return on Monday in one piece. Once done, she stood by the kitchen's back window and stared at the trees.

The pressure was supposed to be over. She was not supposed to continue to have these fantasies of surveillance and menace. It bothered her to think she might not be as strong and resilient as she'd thought, bothered her more that she could not stand being in the apartment one moment longer. Yet there was no escaping the sensations that trailed after her as she headed quickly toward the door: that the ceilings were beginning to lower by incredibly slow inches, that the furniture was more suited to a funeral parlor than a home, that there were whisperings in the corners that could have been the hot water streaming through the baseboard pipes, could have been and weren't.

Her right arm dragged downward. She glowered at her handbag and saw the glove and Homer, returned muttering to the kitchen, where she dropped the former on the table and set the latter on its shelf.

Out again, holding a palm to her throat while she looked up and down the street, seeing for a disturbing second the dark wind chasing her, seeing herself stumbling, seeing her cap cartwheeling along the blacktop. She glanced around without much expectation of finding it in the snow banks, shrugged when she didn't and headed down to the next corner, turned left and walked slowly until she found herself on Centre Street.

The Christmas decorations were gone, the curbs lined with cars, most of the shop windows under the mansard roofs already beginning to display the next season's wares. She considered walking over to Yarrow's to find a book to read, thought seriously about stopping in at Miller's Mysteries to see what curious items were all the rage this month. Miller's, though it had changed hands sometime last year, was a search-and-locate business; if there was something odd, something offbeat you wanted or needed, Miller's would find it, bring it back and give you a fair price. Josh Miller, the original owner, she had known only slightly, had remembered him because he'd been one of the few people in town who hadn't held it against her that she wasn't a native. Now he was gone (though where, she didn't know) and Larry Nesmith had taken his place. A bright, rotund Santa Claus of a young man whose amateur magic was more a drawing card to the shop than his uncanny ability to locate the unusual.

She had almost taken a half-dozen strides in that direction when she stopped herself, almost causing a collision with a woman coming up behind her. No. Nesmith's cheer would be too much for her to take just now, and she made an about-face and virtually marched down to Chancellor Avenue. Stopped at the corner and looked to the building on her right.

Something, she told herself wryly, is trying to tell me something, I think.

The Oxrun police station was a pseudo-Grecian temple of marble and granite, white globes on either side of the solid oak doors, and pale green walls on the inside that somehow seemed standard for every station across the country. A low wooden railing divided the waiting area from the workspace, and just behind it was a large desk raised on a platform. Behind it, two frosted-glass doors for detectives and patrolmen, the detention cells down a corridor to the right and the chief's office down a corridor to the left. Behind the desk a grey-and-blue uniformed policeman sat, working a crossword with a fountain pen. When he looked up and saw Pat waiting he grinned, erupting deep dimples in his cheeks and taking ten years from his age.

"Hey, hi!" he said, rising and coming around to step down from the platform. "Congratulations, too, Miss Shavers. I hear you're taking over the college next year."

She grinned, and ducked her head in thanks. Wes Martin would never know how good it had made her feel to hear something like that.

"What can I do for you?"

She hesitated, feeling abruptly and deeply foolish for giving in to a whim.

"Oh," he said, nodding as though he had read her thoughts. "Oh, you probably want to know if they found the car smasher."

"Yes," she said softly, and had to repeat it when it was evident he hadn't heard. "Dr. Danvers was awfully upset, and so was I, for that matter. Fred seemed to think it was one of the students."

"Well, if it was," Wes said, "they didn't find them. Or him. Poor old Borg must've been there until dawn, and all he got for it was a couple of snowballs down his collar." He grinned again and brushed his fingers through short-cropped sandy hair. "If you want to know what I think ..."

Her hands slipped into her overcoat pocket. "Sure, Wes."

"I don't think we're gonna find them. There were no fingerprints on that hammer-thing, only a zillion footprints in all the snow ... I don't think so, nope. But I tell you, I sure would like to meet the people that could do a job like that. I got a potential mother-in-law I'd like to see made into a dwarf."

Her laugh was dutiful, whatever comment she might have wanted to make forestalled when one of four telephones on the desk rang and Wes excused himself quickly. She didn't know why, but she waited, watching him nodding, grunting once, reaching for a pencil to scribble something down on a pad. There was a long, narrow scar behind his left ear, one that darted under his collar and, she knew, didn't stop until it reached his decidedly un-flabby waist. She had gone out with him several times two summers ago, never once learned the scar's story, and couldn't understand why a man with an advanced degree from John Jay would bury himself in a place like Oxrun.

Bury; and she chided herself for being unfair. It was the wrong word, of course, unless it was applied to her. And before she knew it she felt the depression, and the unease, slipping around her again.

"Sorry," Wes said then, swinging around the desk to take his seat. "That was King's. They need authorization to release a wreck to the insurance company."

"Susan Haslet," she said without thinking.

Wes lifted an eyebrow, one much darker than his hair. "Yeah, how did you know?"

"A guess," she said. "She was a student."

He nodded. "A crime, ain't it. You see some people a hundred years old that should've been buried before they were twenty they're so miserable, then you get someone like this who hasn't even had a—" He stopped suddenly, and looked away to the far wall. "Hey, Pat, I'm sorry. I wasn't thinking."

It took her a moment to realize he was referring to Lauren, another startled moment to realize she didn't feel guilty. "It's all right," she told him, softening his embarrassment with a forgiving smile. "It was a long time ago."

"Well, yeah, I suppose." He looked down at his pad. "Y'know, I'll never understand how King manages to stay in business. He's incredible. Can't keep records worth his soul, changes mechanics quicker man the weather, yet he has the gall to complain we didn't investigate the accident right." He shook his head in disbelief. "I mean, the car—you heard it was just like yours, I guess—it was right smack against a telephone pole, whole right side smashed to hell and gone. So was the left, the door sheared off its hinges. King claims it couldn't have happened, forgetting, I think, a car does tend to spin around when it's hit. Dope. I mean, he's a real dope." He leaned forward on his elbows. "Last year," he said, winking conspiratorially, "he gets a call to pick up some MG that took the woods on over near Harley. On the way back in the tow truck he ends up in the ditch himself, claims to this very day he was attacked by giant gnats." His laugh filled the room, so ceiling-high and wide it almost echoed. "King do enjoy his Coors now and then, he really do."

Pat nodded, trying to join the banter and ignore the weight easing onto her shoulders. But she could not. After a few minutes more she waved and left quickly, afraid he would notice something and try to ferret it without her permission. He was good at that, one reason why she'd stopped seeing him so regularly; she'd found herself telling him things she hadn't wanted anyone to know, not even if the time were right and proper.

He called out a goodbye as the doors closed behind her, and she almost turned to answer, saw the oak swinging heavily into place and shrugged. Stood on the broad stoop and watched the traffic swing out of Centre Street and onto the avenue. Most of the automobiles had snow tires on, but there were still a stubborn few that refused to yield to the blandishments of advertising and had chains on their tires, the rhythmic clanking blurring into a single sound doing more to stir childhood memories than any faded photograph.

A man and woman walked by slowly, arm in arm, heads together, laughing red-faced and slipping on the snow. She recognized them as the editor of the Station Herald and his wife, the Station's head librarian, was about to call out a greeting when she heard, faintly and briefly, the blare of an air horn—a train pulling into the depot three miles into the valley from where she stood. It reminded her of the first day she'd come to Oxrun, stepping down from the coach and slipping on a wet piece of paper. She'd fallen directly into the arms of the stationmaster, first name Herb, last name never known, and had decided it had been a sign. Herb was gone now, to where no one knew, and it struck her that Oxrun seemed somehow to work that way—people lived here and died and were buried in the Memorial Park, they moved here and moved away with great vans filling the street, or they were here one day and gone the next. No fanfares. No notice. As if the Station had decided it no longer had need for them and swallowed them whole, at midnight, without a moon.

She looked up and saw that the sidewalks were empty, the street momentarily deserted.

A dead town. Posing for Currier and Ives, refusing to turn around to reveal the blood in the yards, the corpses in the attics, the ghosts and the demons and the preternatural creatures that stalked the valley no matter what time, no matter the season. She was alone in Oxrun Station; everyone was gone. She took the four wide steps apprehensively, willing a bus to chug around the corner, demanding someone walk out of the Cove across the street to her left, the Town Hall to her right. Her lips tightened. Alone. The last one in the world in a village marked by the past and remaining there forever. Alone.

And someone was watching her.

She knew it wasn't her imagination.

She knew her reverie had not included others.

There was someone watching her. From behind a partially closed door, from behind a curtain, from one of the cars parked along the street. From an alley. From a tree. From the frosted glass behind her.

She spun around and ran back up the steps, shoved open the right-hand door and saw no one inside. Wes was gone from his post, and the police station was silent. Her hand pulled away; the door swung shut on well-oiled hinges. She backed away, felt a heel catch on the edge of the top step and turned, fairly jumped to the sidewalk and hurried east toward home.

She slowed only once, when she passed the Chancellor Inn. Larger now in daylight, gloomy under the overcast, it scarcely seemed to be the place where her troubles had begun. If she hadn't remained at Janice's party for so long, if she hadn't succumbed to Greg's encouragement and the spirit of the others and taken all those drinks, if … if … she slapped at her leg angrily. If wishes were beggars then horses could ride, she told herself, faltered in her stride when she realized how she'd mangled the epigram and laughed aloud. It was a curious feeling; she still could not shake the irrational fears closing in on her, but she knew too that she was on her way to slipping away from them. All it would take would be an overnight bag, a check to cash at the bank, and within an hour she would be at the station, waiting for the afternoon train to New York.

Through the front door, then, and the steps two at a time, fumbling with her key furiously when she heard the telephone's muffled ring. When the bolt turned over she kicked the door inward, not bothering to close it as she raced into the kitchen and grabbed for the receiver.

"Hello?" Breathless, a hand to her chest.

The dial tone, slyly mocking until she slammed the instrument into its cradle and glared at Homer.

"Well, speak up! Who was it?"

A shake of her head and she was in the bedroom, grabbing the small suitcase from the closet, standing for a moment in judgment of the array of clothes before slipping out of her coat and skirt, exchanging the latter for a pair of grey slacks that, she frowned, fit her a little too snugly around the buttocks. She kneaded her thighs thoughtfully, made her choices and pulled her cosmetics from the bathroom. As she crossed the living room she glanced through the doorway to the kitchen, as if expecting the phone to ring again. When it didn't, she shrugged and headed for the landing, stopping again with an exasperated groan when she remembered Kelly, Abbey, and the car. The suitcase hit the floor with an unpleasant thump, tipped over slowly and landed on its side as she returned to the kitchen and ordered a cab. A second daring for the caller to try again, and she went outside to wait.

Fifteen minutes later she was on the platform.

An hour later she was taking a seat in the forward coach, the windows gleaming and clear, the smell of lemon cleanser filling the compartment as the train lurched once, twice, and pulled slowly out of the station.

Her eyes closed as the rails clicked in increasing cadence, opened a short time later when she felt almost physically the weight lifting from her shoulders. She frowned and leaned close to the window, twisting until her cheek was pressed against the pane. There was nothing but embankment and woodland as the train took the hill's slope, and a grey glare that masked all sight of the valley. She knew she should have felt relieved, and gratified that her decision had been the correct one. Paradoxically, however, the dread returned for a second fleeting as a spinning shadow. While she certainly did not appreciate what was happening to her in Oxrun, neither was she comfortable with the sudden release. It was almost as if whatever had been stalking her was bound by the village, by the hills; and if that were so, then it would be waiting for her when she returned.

And if it was, she realized with a start that made her gasp into her palm, then none of it was in her mind at all. It was real. And if it was real, then her father had been right all along.

"You'll suffocate there, Patrice," he'd said after hearing her decision. "I've been there once or twice, and it's no place for a city girl. No place at all. And think of Lauren, for heaven's sake."

"Lauren's with her father," she'd said flatly. "Don't forget, I'm the one who has summers and holidays now."

He lifted his eyes to the ceiling for guidance. So much like her he could have been her reflection. "Patrice, you're not thinking. Oxrun Station is a closed community. You'll not fit in. You are definitely not the small-town type."

She'd gone anyway, and she had fit in for the most part, but he would not listen to her when he heard her reasons for fleeing as abruptly as she had. And she couldn't lie to him. Any story she might devise would be as transparent to him as all her stories had been, all her life.

He would say, "I told you so," and they would argue and she would return.

And when she returned …

She sat back, stripping off the gloves and caressing the smooth leather seat beside her.

My god, she thought. And didn't bother to stop the tear that wriggled out to her cheek.

Chapter 10

It was after two in the morning when the train pulled away from the station, slipping dark engine and darker cars into the black as it crept across the valley toward the tunnel on the far side that would break it away from Oxrun and into the flatland beyond. The platform was deserted. The stationmaster had long since returned home, and the only light came from a single bulb burning behind the locked doors to the waiting room. Slowly, Pat walked toward the stairs, her heels loud on the wood flooring, her breath unseen but felt as it drifted back into her face ahead of a light breeze. The overcast was gone; reluctantly, the clouds had broken into tatters and tails and had left behind stars as cold as the snow.

The parking lot behind the station was empty, and she moved around the corner to escape the wind, holding her case close to her waist. She had called from New York to have a cab waiting, but she wasn't surprised it hadn't arrived. Oxrun Cab and Limousine was a small operation leisurely in its response, perfectly suited to the beat of the village.

And she did not mind. She didn't mind at all.

From the moment she stepped off the train and entered the cavern that was Grand Central Station she felt as if a field of mild electricity had cloaked her gently. Her vision had sharpened, her fingertips tingled, and even her parents' home had seemed less like a sterile museum. She'd wandered around the penthouse without touching a thing, had a drink and stood on the windswept terrace to look down at Central Park. There'd been children playing, a policeman on horseback, the traffic streaming down Fifth Avenue toward the Plaza Hotel. Vibrancy, she'd thought, knowing the thought was a cliché, and she'd hurried back inside to make a quick meal in the white-and-gold kitchen.

She didn't much mind that her parents weren't there; she hadn't come to see them, was relieved there would be no inquisition to ruin her day.

And for the rest of the day she walked. Window-shopped. Ducked out of the cold and into a gallery now and then to warm her cheeks and check the competition. She stayed away from the Spartan. Curtis wouldn't like seeing her, feeling as if she were putting pressure on him to accept her students' pieces for the show in June. As it was, she was already beginning to doubt it would happen. The man, though a friend who'd helped her when she'd started, had a reputation as well, and she knew she could push him only so far.

A comedy double-feature at the Little Carnegie: the Marx Brothers, and Cary Grant, from the ridiculous to the sublime.

A snack at the Russian Tea Room, and when she returned to the street she found herself checking her watch. Twice. Three times as she slipped into a taxi that brought her back to the place where it all began, and all ended.

And she realized then, as she'd never done before, that New York was now no longer her home. As she rode back to the station she smiled to herself, wondering how her mother would respond if she ever told her she actually missed an Oxrun weekend: the quiet, the walks through the Station's own park, the games in the middle of the street, the shops ... and the absence of a feeling of being hemmed in. In spite of her mind's reactions to her struggle and the aftermath, she realized that what Oxrun had given her was freedom from entrapment.

She giggled, again when the cabbie stared in the rearview mirror and accelerated slightly.

She grinned most of the way home, and now broke into a quiet laugh when the old Buick touring car swung into the parking lot and flashed its lights at her.

Yesterday it would have been menacing; this morning, under the stars and in the quiet, it was warm and it was welcome, and she nearly fell asleep on the short ride home.

On the second-story landing, the wall facing the stairwell had been painted an earthen brown and was centered by a large oval mirror framed in elaborately scrolled and gilded oak. Beneath it, a long, narrow table, cherry wood and polished to such a degree that even now it picked up the dim bulb downstairs as if the wood itself were glowing. She paused on the top step and glanced to her right at the Evanses' door. There was no light at the threshold; they were still in Florida. Two paces forward and a turn on the worn fringed carpet, and toe kicked heel, tripping her into the table. The pain was sharp, brief, a scolding for her clumsiness, and when she righted herself, rubbing at her leg gingerly, she saw the envelope floating on the tabletop, her name printed in red ink across its face. She poked at it with a forefinger, thinking nothing at all but a faint puzzlement, and felt a hard bulge. She lifted it by one comer and the bulge shifted noisily, the sound of her station wagon keys clattering together. She nodded. Looked at the floor as if she could see through it to Kelly's apartment below. A grin. Perfect, she thought as she stuffed it into her pocket. Absolutely perfect.

A touch to the thermostat, and within moments the pipes in the baseboard heating system began to pop and slam. From the workroom a sound almost like hissing. A floorboard near the

99

center of the living room creaked when trod upon. The draperies had all been drawn, and an imperfect meeting of the French doors set the fabric whispering against a draught. The refrigerator hummed sporadically. Wind in the attic. She pulled off her boots and left them by the front door, the soles of her feet rustling through the nap of the carpeting she walked over.

The sound of her breathing.

Not exactly a symphony, but so familiar as to be inaudible until she stood at the side of the bed and listened, and smiled.

The canopy in swirls of green and yellow billowed darkly above her. Here the draperies had been tied back, and the streetlight was gentle in the bedroom air; soft, like smoke. She lay with her hands cupped behind her head, knees drawn up somewhat to bulge the floral quilt. There was a light but not unpleasant scraping at the corners of her eyes, a lulling rhythm to her breathing; yet she would not allow sleep to overcome her now. This was a day not to be released without some moments of savoring, without some leisurely reflection. She understood that something in her life had been altered, though exactly what and for what reasons were still elusive. The fear she had felt leaving the Station had been replaced by something she could only call a sense of well-being, a sense that bordered almost on belonging. But not quite ... not quite. Almost, but not quite.

Her smile was languid. She could feel it at her lips, a reaction without strain.

Her buttocks shifted against the cool sheet, her toes wriggling as though trying to dig in.

Well-being; belonging. She did not frown and she did not struggle. It was only a feeling, and one she knew she would never really be able to put words to in proper fashion. It was an abstraction. An impulse. And an undercurrent of determination that slipped very close to anger—for whatever it was would have to be protected or she would be vulnerable again to the memories that didn't deserve the power they'd had. They were memories, nothing more.

Memories …

Her eyelids fluttered and lowered. Her legs straightened so slowly she scarcely noticed their moving. And her arms slipped in stages down to her sides.

She slept. Without dreams.

Woke when she could no longer hide from the sun. A stretching, then, and a groaning, and absolutely no guilt at all when she saw that the time was less than ten minutes to noon. A roll onto her stomach, a thumping at the pillow, the muffled squeal of a child behind the scrape of a sled's runners. With one eye she peered at the window, saw the hard blue of the sky and the shadows on the sill. The eye closed. She sighed. She smiled into the pillow and suddenly vaulted from the bed.

By one, she had showered and dressed, had washed and dried the dishes from a breakfast she'd almost gulped down so as not to see the calories from the eggs and toast and bacon. A muttering as she replaced Homer on his shelf by the door. Then she drifted through the apartment to pull back the draperies and flood all the rooms with brilliant yellow light. When she was done, she paused in the center of the living room for a moment, remembering she had come to some sort of conclusion just before she'd fallen asleep. It eluded her, however, and it didn't bother her. Whatever it had been had taken root somewhere, and it must have been good or she wouldn't have felt so fine, so loose, with so much ready and patient energy.

She nodded once, sharply. Today she would finish Greg's gift. Or come as close to it as she could. She didn't know why, but it felt right she should work on it—not the sculpture at the college, but the statuette in her workroom. When he had first seen Homer and had heard the story behind it, he'd laughed and touched it gently, hoping (he told her) that some of its luck would rub off on him. She'd never forgotten it, nor had she forgotten the pleading and the frustration that had briefly darkened his face. It had taken her some while before she'd decided to make a copy, some while longer before she knew it would be a mirror image of the original instead of an exact duplicate.

She nodded again. Yes, it was right. His increasing dreary moods and periods of self-doubt, his virtual surrender to his students in lieu of working on his own—who knows, she thought, he may even break out of his slump and stop feeling so jealous.

The telephone rang. She turned casually and took her time walking to the kitchen. It didn't matter if whoever it was hung up before she got there; if it was important they would call back, and if not she didn't want to hear it. Not today, when everything was so fine.

As she lifted the receiver she almost yawned, and nearly choked on a laugh when she heard Greg's voice.

"Well, speak of the devil."

A pause. "Pat, are you all right? I mean, do you have company or something?"

"Nope," she said, reaching out for the nearest chair and pulling it toward her. "I'm alone and getting ready to do some work."

"You didn't come in yesterday." No accusation, not exactly a question. "Luckily, I was able to come to your rescue and keep Danvers from raising the roof."

A palm clapped to her forehead. "Oh my god, I forgot about him completely. I was going to call—"

"I know, I know," he said, a rim of laughter in his voice. "It was a good thing Harriet saw me first. When she told me, and when I called you and you weren't home, I sashayed into the schmuck's office and told him you had an interview in

Minneapolis, contracted a vicious form of typhoid on the way and wouldn't be in until Monday. I'm not sure he bought all of it, but at least you'll live through the weekend." His laughter broke loose, then, while she grinned at the window. "Seriously, though, are you okay, Pat? I mean, there's nothing wrong, is there? I was ... well, I hate to admit this, you realize, but I was worried about you. And when I dropped by after classes you weren't there. Did you, uh ..."

"Yes," she said, drawing up her legs to set her heels on the cushion's edge. "Yes, I went to New York. I had to, Greg."

"You could have called me."

It took her a moment to say, "No. Not this time. I guess it was all that pressure and stuff, too much drinking, too much imagination. I mean, I was beginning to think there were spooks and goblins out there to get me, and every one of them had Ford's fizz painted all over them."

"Fizz? Did you say fizz?"

She pushed her free hand back through her hair. "Fizz. An old Cagney term for puss." She waited, but he made no comment and she stuck her tongue out at the receiver. There were times when she wondered if his sense of humor passed only in one direction. "Anyway," she said into the silence, "I had to get away for a while. I thought I'd be gone the whole weekend, but ... I came back. Late. Greg, so many things have happened lately, and somehow I lost the ability to handle it. So it was either go down to the city or lock myself in a closet."

"Yeah," he said, "I know exactly what you mean. So. Are you okay now?"

"Fine," she said. "Just fine."

"Good. That's good."

"It sure is."

"Great." Her grin became impish. If there was something else he wanted to say she wasn't going to drag it out of him.

He'd have to do it on his own. "So what are you going to do today?"

"Work," she said, glancing over her shoulder to the hallway. "A project I have here that's pretty important now."

"Oh really?" And she frowned at the abrupt frost on the line. "Got yourself a commission or something?"

"No," she said sharply, not caring if he bridled. "No, it's not, Greg. A private thing, and something I can't talk about until it's done, all right?"

"Sure, sure. I know what they are."

I'll bet, she thought uncharitably.

"So."

"Buttons," she said.

"Huh?"

"Sew buttons. Something my mother used to say when I was a kid."

"Oh." A crackling, then, and she was puzzled until she heard it again; he was opening a pack of cigarettes. "Say, Pat, is this work of yours going to last very long? I mean, I don't suppose you'd be done in time to catch a show over in Harley. Maybe a couple of drinks after?"

She almost accepted, but she sensed a fine edge on his temper and did not want to spend the evening walking on eggs. Especially when she knew her present mood wouldn't fade.

"Pat?"

"Greg, I'd like to, really, but I want to get this done as soon as I can."

"It's really that important."

"Yes. At least it is to me. And as long as I feel like working again, I don't want to waste it." Her laugh was forced. "You know how it is, Greg. Strike while the iron's hot or it all turns to crap." She waited. He said nothing. "You do understand, don't you?"

"Sure I do, Pat. You know I do." A rustling, then, as he changed hands. "Well, look, I'll—hell, there's someone at the door. Hey, I'll call you tomorrow, okay? Maybe we can go for a drive, watch the snow buggies tear up the wildlife, okay?"

"Sure, yes. As a matter of fact, I'll probably have cabin fever by then, so I'll need to get out. Call me around noon, okay?"

"You got it, Pat. And Pat ..."

"Yes?"

"I, uh ... I'm glad you're all right. You really had me worried for a while there."

"I had me worried, too. Talk to you tomorrow."

The connection broken, she lowered her feet to the floor again and leaned back until the chair tilted, bumped against the doorframe. Her ankles hooked around the legs. It was incredible, and not a little enervating, what an admixture of feelings she had when she spoke to him over the phone. Motherly and antagonistic, challenging and daring, exasperation and quiet. She was positive he'd been about to tell her at last that he loved her, and had backed away as he had every other time. Now, however, she did not feel angry, nor relieved. Angry because he'd failed to give voice to his feelings; relieved because it had always produced in her a need to run, to fend him off, embattled as she was with memories of Leonard and their idyll that had died so suddenly. He'd never harmed her, never cheated on her; what they had had simply eroded because they'd no foundation except short-lived romance. And when Lauren had been born ... and had died ... not even joy or sorrow could pull them together for more than a moment.

It had been, simply put and simply meant, a mistake.

And she didn't want to make that mistake again.

The chair thumped back to the floor and she rose, grabbed Homer from his perch and wandered into the workroom, shaking off Greg and the call and a fuzzy image of Leonard the moment she stepped over the threshold.

Into a room small and oddly shaped, hooking around into an el at the back, a narrow windowed space that could easily have been made into a closet if it hadn't been for the door leading to never-used back steps. That part of the room was behind the mirror on the landing, and she knew from a single visit that Mrs. Evans had turned her identical space into a sewing room filled with bolts and scraps and the smell of a hundred spools of thread.

The floor was covered by the cheapest rug she'd been able to find, one that wouldn't mind being layered with fine dust. The walls were papered in stripes and roses, the left one partially stripped until she'd given up and left it. Pedestals, workbench, an easel, rolls of canvas and stretching boards—this was a haven for comfortable chaos. Neither the window in the el nor the one practically jammed against the wall shared with the bathroom were curtained or shaded, and the sun just starting its winter dive to the west filled the room so brightly she had to squint until she could see.

Greg. She shook her head once and pulled a smock off a wall peg, shrugged into it and set Homer on a tall barstool, just to the right and behind a matching stool-and-wide-board that held a fifteen-inch cube of grey-white marble. Most of it had been chiseled and chipped to sharp pieces on the floor, leaving behind all of Homer's mirror-twin save its hind legs. Its body was already as detailed as she'd wanted, its face complete but for the eyes and the teeth. She stood in front of it and stared over at Homer. "Doesn't have your personality," she said, grinning as she rubbed her palms together for starting. "And if he doesn't like it, you know I'm going to use it to bash in his head."

She walked around the stool slowly, a finger reaching out now and then to remind herself of a correction, of a speck in the stone she considered polishing out. Then she reached for a rag and dusted lightly its cocked head, looked down at the block where its feet were still embedded. That first, she decided, and the face last. Because once the face was done she would want Greg to see it, and she didn't want him spoiling things by making jokes about her method. It was bad enough he pulled every chestnut from the fire—This looks easy; all you do is chip away everything that's not what you're doing; it would be worse if he didn't appreciate both the work and the hope behind it.

"And that," she said to Homer, "is why we haven't been in here for a while. You know, a shrink would love me, he really would. Avoidance-approach, isn't that what they call it? God, it's been so long, Homer, I can't even remember."

She leaned closer, blindly reaching out to pick up the chisel.

"You know, pal, I'm glad you didn't go with me yesterday. You'd hate the city. Too big, too noisy, they'd want to run you through a Xerox and stick you in a Times Square shop window for the tourists or something. Better you should stick to the kitchen, you know?"

She started at the uncompleted block, envisioning the paws, matching them with Homer's, searching again for flaws that might crack the entire piece to dust.

Then she blinked and straightened and stared right at Homer.

"What... ?"

The chisel dropped to the floor unnoticed as she turned and hurried back to the kitchen. Stood in the doorway and saw herself coming in for breakfast. At the stove. At the cupboards. Pushing Homer aside while she ate and had her tea. Pushing

Homer aside while she cleaned up afterward. Setting Homer on his shelf ... setting Homer on his shelf ...

"No."

She walked around the table, searching the floor, the counters, even looking down the crack between the refrigerator and the stove.

"No, damnit!"

But yesterday (yesterday, or a hundred years ago?) she had run upstairs with the glove she'd found in the box, with Homer in her handbag. Homer had gone to his shelf, and the glove had been tossed onto the table.

Now the glove was gone, and Homer had been moved.

Chapter 11

Less than twenty minutes on her hands and knees in kitchen and bedroom convinced her she'd not find the glove, and it took far less than a second to dispel any thought that she'd been mistaken. It had been there. On the table. And Homer had been placed on his shelf before she'd left.

Which meant that someone had been in the apartment while she'd been in New York.

She dropped heavily onto the sofa in the living room, hands clasped between her knees as she stared blindly at the coffee table. A pile of magazines on the right, ashtray in the center, a half-read paperback novel on the left. She saw none of it. There was only a streak of enhanced light from the windows arrowing across the dark wood to the filigreed raised edges. It blinded her, but she did not turn away. It shimmered, seeming to drift away, then winked out and back when a large bird passed between it and the sun. She saw none of it.

What she saw instead was a shadow, features and edges indistinguishable as it slipped through her home— her home! — and made its way into the kitchen where it picked up the glove and moved the statuette from one place to another. Again and twice more she followed it, shaking her head in bewilderment because it made no sense, no sense at all. There was no question, of course, but that it had to have been Oliver. Without a single bit of his trappings he was more like a child than a twenty-one-year-old student flirting with manhood. She recalled a day last spring when he'd come to class without his Stetson, trembling like an addict without his drug. Someone on the quad had snatched it on the run, and it wasn't until Ben had tracked the prankster down and retrieved it that Oliver had been able to think straight, to work. Pat hadn't quite understood it then, and she did not understand it now. He was much too old to rely on such charms, certainly too old to continue retreating into a romanticized era where his own ungainly size would have been a symbol for strength, not ridicule. He was much too old, and yet obviously not old enough.

Her hands slapped her thighs and she rose, hesitant until she saw his traipsing through what was hers, without her permission, breaking in like a common criminal for a lousy goddam glove.

She called Harriet, learned the two boys were with her, and instructed the three of them to remain where they were until she arrived. Her coat fought with her, her hands fumbled through the pockets until she remembered the wind had taken her cap that night. *Well,* she thought as she stomped angrily down the stairs, *at least I'm not calling it a monster anymore.*

Across the street and up the block to High, over to Fox Road and she stood in front of a Victorian much like her own on a much smaller scale. Evergreen shrubs lined the porch that ringed the house, and the pines in the front yard were a good thirty feet over the roof. Harriet was standing at the front door, waiting, smiling anxiously and rubbing her hands together against the chill.

"Hey, Doc," she said as Pat took the steps. "We're—"

Pat brushed past her and turned right into the parlor, a room turned into a tropical forest by hanging ferns and potted rubber plants, the greens of the carpet and furniture, the tinted shades that as far as she knew had never been lifted. The house was warm, too warm for her taste, and she had her coat unbuttoned before she'd stopped walking.

110

Harriet hovered at her side, confused, her left hand pulling at the buttons of her plaid shirt, then dropping to rub against the snug fit of her jeans. Ben was sitting in a large wing-back in front of the far side windows, his legs crossed, a glass of dark liquid in his hand. He smiled, though a glance to Harriet asked the obvious question. Oliver was by the fireplace. Cowboy shirt, jeans, black boots, and his gloves poking from his right hip pocket.

"Hi, Doc," Ben said, shifting as though to rise. "You weren't in class yesterday. You're not sick, are you?"

"No," she said. She stared at Fallchurch.

Oliver tried and failed to meet her gaze, half-turned to poke a pointed toe at an andiron.

"Oliver, how could you," she said quietly. "How could you do it?"

Harriet moved past her to sit on the couch, straggles of hair slipping over her eyes. She licked at her lips, looked to Ben, who shrugged and sat back, sipping at his drink.

"Oliver."

"I'm sorry, Doc." The voice was much smaller than the body from which it issued, just barely under control and its sentiment totally false.

"If you're sorry, why did you do it in the first place? Why couldn't you have waited? Is it that damned important? I mean really, Oliver, is it that so goddamned important?"

Harriet gasped, and Pat glared at her, wondering if she had been there, too.

"Yes," Oliver said then, stronger, jamming his hands into his pockets and leaning his shoulder against the mantel. "Yes, it is that important. And if you don't mind me saying so, Doc, it seems to me you should have known it."

Unbelievable; it was absolutely unbelievable. And in catching the look that passed between Ben and the girl it was

111

evident they were on Oliver's side, condoning the break-in in spite of the trivial reason.

"I'm sorry," she said coldly, "but I fail to understand how—"

"Aw, shit, Doc," Ben said in disgust, thumping his glass down on the floor beside his chair. "Jesus Christ, you know damned well how we feel about this. Unless you're so wrapped up in your new department that you don't notice us anymore."

"We?" she said, ignoring the jibe. "We?" She looked to Harriet, back to Ben and lifted a hand. "What … what do you two have to do with—"

"I told you," Oliver said. "Didn't I tell you she didn't care? Didn't I tell you, huh? She can't even see us anymore. We're just faces now, just like the rest of her students. Hell, I told you."

Pat put a hand to her forehead, the other gesturing for silence just as Ben started to speak. "Wait a minute," she said. Her eyes closed briefly, opened, looked at each of them in turn. "Wait a minute, just wait one little minute here. Why do I get the sudden feeling none of us know what we're talking about?"

"The call," Oliver said, almost sneering. "As if you didn't know." He moved off the hearth and stood in front of Harriet. "You couldn't wait to tell her, right?" Harriet denied it with a shake of her head. "Couldn't wait. Soon as I hung up you called her, right? Before we got here, and now …" He waved a disgusted hand toward Pat.

"What call?" Pat said.

Oliver opened his mouth, closed it, a fish gulping air. "The … call."

"Oliver, I don't know anything about any call. I was talking about your glove."

He slapped quickly at his pocket, pulled out his gloves and held them toward her. His bewilderment was comical as he showed them to his friends, and Pat took the moment to sag into an armchair that faced the front windows. She folded her hands loosely over her stomach and crossed her legs. Behind her, a fern tickled the back of her neck.

"You don't know about the call," Ben said.

Pat shook her head. "But as long as you're all talking about it and getting angry at me for it, you might as well tell me what it's all about, don't you think?"

"Oh … shit," Oliver said, his shoulders sagging as he skirted the coffee table and dropped to the cushion beside Harriet.

"Never mind," Pat said wearily. Her head tilted back until it rested against the chair and she was looking at the plaster ceiling. "I think I can guess."

"It's not that we doubted you," Ben began; but when she looked at him without moving her head he cut himself off and glared at his knees.

"But you do," she said quietly, knowing she sounded like a teacher about to scold, knowing how she sounded and not caring at all. "You doubted—and maybe you still do doubt my intentions—so one of you—Oliver, I'd say—called Mr. Curtis at the Spartan Gallery either yesterday or today. I imagine you thought your earnestness would goad him into a decision in your favor. Knowing Curtis as I do, though, he was probably very polite and gently enthusiastic and told you he would let you know his decision before very long. Then, as an afterthought, he suggested you get in touch with me and have me call him at my earliest convenience. Preferably on Monday, if it would be all right with me."

"Christ," Ben muttered, "you must have been standing right next to him."

Pat couldn't answer for a moment. She searched the ceiling and the hearth for strength, lowered her gaze to Harriet and asked her with a look why she had allowed Fallchurch to make such an ass of himself. Harriet, however, did not hear her; she had taken Oliver's hand and was patting it maternally. *God save me,* she thought, and reined in the anger that was too close to explosion.

"You may have blown it, you know," she said, looking down to her hands. "Curtis does not take pressure well. He doesn't take it at all."

"I didn't threaten him or anything," Oliver said sullenly. "I was polite."

"That and fifty cents will get you a cup of coffee in the luncheonette," she told him.

"Great," he said. "I can't drink the damned stuff."

There was a pause during which Pat considered screaming and wringing the boy's neck; the contemplation wrested from her when Ben began to laugh. A nervous, high-pitched laugh that infected his friends and caused her to smile. Incorrigible, she decided as she covered her mouth with a palm. I don't know why I bother to put up with them.

She waited until they were done, then pushed herself out of the chair and bunched her hands in her coat pockets. "Now listen to me, you three," she said, her stern tone only half mocking. "I can honest to god understand your impatience. I'm not that old that I don't remember, as someone reminded me only a couple of days ago. But you really are going to have to trust me. God knows what Curtis will do now, but I'll call him first thing Monday and mend any fences that might have been knocked down. Meanwhile, keep your minds on your work, okay? Leave the arrangements to me. All right? All right."

She left with an upward jerk of her head and walked slowly back home, enjoying the sharply fresh air and thinking of the harsh city odors she'd once thought were so wonderful, until she'd had something much better for contrast.

With her head down and taking short, less purposeful strides, it took her nearly five minutes before she was at the front walk, watching as Linc Goldsmith used a short-handled broom to knock snow off the porch railing. "Beautiful day," she said brightly as she headed for the door.

"Some say," Goldsmith muttered. He was bundled in a faded hunting jacket and heavy corduroy trousers, a pumpkin-covered hat jammed down over his head, ear-flaps untied and angled out from the sides. His long bony face was pinched red from the cold, his hawk's nose threatening to stab into a thick upper lip.

"Why, Mr. Goldsmith," she admonished. Futile, she knew, but she felt too good to resist. "I mean, how can you say that when the snow had stopped, the birds are out, the children are playing … it's almost like Christmas, wouldn't you say? A brisk walk for the blood, a cup of hot soup."

He stopped and turned his head slowly toward her, the beak of his hat shadowing his eyes. "Easy for you to say, Miss. You ain't got the damned kids tramping all over the place."

She looked down at the yard, at the foot-plus deep snow untouched except for a few bird tracks and a place near the hedge where a dog had floundered. "Hardly tramping all over, Mr. Goldsmith."

"Not now," he said, as if she should have known better. "Night. Have t'get my sleep and they come around banging at the walls, climbing to the porch." He spat over the side, dark tobacco juice. "Oughta all be home. Not like the old days. My old man'd switch my ass bloody if I ever came home with some neighbor complaining. Ain't right." He glared at her, his jaw working slowly. "You teachers oughta teach 'em better. Give 'em values. Soft is what they are. Soft in the heart, soft in the head."

She tried to remain solemn, to at least take him seriously. But with his faded straw hair jutting out from under the cap, his oversized coat, and his cuffed and uncreased trousers he reminded her too much of an overworked scarecrow. And dire grumblings from a scarecrow were not exactly a prophet's strength.

"I do my best," she told him, with a smile so wide she could feel her cheeks ache. "But none of us are perfect."

"Could work at it, though," he said, turning back to his work.

A snort meant for a laugh and his shoulder began to shake. Pat groaned loudly to show she'd heard him and stepped inside, closed the door. It was Homer's turn now, and his reflection she was making. But she hadn't taken two steps up when Kelly's door opened and Abbey beckoned her back down.

"What?" she said, slipping out of her coat. "Never mind, don't tell me." She put a finger to her chin and considered the front door. "Kelly has met this absolutely fabulous man in Harley. He's rich, owns a bank, and he has a twin brother. Naturally he's much too busy to come pick you guys up tonight, so you agreed to meet them in town. And naturally, Kelly is too chicken to ask me to borrow my car because King's still hasn't finished with whatever needs fixing." She looked back and grinned. Abbey was laughing.

The brakes, Abbey signed, her expression doleful and resigned. *The mechanic says if we don't have them repaired now we're going to end up in a ditch if we drive the car again.*

"And the man with the bank?"

No man. We just want to go to the movies. Kelly thinks the manager is cute.

Pat couldn't help the laugh that bubbled in her throat. "Well, is he?"

Abbey shrugged, waggled her hand. *He was so-so.*

"Does he have a brother?"

Pat, that's not fair.

"You know," she said, "I really ought to start charging you guys rent or something. But sure, why not. I'm not going anywhere tonight. I'll get Goldsmith to let me in." She fished in her pockets. "Nope. I'll bring them down later, okay? Give me a couple of minutes and I'll let you have them."

Abbey beamed. *I'll pay you back.*

"You do and I'll cut your throat. Just tell Kelly I want an invitation to the wedding."

A spurt of laughing applause followed her up the stairs, continued until the door shut and her coat was on the rack. Then she sighed and decided she was hungry again, made herself a sandwich for lunch and, thinking of her breakfast, forced down a small salad. Once done, she rolled up her sleeves and went into the workroom, lost almost an hour before she remembered the keys. Telling herself she needed a break anyway, she dusted off her hands and brought the keys down to Abbey's. When she knocked, however, there was no response; when she rang the bell (which would activate a series of bulbs throughout the apartment) Abbey didn't answer. She shrugged and ran upstairs again, grabbed an envelope from the secretary in the living room and stuffed the keys in, put Abbey's name on it and left it on the table by the front door. Tit for tat, she thought, and grinned when she imagined what her mother would say.

"Patrice, you mean to say you actually leave your car keys right there in the foyer? Right there where anybody can pick them up and steal your car? Honestly, I just don't know what you're thinking of."

And if Pat mentioned friendship and trust and Oxrun Station, her mother would only scoff and triple-lock the penthouse door.

"Score one for Oxrun," she said as she returned to the workroom, and lost time again until the dark arms of the trees had snaked across the floor and set her eyes to blinking.

She stepped back and wiped the back of her hand over her face. It was nearly done at last. Tomorrow. Perhaps tomorrow, if she could bring herself to work for another five or six hours. There were only the teeth left, and the way her eyes were stinging she knew she didn't dare attempt to do them now. One slip, one chipped tooth, and the whole thing would be ruined.

"Lucky boy, Homer," she said, returning the statuette to its place in the kitchen. "Only a few more hours and it'll be all done."

She yawned, and stretched. A nap on the sofa, she decided. *An hour, and then I'll cook me some dinner.*

But just as she lay down she sat up again, quickly. "Damn!" They'd done it to her again. Oliver and Ben and Harriet, by making that ill-timed telephone call and thinking that was what she'd gone over about, had sidetracked her from demanding an apology from Oliver.

And it was curious, very curious. As she recalled the confused conversation and saw Oliver standing next to the mantel, she could not bring to mind anything in his face that even hinted of guilt once the matter had been straightened out. Almost as if he'd not done it at all.

A mystery, she thought, a sudden great yawn making her jaw pop. *God, I hate mysteries!*

But her legs were already too relaxed to support her, her arms too heavy to do more than flop. The glove, then, was something she would have to face later. Right now she would rest. After all, it wasn't as if something had been taken, something that was hers.

And when the telephone rang, she muttered, "Go to hell," and slept.

Chapter 12

The knocking was light, and persistent. Pat didn't want to hear it, but it refused to leave, becoming louder, more frantic, adding to it the faint call of her name. She groaned and sat up, wincing at a sharp tug in the small of her back. The heels of her hands pressed hard against her eyes to drive off sleep, and what felt like a thin layer of cotton over her teeth made her want to spit. It was a stupid thing, taking a nap in the late afternoon; she never felt rested afterward, and though this was one of the few times she'd awakened without a headache she still felt as though a rubber hammer were working hard to rectify the error.

It was dark. And when she swung her legs to the floor and stood, a shin cracked against the coffee table. She swore and reached behind her, fumbling along the outline of the sofa until her hand found the brass pole of the floor lamp. A tug at the chain and both bulbs glared on, shutting her eyes against imagined pain while her free hand rubbed angrily at her leg.

"All right!" she called when the knocking started again.

She walked slowly to the door, massaging her back, her neck, shaking her head vigorously until she thought she could at least pretend successfully to be human again. She wondered at the time, certain that more than her allotted hour had passed and hoping it wasn't so late that she'd be awake until dawn because she'd slept so late now.

"All right, all right," as her hand reached for the knob and slipped off. She glowered at it, tried again, and pulled the door

119

open. Harriet was in the hallway, coat open, hands ungloved, and her eyes puffed from hard weeping. Pat immediately reached out for her and took her into the room, closing the door softly and guiding her to the sofa. The girl slipped out of her coat awkwardly, her head stiff and her gaze steadily on the magazine pile while she swallowed several times and rubbed a trembling hand across her lips.

"Coffee," Pat said, and without giving Harriet an opportunity to protest she hurried into the kitchen and set the kettle on the stove. A choked-back sob drifted after her. She pinched hard at her cheek to bring herself more awake, drummed her fingers on the stove to hurry the boiling. There was, however, no real rush to get back; she could have guessed easily what had happened, that one of the boys had attempted something with Harriet that Harriet wasn't prepared for. For all the girl's outward worldliness in a campus situation far different from her own, she was still a small-town girl whose parents demanded values much of the rest of the student body had long since replaced with values of its own. It would come as no surprise to her to learn Harriet was still a virgin.

The water boiled, the kettle shrilled, and within minutes she had cups, sugar, and creamer on a tray.

Harriet was leafing through a magazine, looked up sheepishly and sniffed. A wadded tissue was buried in one palm.

"Drink," Pat said. "You look like you're freezing to death. My god, girl, how long have you been walking out there?"

"What time is it?" Harriet asked, holding her cup in both hands and sipping. Then she glanced at the watch on her own wrist. "Eight. About two hours, I guess. Give or take."

Pat dropped into the far corner and pulled one leg to the cushion. Watched silently, wondering if perhaps she should have added some brandy to the coffee. Harriet's face, she could see now, was less ravaged by her weeping than it was by the brutal dry cold — her cheeks were flushed as if burned, her lips cracked and chapped, her red hair tossed and tangled by too many encounters with corner-winds she hadn't bothered to duck. A glance up to the windows. Beyond, the air was black and brittle, cold just looking at it, without need of a wind to bring the temperature home.

Harriet set her cup back on the tray. "Thanks," she said.

"No problem. What's the trouble?"

The girl hunched over her legs, hands gripping her knees tightly, leaving them to clasp into a single large fist. "After you left today."

"Oh."

Harriet suddenly gestured angrily at the air. "It isn't fair! They think you owe them something. They think it's your job to make them rich and famous. All they've talked about for the past four months is that dumbass show in New York." She turned to her, and her eyes had narrowed in rage, in sorrow. "I wish you'd never brought it up, Doc, I really do. It's not that I'm ungrateful or anything, but ..." She gestured again, helplessly. "You know how they are."

Pat inhaled slowly and puffed her cheeks, blew out the breath loudly and rapidly. "I know how they used to be, yes. Assuming, of course, we're talking about the cowboy and Ben. I know they used to be eager, and enthusiastic, and they used to listen to advice even if they didn't like what they were hearing. I know they used to have a grip on the stage of their development, and they used to believe that they had a definite large slice of raw talent that needed to be directed. It goes without saying this all applies to you, too."

Harriet lifted a shoulder in an apathetic shrug. "Yeah, well, they're not that way anymore."

"Are you blaming me?"

There was no need for an answer.

"Oliver said he wouldn't have felt so stupid talking to that Mr. Curtis if you'd've taught him how to deal with people like that. He said the guy was pretty close to being rude to him, and Oliver almost hung up on him."

"Oh my god, he didn't, did he?"

Harriet shook her head. "But he said he felt like it. And he says ..." Her hands twisted in her lap, her head bowed.

Pat watched the display for only a moment before lifting her gaze to the windows. The lamp behind her cast little light beyond the sofa and the table, and the panes were gauzed rectangles set in winter-dark ice. It occurred to her rather incongruously that she ought to take the curtains down at least and have them cleaned before they yellowed, maybe even take the draperies to the cleaners. She couldn't remember the last time she'd done it.

Harriet was saying something, looked at her reproachfully when she realized Pat wasn't listening. Pat smiled weakly, nodded for her to continue.

"We've been arguing almost since you left, you know."

"I hope," Pat said, "someone took my side."

"I did." The pain, then, the effort it had cost her to say those two words, and Pat wanted to embrace her, to rock her, but did nothing.

"Well? I guess you're here either to warn me or ask me a favor. A little of both, right? Would you rather have some wine instead of all that caffeine?"

Harriet, startled into a brief smile, shook her head. "Ben said he was beginning to think we were getting a raw deal, that we should stop listening to everything you say and get things like shows and stuff done on our own. He said we were good enough, we must be or you wouldn't have started all this. I told him he wouldn't know the first place to start and he said he could always ask Mr. Billings. He said you weren't the only one in the world who knows how to do this stuff."

"He's right," Pat told her. "He's absolutely right. There's no reason at all why any of you should take my word as gospel, ever. As an expert, yes, but not as law." She waited, but there was no reaction. "There's more."

"Oliver wants to quit school and live in New York."

Pat opened her mouth, but the sound that broke out was more like a croak than the oath she wanted. She stood and paced out of the lamp's glow, back again and stood in front of Harriet, the table between them. "Oliver Fallchurch, if I may use my professorial rights here, is an addlepated adolescent whose grasp of the realities of the field he thinks he's chosen is virtually nonexistent in any context whatsoever."

Harriet stared at her, obviously fighting a grin. "What?"

"Ollie is a shithead," she said. "He wouldn't last a week in New York. What about Ben?"

Harriet shrugged. "Sometimes he agrees with Oliver, sometimes with me. But he's mad, Doc. He's really mad. And I don't understand it because you never promised anything for any of us, except that you'd try this Curtis for us. That's all you ever said, right?"

She nodded.

"Well, that's what I told them. And the next thing I knew we were running all over the place yelling and screaming and Oliver was punching out my mother's ferns ..." She stopped and giggled. "You ever try to punch out a fern?"

Pat sighed her relief and sat again, closer this time, feeling less at bay. "Harriet, you know there are times when you're not nearly as dumb as you let people think."

The girl started as if touched by a flame, rubbed a hand gently along one cheek.

"So what do you want me to do, Harriet? Do you want me to talk to them?"

"No!" Her hand shifted to cover her mouth. "I'm sorry; I didn't mean to snap at you. But when they left they were ready to kill, if you know what I mean, and I just wanted to let you know. Maybe by Monday they'll be okay, I don't know. Maybe. I just thought you should know because—"

"I should be prepared for the worst?"

Harriet looked at her, the lamplight bleaching her color, yet sifting shadows into her eyes. "Yes," she said quietly. "Something like that." Then, before Pat could react, she was on her feet and rushing toward the door. One arm caught in a sleeve as she tried to fling on her coat and she cursed at it loudly, glancing fearfully back over her shoulder as if Pat might come after her.

Pat, however, remained where she was. As suddenly angered as she was over the girl's dramatics, she knew better than to follow. All she would get now would be more of the same, only this time couched in typical Trotter hysterics. And when the door slammed shut, she rose and walked to the French doors, pulled aside the curtain and watched as Harriet darted into the street to the opposite sidewalk, running in spite of the patches of snow still on the pavement, her coat flapping behind her, her arms close to her sides. She was gone in seconds.

A week ago, even a couple of days, and she would have been scrambling for the closet to hide in, or for the telephone to call Greg and demand protection and sympathy for the collapse of her world or the destruction of her enemies. She might even have had a glimpse of something lurking in the early-evening darkness, out there beyond the trees, waiting for her and watching.

But that was done now.

124

All she could do was feel an understandable twinge of self-pity for what she believed was her own failure in properly preparing the trio for what lay beyond Hawksted's walls, and a certain amount of disgusted anger at Oliver's childishness and Ben's fickle loyalty. She would talk to them, but she would wait until Monday when her temper had calmed and her mood stabilized. For now she had work to do. Homer and his twin. And she would be damned if Oliver was going to take Greg's pleasure from her.

By midnight the grizzly's canines were finished; by one her eyes had grown so tired they felt in danger of crossing. She grinned at her work and swept the dust and the chips onto the floor. Tomorrow would be soon enough to take care of the cleaning. Then she wandered into the kitchen and pulled a bottle of brandy from the cupboard over the refrigerator, filled a juice glass halfway and toasted her reflection in the dark-framed window. As she lifted her glass to drink, however, a tiny piece of marble fell from her hair into the liquid. She blinked at it stupidly, sighed and fished it out with a finger. Not exactly the most sophisticated method of taking care of a problem, but one she was used to, forever finding chunks and fragments of stone in her purse, in her car, even in her pockets. It was an occupational hazard, and one of the tiny-reasons-made-huge that had caused Leonard to leave her.

Greg, on the other hand, thought it a fascinating characteristic, an identification of her which belonged to no one else. He had, in fact, been with her and the trio on several afternoon excursions to the quarry. And he'd confessed to her once that, like the trio, he'd gone back there on his own, alone, just to stare at the gaping hole in the hillside, just to wonder about things that to someone else would not be important.

Leonard would have called it a rock pile, she thought without malice; *a rock pile, and nothing else.*

The smile that parted her lips grew slightly melancholy; she'd been thinking an awful lot about her ex-husband these days, another sign of the pressure she'd finally dug out of with her trip to New York. There was no affection there, however, except one for a distant, onetime friend one seldom saw anymore. A wondering, as she did every other June about those in her high school graduating class. Which of them had become real estate salesmen, which policemen, which outlaws. Which of them, like her, had finally shucked the conventions taught so diligently by her teachers and had discovered there was a living out there in the world that was defined in a much larger sense than by the size of a paycheck or a white-cottage mortgage or the number of children one had before one was thirty.

Not many, she guessed as she replaced the brandy and set the glass in the sink. Not many at all.

There was a knock on the door as she moved slowly toward the bedroom. She stopped, listened, thinking perhaps it was Harriet returned with another episode to be unburdened of. A glance at the digital clock on the nightstand told her it was almost two, and a moment of tension stiffened her spine until she heard a voice whispering her name. She grinned and took her time answering. Laughed aloud when she yanked open the door and Greg took a step backward, as if expecting a blow.

"You do know what time it is," she said, stepping aside and waving him in.

"I am not drunk," he insisted, heading directly for the sofa without taking off his coat. He sat primly, hands in his lap, knees and ankles together. "I am not drunk."

"I believe you," she said, still grinning, the scent of bourbon strong in his wake. "But I repeat: you do know what time it is, don't you?"

He nodded, and leaned back, his hands slipping to the cushions on either side of his hips. "I was enjoying a small tot, as it were, in the Inn, as it were, when I thought about you cooped up here all day. I decided it was time you were liberated." He struggled out of his coat and dropped it on the floor. His shirt was dark flannel, opened midway to his abdomen, yet he still slipped a finger under the back of his collar and tugged at it as if he were being choked. "I said to myself that it wasn't fair you should be abed on a Saturday night. At least not alone."

"Greg," she said carefully.

A grandiose wave was meant to dispel her objection. "I am a dear and close, though not so old, friend, am I right? Who else to lay your troubles to? Who else to spill your guts to in such a time of tribulation?"

"You've been taking lessons from Danvers on the sly, you bastard." She sat beside him, just out of reach. "Greg, why didn't you go home?"

He closed his eyes, his head resting on the sofa's arched-wood back. "I missed your voice."

"You have a telephone."

"I might have gotten you out of bed."

She coughed back a laugh.

"Your car is parked at the curb," he said then, his voice quiet, the words not quite slurred. "Dangerous. You should keep it in the driveway."

She frowned for a moment, shook her head to rid herself of the curious impression he was at once scolding her and sounding relieved. She leaned closer to him and touched his arm. "Greg, what is it? Is it that girl, Susan?"

"Who?"

"Susan. Susan Haslet. The one who was killed in the accident."

His face creased in an effort to think. Then: "No."

She couldn't resist it—she slid next to him and kissed his cheek lightly, laid a hand on his chest and slipped her fingers under his shirt. "What?"

He stirred, but kept his eyes closed. "I was thinking," he said.

"Good."

"I was thinking about you. I was thinking ... I couldn't figure out why it was that so much of your work sold when I can count on the fingers of two hands how many of my things have left my easel. I was thinking that maybe you had some kind of potion, something you gave buyers to loosen up their wallets. I was thinking ..."

When he paused she pulled away, not shocked but somewhat pained at the bitterness that had crept into his tone. He sounded so much like Oliver it was uncanny, and she had to resist the urge to slap him as hard as she could. An urge that passed the moment she saw his lips grow taut as he fought to bury a smile.

"I was thinking all that, you see, and decided it was sour grapes." His eyes snapped open, and his hand slipped to the back of her neck. She did not resist. "You asked me if I'd been drinking."

"Shut up," she said, and kissed him.

"I was," he said, making her laugh and back away. He sighed loudly. "Drinking and expostulating and making a damned fool of myself so I decided I needed some salvation." His hand went to the top button of her shirt. "You either have a hell of a case of dandruff or you've been working."

She grabbed his hand and pressed it hard against her breast. "If you don't shut up, Greg ..."

His lips brushed her cheek, her ear. "You work too hard." Moved to the side of her neck. "Much too hard." To the hollow of her throat. "You smell like stone." Hands unbuttoning the shirt, lips to the rise of her breasts. "All work and no play." Her bra parted in the front. A chill across her flesh, pleasant, anticipation. "You need someone to protect you against all work and no play." She shrugged the shirt off her shoulders, concentrating on his touch while her hands moved to pull his shirt from his waistband. "I decided it was all sour grapes and I'm going to accept your favor for the next joust." Lips. To her own, to her chin, to her throat.

She let a small groan slip from her, laced her hands through his dark hair as he slipped past her breasts to her stomach. She pulled up her legs and worked them to either side of him, waiting, waiting, until the warmth of his breath against her stomach made her swim out of the dream she thought she'd fallen into.

"Greg?"

He turned his head slowly to rest his cheek on her navel.

"Oh ..." She would have said "damn," but he wouldn't have heard her.

Chapter 13

The snow untrapped by the shadows of the trees was brilliant, daystars caught in a crust of white that spread unbroken over the fields beyond the village. Skeletons of orchards, stands of pine, a few shaggy-coated horses were the only dark elements in an otherwise pristine valley. Even the ridges thrown up by the plows on the verges had not yet been completely contaminated by passing traffic; and out here, along Cross Valley Road, the odds of that happening were considerably small. Most of the homes east of this road were farmhouses, most of the people either members of the stoic and hardy few who refused to give in to the larger combines in other parts of the state, or recent settlers who allowed the fields to go to seed, content only in the block-style buildings and the fieldstone fireplaces and the open spaces where their children and their imaginations would run without danger. There were a number of spurs off Cross Valley, each digging closer to the back wall of hills, only one of which had a name— Pointer's, over which Greg drove his VW with confidence born of the extremely lucky and the marvelously foolhardy.

Pat adjusted her sunglasses, muttering every time the loose temples allowed them to slide toward the center of her nose. She had kept her coat buttoned snugly, her muffler snugly wrapped, since the car's heater had given up working just after they'd thumped over the railroad tracks. The windows, then, had been cracked to prevent the windshield from fogging, and though the day was gorgeous and the breeze bracing, she didn't really care to add pneumonia to the outing.

The outing itself was startling enough.

Sometime during the dark morning hours she had managed to get Greg undressed and into her bed. Her mind fuzzy with sleep, her lips working at a laugh that never quite came to surface, she'd fallen in beside him and snaked an arm under his neck. Drifted off, and had awakened with his left palm cupping her breast. She'd kissed him and he'd moaned in his sleep, kissed him again and let her hand slip tickling between his legs. Kissed him a third time, tasting the inside of his lips with her tongue and opening her eyes to find him staring at her. She'd almost laughed, held it in check until he had realized he was awake and made love to her. Gently. So slowly she wasn't sure he would be able to finish. But he had done it. And had done it again. Then rested her head on the center of her pillow and had padded off to make breakfast.

Two hours later he suggested they forget whatever plans they had decided on for the day and drive out to the quarry. She had refused him admittance into the workroom, and his none-too-subtle curiosity was sufficient reason to get him out of the house. When she agreed, shoving him back toward the kitchen, he nodded as if he'd known it all along and proceeded to organize a gathering of sustenance, the prime ingredient of which was a Thermos filled with brandy.

"Unless," he said loudly over her halfhearted protests, "you believe that Connecticut has a contingent of St. Bernards. My dear, suppose we get lost, huh? Suppose the wilderness engulfs us and we are trapped in the vicious and uncaring arms of an unrepentant Nature."

"Oh my god," she said, "you've been reading Jack London again."

"You can bet on it, love," he said, and had hustled her out the door almost before she'd had time to snatch up her keys.

The quarry had been her idea, for no reason other than she enjoyed the quiet. Greg had protested mildly, had yielded when she threatened to be "in a mood." Now they had climbed into the forest, the road losing its blacktop and becoming a concrete-hard dirt trail barely wide enough to allow the car through. Branches scraped over the roof, shrubs scratched the sides, and she winced whenever they passed over a low thicket of browned weeds topped with spear-tips of ice. The rattle made her nervous; they were already a considerable distance from the nearest house, and she didn't relish the thought of the VW breaking down and forcing them to walk all the way back. With civilization so near, she had forgotten how desolate this area of the hills could be.

And how quiet now that Greg had stopped his chatter and was concentrating on keeping the vehicle from dropping into a ditch or colliding with a boulder cloaked with heavy snow.

The road banked sharply to the right. Widened, and the young trees to either side marked a place once cleared and used. A series of five old sheds on the right had been weather-stripped of their paint, a sixth and seventh had collapsed in the past from the weight of the seasons. On the left were two chimneys, nothing more. A half-mile further on and the road dipped, all that remained of a railroad spur that had taken quarry blocks down to the depot for shipping. She had once spent an entire Saturday trying to locate the tracks, had concluded someone had ordered the rails and ties taken up once the mining had ceased.

And then, abruptly, the road climbed for a hundred yards, leveled, and Greg braked slowly to keep the car from skidding.

"God," she said breathlessly as she pushed open the door, "I should have come out here sooner."

The Bloodwind

The abandoned quarry was two hundred yards across, less than one hundred wide, and a sheer drop from where she stood of sixty or more feet to the surface of the water. The sides were sheer-faced stone still showing the marks of explosions and cutting, inter-spaced with saplings and brush that somehow made it all seem much more forbidding. The woodland came directly to the edge, save for this one area where Greg had joined her, an open cage, she had first thought, to keep in whatever lived down in the pool.

During the summer she had expected to find any number of students and local kids using it for swimming, but not once during any of her visits had she discovered signs that even picnics had been held here. It had been abandoned, then, not only by the miners, but also by the village; a short-lived enterprise that had yielded low-grade granite and a few tons of marble unobtainable elsewhere and quickly snapped up for the village's municipal buildings.

The snow crunched beneath Greg's workman boots. He stood behind her, one hand on her shoulder.

"You really do like it here, don't you?"

She nestled her head back against his chest. "Yep," she said. "It's a getaway place, if you know what I mean. A good place to scream when throwing dishes doesn't work."

He chuckled and squeezed her shoulder tightly. "For you, maybe. For me it's kind of spooky, don't you think? I mean, all the times you've brought me out here, I've never seen a single animal or one lousy bird."

"No kidding," she said. "I've never noticed."

The road angled downward slightly, leveled again at the base of a six-foot grey boulder the wind and the rain had scoured into the vague shape of a throne. At its front there was a wide seat and armrests, and Pat quickly dug and brushed off the snow so she could take her place and stare out over the quarry. Greg, who distrusted the slippery ground that only ran another eight feet before it plunged over the edge, stood to one side, his hands deep in his pockets, his chin tucked into his muffler.

"Crazy," he muttered.

A faint echo. Fainter still, the chorus of intermittent voices the wind wrung from the gaps that pocked the walls.

"There," She said, pointing to her right. "Over there is where I found the stone for Homer. I nearly killed myself climbing down when I saw it." She smiled at the memory, fear gone and replaced by amazement. "It was wedged in a crack, but I knew what it was as soon as I saw it. I had to have it, you know what I mean, Greg? Nothing was going to keep me from getting it."

Greg leaned forward at the waist, squinting. "You're right. You could've been killed."

A silence, then, as he pulled out the Thermos and poured a dollop into its red cap. He passed it to her and she drank, hugging herself delightedly at the fire in her gullet. She sighed her content, not wanting to frown when she saw how uneasy he seemed, as if the drop to the white-covered frozen surface were pulling at him with invisible, tempting fingers. They hadn't been here together since last fall, last October, but she was positive he hadn't reacted this way then. Not that it mattered. He could have been covering up in order to impress her. This made it a good sign, that he was relaxed enough not to have to play foolish courtship games.

"It's like you told me once, about your paints," she said, quietly, not wanting to disturb the quarry's soft singing.

"What?"

She grinned. "Sorry. What I mean is—you're always telling me how involved you get in your work, how the paints sometimes feel as if they're alive, directing the brush to the right places. Like you don't even have to think about it."

"Rare," he said, making her realize then his frown was merely a squinting against the snow glare. "It doesn't happen very often."

"Oh, not with me," she said. "Not with me. Once I get the stone the way I want it, once it's checked out for flaws and I can really see what I'm going to do in there … well, it's like there's blood there in veins no one can see but me. When it's all done it's almost alive, figuratively. If it isn't, it's just stone. And it looks like just stone. And it sits there like a lump, just waiting for me to smash it."

As she'd spoken she'd begun to lean forward, and the slight downward slope of the seat soon had her slipping until she gripped the broad armrests and yanked herself back.

"You think that dumb bear's alive then?"

She laughed. "To tell you the truth, there are days when I wonder. I'm just glad he can't talk."

"Ah hah," he said, slipping behind the throne and peering over its top at her, making her twist and crane to see his grinning face. "You tell secrets to it, do you?"

"Everything. No holds barred."

He crossed his forearms on the top and rested his chin on it. "Y'know, Oliver told me once there are people who believe, who used to believe that stone has a life force just like trees and grass and people. I think he was going to try to make a statue of you and ravish it at night."

She stuck out her tongue at him. "He has Harriet, and dozens of other nymphs, my dear. He certainly doesn't need a woman almost twice his age."

"Ah, but he's mad about you, you know. He really is."

"Greg, please."

135

"No, I mean it. You should hear him and Ben arguing about the right way to get into—"

She scooped up some snow and tossed it at him, slid off the seat and hurried around it. He was laughing, brushing the snow from his collar and hair. His smile drained with the mirth in his eyes, however, when he saw her standing there, hands on her hips.

"What do you have against Oliver and Ben?" she asked. "It seems that all you're doing lately is running them down. It isn't fair. It really isn't fair."

The day was spoiled. The serenity of the quarry had been shattered by his unthinking jibes: If he'd only been sober last night, if he'd only been there when Harriet had come crying to her, maybe he wouldn't feel quite so … so damned superior.

"Hey, Pat, wait a minute."

From mirth to confusion to sullen anger.

"No. No, I'm not going to wait a minute. I want to know what they've done to you that you're so mean to them now. As I recall, you couldn't get enough of their company last year. Whenever they weren't talking or working with me they were having coffee in the Union with you. Now, all of a sudden, they're my enemies, they're against me, they're using me … what the hell's going on, Greg?"

He straightened, his gloved hands bunched into fists. "Nothing," he said flatly, "is going on, Pat. I told you last week not to give them so much credit, and I mean it. They're kids. I don't care how old they are, they're kids."

"Shit," she said, turning upslope toward the car so she wouldn't have to look at him. "Crap. Bull. What's the matter, was Oliver or Ben making time with that … that Susan Haslet or Abbey Wagner? Were they cutting you out of something, Greg?"

And as soon as she said it she bit hard on her lower lip, spinning around to apologize and seeing that an apology would do her no good at all. He stared at her as if she'd struck him, his eyes without expression. Then he started toward the car along the wind-cleared road, pausing at the higher level to look back at her.

"You coming?"

He made it sound as if nothing would displease him more, and her rage boiled through her shame just long enough for her to shake her head and give him her back. She heard him leaving without even trying to get her to change her mind, heard the VW sputter to life and the rear tires whine until they found purchase as he U-turned and drove back into the forest.

The sound of the engine lasted for quite a long time.

And when it was finally buried by the relentless press of silence she reached up a hand and brushed a tear from her cheek. What she had done had been spiteful, petty jealousy, damned close to ghoulish. Greg loved her, and she had struck out at him when he'd hit too close to home with his criticisms of the trio. Too close. Much too close for her to think of any effective denial, hitting out instead like the child she'd thought she'd left behind decades ago.

She punched at the air.

She kicked at the snow the wind hadn't been able to dislodge.

She walked back to the boulder throne and leaned hard against it, staring across the quarry until her gaze finally sidled to the place where she'd discovered the stone for Homer. She wished she had him now, if only to crack over Greg's head.

"Hell."

The two of them. What a hell of a pair. Both so frightened of each other they couldn't have a simple conversation without either shying away or turning to sarcasm. If one of them didn't say "I love you" damned quick, the next time they met they might do permanent damage. But the way he'd acted today, she'd be damned if she'd be the first.

Then, to the quarry: "Did you hear that? Did you hear what I just said?" She kicked the throne in disgust. "Damn, I sound just like him."

It occurred to her then not to finish his statuette; then to finish it and give it to him anyway, just to see the look on his face.

It also occurred to her that she'd better calm down before she did or said anything that would drive him away. That she didn't want.

She slumped onto the seat again and stared glumly at the far wall. She had certainly done it this time. All he'd been trying to do was caution her against too deep an involvement, and she'd turned on him as if he'd accused her of murder. As usual, she'd reacted strongly to any hint of weakness in herself, a weakness she knew was there but couldn't tolerate showing to others.

Like bragging, for god's sake, about fearlessly climbing halfway down the quarry wall to get the stone that became Homer. What had happened was far less flattering—she'd been walking along the edge and peering down into the dark water for signs of life, for hints of fish, when her foot had slipped and she'd fallen. Luckily, the ledge had been there, jutting nine feet at an upward angle over the pit—nine feet out and six feet wide. She landed on her rump, and once the pain and the dying-fear had passed, she'd seen the crack in the wall, and she'd seen the stone. Two large halves that, with the aid of a rope from the car, she'd hauled up after wrapping them in an old burlap sack. The one half had been Homer's grey-white; the other, Greg's, was the same, only the grey was slightly darker. That one she had given to him in hopes he would try some sculpting of his own, but when she'd initially had the notion for Homer's twin she'd managed to wheedle it back from him without explaining why. Had almost despaired when he'd told her he'd given it to Ben.

But Ben apparently hadn't taken it. They found it at his workspace in her Fine Arts studio, and so anxious was she to begin work on Greg's gift she'd had no compunctions at all about taking it without asking. It had been one of those I'll-talk-to-him-tomorrow things, when tomorrow never comes, and Ben had never mentioned it and she only remembered it whenever she was here at the quarry.

Here at the quarry, trying to work up enough energy to start the walk home.

Her anger rekindled.

Idiot! Didn't he know she could freeze to death before she reached the nearest farmhouse? What did it matter that she only had to follow the road downhill; my god, it would be dark before she broke from the forest, and suppose there was no one home? Suppose there was another storm tonight? She scanned the sky quickly, her nervousness rising until she convinced herself the haze to the south was only the weak sun's discoloration, not a forming cloudbank.

Enough, she ordered then. Enough. Take it easy. And get off your ass before it freezes to the rock.

She leaned forward to stand. Stopped when she saw a band of powdery snow trail off the quarry's rim. It scattered and swirled, was followed by another on the opposite wall. A third. A fourth. As if the ground were tilting and dumping its load.

Then she felt the wind.

And heard the deep-throated grumbling.

Chapter 14

*E*arthquake, she thought; but when her concentration shifted briefly to her hands, her feet, she could feel no vibrations through the stone, the ground. A glance to the sky, and the blue had hazed over; a glance to the woods on either side of the quarry, and the trees were immobile.

She wanted to move, to get off the throne and start running up the road. Maybe Greg had cooled down and was turning back. Maybe there was a truck coming up the trail, a farmer or some kids out for some illegal hunting. And maybe it was simply a stone shifting under pressure of the cold.

The wind flicked like the tip of a whip against her cheek, and it took her a moment to realize its direction.

South; from across the mouth of the quarry and directly into her face.

The snow tails fell more strongly, slipping from between cracks and shrubs, falling toward the covered ice. White waterfalls now that began to swerve away from the ice as if repelled, sweeping toward the center and billowing upward again, twisting, writhing, shaping themselves into a funnel that climbed slowly toward the haze. Pouring from all sides, and lifting from the bottom, until the black surface was clear, reflecting nothing of the turmoil above it and allowing her to see nothing below.

She was mesmerized.

She knew it was a phenomenon of the wind, of the shape of the quarry, of the powdery substance of the snow, and despite the sub-aural grumbling she was intrigued, wondering how high the fattening pillar would rise before either it collapsed under its own spinning weight or the wind finally shifted direction. It was now midway to the top, and still the snow fed it. She looked down to her feet and saw the flakes shifting away from her, curling around her heels to ride for the edge, saw patterns of white streaming around the sides of the throne, moving so rapidly she had a moment's illusion the stone was traveling backward. She closed her eyes, opened them quickly, and saw that the revolving pillar had begun to change color.

Fascination died.

There were flecks now in the white, flecks of deep red that blurred into a pink too much like watered blood. She shrank back, pulling one leg up protectively, pushing herself with her hands until she was almost standing.

Deep red. Deeper.

And the grumbling grew louder.

The pillar rose higher. She thought for a panicked moment of cinema effects, twisted spires of flame that yielded no heat and cowed the actors just the same.

But this was cold. A dull and lifeless cold shading from white to red without benefit of the sun, without a fire nearby. Her other leg drew up and she was crouching, trying to watch the snowfall and the funnel simultaneously. She grew dizzy. Her lips dried, her eyes burned, but when she lifted a hand as if to ward off the vision she realized it wasn't the snow that had turned red, it was something inside the spiraling fury, something lifting itself ponderously from beneath the black ice.

A movement contrary to the pillar's spin, a flash of dark red that caught her eye and was lost before she could follow it.

Mesmerized; drawing her legs and arms closer inward, kneeling and hugging herself, until a second flashing movement galvanized her. She did not cry out (though she

141

thought she heard a scream), and she did not scream (though she thought she heard herself cry out); she launched herself over the throne's left armrest and landed with her back to the quarry, on her knees and slipping toward the edge. Her hands grasped at the frozen ground, claws searching for purchase, while her back strained and her legs fought to bring up her feet. Slipping again, and her right foot came up against a stone. She used it. Without thinking she let all her weight rest against it, suddenly straightened her leg, and flew several feet in the air before she landed on hands and knees, crawling frantically, legs pulling up almost to her waist until she was up on her toes, on her fingers, up on her feet and racing for the crest.

The wind ignored her. It grumbled and shrieked behind her, magnified by the quarry's throat, smothering her bird-weak prayers and sending daggers of pain into her ears.

At the top, turning and not wanting to turn, seeing the pillar rise above the quarry, seeing within it a creature deep red still masked by the white. Yet it was there. She could see it. She could see ... something ... an arm, a tentacle, a limb of some sort thrashing about as if seeking a way to smash through whatever held it. A flare, then. An eye. The vague outline of a head turning like a beacon; turning, stopping, and she knew it had seen her.

It bellowed.

Whatever head it had, whatever throat it had, it raised the one and stretched the other and it bellowed its challenge, unmistakable and enraged. Immediately, the snow lifted from the ground and blinded her, made her windmill her arms as her boot came down on a patch of ice. She stumbled forward, sideways, and fell. Sprawled. The snow climbing over her, insects of ice that slipped down her collar and into her ears, into her eyes, past her clenched lips and into her mouth. She tumbled, slid, tumbled again the full hundred yards down to the trail. An elbow cracked viciously against the ground and she screamed, feeling the numbness climb to her shoulder; her forehead glanced off a rock, and there were more colors than white, none of them red, burning Catherine wheels through her vision until she cried again; her knee; her back; and the snow swarmed around her, no longer soft, no longer gentle, striking her like pebbles even after she regained her feet and started running again.

The trail rose, and she sobbed. She was heading in the wrong direction. She turned helplessly, looked back once over her shoulder and saw something ... red ... climbing over the crest.

It bellowed.

It challenged.

She flung herself forward, only half-thinking that the snow-cloud meant to stop her could also hide her for a while. And immediately the thought came, the snow settled. Like dust, ghost-dust, it drifted out of the sky and back to the ground, and she swerved off the trail and raced toward the woodland. Out of the open, she thought; get out of the open. It made no difference that a thing that size would snap the trees to pieces, like so many brittle bones; if she were out of the open there would at least be the slim chance of safety, the smallest hope of escape. Anything else would be unthinkable, and deadly.

The sheds blurred past her, and behind the last one in the row she stumbled over something buried beneath the white. She fell heavily, her mouth filling with snow that stung her cracked lips, her shoulder striking the rear wall to black her out for a moment. And when she awoke her face was pressed hard against the rough, gapping wood, and one hand was thrown up to blot out the sky, the other pushing against the shed to bring herself to her feet.

Die, she thought; *oh god, I don't want to die.*

143

She listened for the space of a dozen heartbeats, a dozen shuddering breaths.

And heard nothing, not even the rasp of air in her lungs.

Quickly, then, she shifted position into a crouch. Blinked snow glare and pain from her eyes and scanned the area immediately around her. Pine saplings weighted and bent. A rock breeching the crusted white. Twenty yards, she estimated, between herself and the trees. But she did not run.

She listened.

And heard nothing. Not even the wind.

Her hands dipped into her pockets, clenched around several hard lumps she pulled out absently. Once again she'd managed to bring pieces of Homer's duplicate with her, and she tossed them aside angrily, did not see them land when a second thought turned her gaze.

There was an impulse, then, short-lived and futile—to scrabble through the snow to find the stones again. David and Goliath. Parts of her she shouldn't lose, parts of her now lost forever.

Calm, she told herself sternly when she felt herself slipping. *Damn, Pat, be calm or we're dead. We're dead.*

There was a mask of perspiration gleaming on her face, an ice-river slithering slowly down her spine. Though she clenched her jaw as best she could, her teeth chattered uncontrollably, and her left knee jumped spasmodically until she clamped a hand on it and held it there tightly. Lifted it, waited, then brought the hand to her mouth and bit down on a knuckle. It was then she realized she had been holding her breath, and she slipped it out in white spurts, breathing through mouth and making her teeth ache. She swallowed, and winced at the sandpaper that had abruptly lined her throat.

She thought she could taste the warm salt of blood.

The woods, silent; the sky, lowering.

The shed creaked under the weight of its snow, and she held her breath again, staring at the nearest plank as if it were ready to split open and spill the creature into her lap.

The woods, silent.

In a moment so swiftly passing it was gone as soon as she noted, she could feel every inch of her skin pressing damply to her clothing: her breasts to her shirt, her stomach to the waistband, thighs to her jeans, calves to her boots, toes so cold they felt nothing at all. It was as though she were suddenly naked, and she moved a few inches to kill the sensation before it overwhelmed her.

Then she listened, and heard nothing.

Gone. Oh my god, it's gone. It has to be gone. Please; please let it be gone.

Yet she dared not move. If it was just waiting, somewhere out there waiting, it would see her the moment she broke into the open. It wouldn't hurt to wait herself. To rest. To think. But she felt as if all logic circuits in her mind had shorted out, had consumed themselves in sudden explosions of sparks that denied her the reason she needed to know what was happening. Because what was happening, of course, wasn't real. It couldn't be real. She couldn't have had a silly fight with Gregory and elected to walk home in the middle of winter through the middle of a forest with ninety feet of damned snow on the ground. And she couldn't have been sitting on that stupid thing she called a throne, muttering to herself and feeling sorry for herself. And she certainly hadn't seen the snow suddenly drift off the edges of the quarry and form itself into a tornado-like barrier around a deep-red, blood-red, night-red creature that just rose from the ice like some stage trick on Broadway. She hadn't felt the wind. She hadn't heard the grumbling, or the shrieking, or the bellowing that was a

145

challenge. She knew she hadn't, because it couldn't have happened.

Not in the middle of a Sunday afternoon, in the twentieth century, in Connecticut, of all places.

She uncurled a fist that had been pressed tight against her chest. She stared at it, daring it to contradict her, demanding it prove to her she wasn't losing her mind. Weeping suddenly and silently because if none of it had happened, then her mind was indeed lost. And she would rather believe in night-red beasts rising from quarries than lose what she had protected for nearly forty years.

It snorted, a snuffling as if a muzzle had been plunged into a snow bank and yanked out again.

The tears stopped abruptly, and the hand returned to her chest. Feeling the heart pounding through its own rabbit quivering.

A footfall. Something wide, something heavy pressed into the snow.

She turned slowly to put her back against the shed wall, her hands spread against the wood and her arms slightly bent. She would run, but only at the last moment. Surprise was a weapon she would be able to use only once, and even then there was no guarantee it would work at all to save her.

What was it? What the hell was it?

The shed trembled as something brushed heavily against it. Snow drifted languidly off the canted roof and into her face. She shook her head, not wanting the dead cold lying on her skin, blinked rapidly to clear her eyes as she tried to judge from which side it would come. Left, and she would charge off to her right, through a hedgerow there, and angle toward the road; right, and she would go left, seemingly heading back for the quarry, but ducking around a broad stand of fir to charge

146

straight down the hill as fast as the snow and the slope and the trees would allow her.

The haze deepened, greyed, filling the air with tiny black specks.

The shed trembled again. Something sharp rasped across the front. Then it stopped. Everything stopped.

Slowly, her back arched, her shoulders drew together; any minute now she knew a lance, an arrow, a spike would crash through the weather-weakened wood and into her heart. She would die before she was able to cry out, to scream, to do anything but open her mouth to let out the blood. The thought paralyzed her, and dried her mouth until it felt coated with sand. She shook it off, and replaced it with another—that the shadows creeping across the snow in front of her would suddenly become three-dimensional. They would prance over the white without making a track, pointing claws and fangs directly to her position, cackling like witches, hissing like snakes, dancing to show her where she would find what others would call her grave.

Shadows. The shadows.

Since the sun was already setting, and since she was facing west, it wasn't possible that shadows would be stretching out before her. It couldn't be. It was impossible. Just like the snow and the night-red and the bellowing and—

She felt the shed trembling again, creaking under the slow application of a weight it couldn't bear.

The shadow.

A head, huge shoulders that seemed almost feathered, and the limbs she had seen now raised so high their black reflection reached the trees.

There was so little time to react she didn't realize she was running until she heard her boots crunching harshly through the crust, and she had no idea of her direction until she found

147

herself plunging through the underbrush, arms high, chest outthrust, legs pumping maddeningly slowly as she fought to break through.

She screamed only once—when she heard the bellowing, and the explosion of splintering wood. It had known she was there, and it had tried to crush her.

The scream, however, was a release. It spurred her through the hedgerow and guided her around the boles; it goaded her through drifts that had piled against fallen logs, lashed her into anger when her boot caught against a root.

Behind her there was silence.

Temptation, then, to slow down, to turn, to see if pursuit had been directed another way or cut off entirely. It passed. There were too many obstacles coming at her, too many opportunities to trip her, to kill her, to slam her unconscious; she needed all her attention just to keep herself alive simply in flight—if anything on her trail was determined to have her it would have to run as she did, and catch her on the fly.

Running. Her whole life running. Her lungs protesting by filling her chest with knives, her legs begging mercy by turning themselves to lead; her eyes watering, the tears freezing on her cheeks, her lips splitting open and the blood salty on her tongue; her head slumping forward and lolling on her neck, her arms flapping like broken wings and upsetting her balance against the wind in her face. Her coat dragging her down. Her boots grafting to the ground. One knee buckling until she screamed at it to straighten. No thinking. It was too hard to think. Downward was the only direction, and the hell with the road.

Running. At least she thought she was running, but the trees weren't speeding past her as fast as they once were, and it was getting harder to kick through the drifts that seemed too wide to go round, and the wind was easing, the wind of her own making, and her mouth wouldn't close and her eyes kept blinking and she was positive someone had cut her hands off at the wrist and her feet at the ankles. A clearing was wind-cleared, and the hunched brown grass was more trouble than mud; a birch grew too fast and smacked painlessly against her left arm; ruts and depressions broke the evenly laid snow, and it took her almost five minutes to see she'd reached the road anyway, was taking it down its center and not caring if she was seen.

Running. No. She glanced down and saw her toes flash out, disappear, and she knew she was walking.

She stopped.

She turned.

The hill was above her, the road swinging off to the right, and she sensed more than felt a grin spreading open her lips, showing her teeth, drawing more blood. She didn't care. She didn't mind. Right now bleeding to death would have been infinitely more desirable than what she'd just averted. What did it matter that she could hear the grumbling up there? What did it matter that through the snow glare between the trees there were darts and winks of night-red?

"Oh."

Not a moan, not a revelation, not a marking of despair.

Simply: "Oh."

She turned; she walked; there was no question of running because the running was no longer there. There was only the sound of her boots on the road and the night-red behind her and an occasional whimpering she could not restrain. Yet she tried. She urged herself into a trot that lasted ten paces; she berated herself into a trot that lasted ten paces more. She raised her eyes (her head was too heavy) and watched the clouds thicken, promising her more white unless she returned home

149

now; she opened her mouth and tried to widen her lips, but the curses were weak, too weak to encourage.

Maybe, she thought then, it doesn't want to kill me. Maybe it was sent to protect me instead. It could have killed me before. A couple of times. Lots of times. The night I was drunk and came home from the Inn. The night I was promoted and took a walk and it chased me and made me lose my hat. I could have been killed then. It could have gotten me then. So why should it want to kill me now? What I should do is, I should turn around and ask it what it wants. Maybe it speaks English. Maybe I could use sign language.

She stumbled.

Maybe it's as afraid of me as I am of it. Like bees. Mother always told me not to worry about bees because they were always more afraid of me than I was of them. Just ignore them and they'll go away and they won't sting you. So maybe—

She stumbled, and fell to one knee.

—I should ignore it and it will go away. It doesn't really want me because if it did it could have done it a million times already. And the bigger they are the harder they fall and oh God I'm so goddam fucking tired! So tired! So—

She knew she was down. Hands and knees were buried in the snow. The wind had risen and was tearing at her hair. She looked up and saw the farmhouse beyond the fence. A beautiful fence. Rail-and-post and coated with untouched white, four chimneys above the peaked roof, a gable in each corner, and smoke curling from a fireplace and merging with the haze. She could scream.

The rumbling.

She could scream and the people inside would rush out and see what was the matter and the night-red thing, the thing born in the bloodwind, it would climb back up the mountain and she

150

would be safe. It had to be that way because she was too tired for anything else.

The rumbling, now a bellow, and something thundering down the road.

On hands and knees she turned to face it.

She couldn't scream. Her throat was dead, her lungs were dead, her mind was so filled with pleasantly warm cold that all she wanted to do was lie down and let it, the night-red, the bloodwind, pick her up and bring her back to the quarry where it was warm and black and she'd never have to think again. That's the way it would have to be. Since she couldn't scream. Since the people in the farmhouse would never come to save her.

A part of her, a place so deep now she hadn't known it existed, told her to get mad, to get moving, to stop feeling sorry for herself and accepting everything she couldn't handle as inevitable. The red thing that had come out of the snow pillar wasn't moving as fast as it had been. She still had a chance. She ought to get up off her ass and start running again. She was rested. She knew it. She wasn't that tired. She knew it. She ought to do something instead of kneeling in the snow like a goddamned idiot and ending it all at the hand/ claws/fangs/of something that didn't exist in the first place.

With a shove that almost sent her sprawling onto her back, she lurched to her feet.

The red-beast rounded the last bend.

She stumbled in a circle and began trotting toward the farmhouse. And once she realized she could trot, she began to run. And once she realized she could run, she lifted her arms and she lifted her face and she lengthened her stride until she could barely feel her boots crashing beneath her. Could barely feel the knives slicing madly at her lungs. Could barely feel the wind as it split open her chin.

And she just reached the gate when the red-beast caught her.

Chapter 15

An arm grabbed Pat around the waist as her legs gave way and she sank toward the ground. She tried to strike out, to scratch, to lift her knees, but nothing would work. The arm gripped her too tightly, held her too closely. And there was a roaring in her ears. A sharp cacophonous display that forced her to squeeze her eyes shut tightly, to bite down on her tongue to keep from screaming. Because above all, and for no reason that made itself plain to her, she did not want to scream. She did not want to give it the satisfaction of knowing her fear. She was sure it could smell it—in the perspiration that had drenched her clothes, in the stench that rose from every pore of exposed skin; but she would not allow it to hear it from her lips. A foolish thing, inconsequential, but as she was dragged away from the gate through the cloud of white, of red, of swirling colors that matched the buzzing swarming over her, it mattered. Later, if there was a later, she would attempt to understand it. Now, however, she had to keep her silence. Even in the hissing in her right ear, the hissing that was insistent, almost vicious, she had to keep her silence, keep herself in the dark behind closed lids so she could not see at so close a range the thing that belonged to the arm fastened so snugly around her waist.

She was lifted.

Her feet left the ground and she was swung gently through the air. Gently. Carefully. Set down again, and the arm slipped away and her back rested against something firm, something that gave when she pressed against it. She held her breath. The hissing, the buzzing, the roaring had vanished.

She opened her eyes and saw the star-shaped patterns of frost on the windshield.

And as she slowly, incredulously, gazed around the inside of the car, her hearing returned—to the creak of warm metal snapping against the cold, to the steady blast of the heater breathing summer on her legs, to the voice beside her laden with concern.

"Doc? Hey, Doc, what's the matter? Why'd you run like that, huh? God, I could've run you over."

Focus. Snow glare receded and the fencing shimmered into sharp relief, the outline of the red sedan etched in a white background, the scratches and worn padding of the dashboard, the faded jeans and sheepskin coat, the stubble-shadowed face lean and leaning toward her. The single gloved hand on the steering wheel. Beneath a hunter's cap whose earmuffs had been tied over the crown, Ben's eyes were dark, searching, filled with a hope that she would smile and cure his worry.

"Doc?"

She began to tremble. Her legs, her arms, until she clamped them all together and hunched over, ignoring the exhaust-tinged air forced to the floorboards.

The engine fired and the car eased forward.

"I'd better get you to a doctor," Ben said, though his gaze refused to stay on the road. "You're sick."

"No." It was a whisper, harsh and unlike the voice she thought she had. "No, please. I'm all right. You frightened me, that's all."

From his silence she knew he didn't believe her, but she said nothing until he'd turned onto Cross Valley Road. The snow banks here thrown up by the plows were nearly as high as the roof of the car, and when they crept onto Williamston Pike and headed in toward the village, she forced herself not to panic when brief gusts of wind buffeted the vehicle, and sent trails of snow lifting toward the trees.

Finally, thawed, her toes and fingertips stinging, she sat back and laid her hands flat on her thighs. "Ben, what were you doing up there? You were up at the quarry."

He nodded.

Ask him the other one, she ordered herself then; *ask him, damnit, ask him!*

"Why?" It was the wrong question. Courage; she needed courage.

"Well, we didn't exactly welcome you with open arms yesterday, you know." Guilt and apology were genuine, she was sure, but she couldn't help a glance to see if his eyes mirrored the tone. "And then Harriet told me this morning she'd seen you last night." He sighed, loudly. "She shouldn't have done that. We were just letting off steam. You know how Ollie is. His mouth is bigger than any brains he has." His smile broke, held, faded quickly.

"The quarry?"

"I went to your place to talk a little." A shrug, not quite an apology this time. "You didn't answer, and when I came back outside Doc Billings had pulled up. He was in a real foul mood, and he told me where you were." He grinned, and it held. "I almost hit him."

Ask him. Ask him!

"Did ... Ben, did you see anything up there? I mean, while you were up there did you see anything unusual?"

"What's to see this time of year? The sheds and a hole in the ground, that's all. God, we have any more snow, Doc, that thing'll fill right to the top when it all melts."

She stared at him, startled. He's lying. She knew he was lying. He couldn't have missed the wreckage of the shed the

155

beast had crushed, or the gap in the ice through which it had risen. He couldn't have. It was impossible.

He looked to her, back to the road quickly. "Hey, did I say something wrong?"

On their left the first signs of the park's spear-tipped iron fence rose from the snow. The pike lifted, fell again, and the library on the corner of Centre Street seemed to act as a signal. He slowed, indecisive.

"I don't know who your doctor is, Doc."

"It's all right," she said stiffly. "Please, if you'd just take me home, I'd appreciate it, Ben."

"Are you sure? You look like—"

"Please!" She stared straight ahead, afraid of what he would see in her expression, in the way she held herself so rigidly.

"Sure, Doc. Whatever you say."

He sped up, nearly sideswiping a bus that had lumbered out of Centre onto the pike. He did not apologize for the near-accident, however. He only held his speed until he reached Northland, turned left sharply and braked almost angrily in front of her home. They sat for a moment in strained silence while she sought the words which would ease the tension.

It was, finally, simple enough: "Thank you, Ben. And I'm sorry I snapped at you."

He dismissed it with a casual wave. "No sweat, Doc. I'm surprised you're still talking to me, after what freckle-head told you."

"It's just that I had a scare," she said, as if she hadn't heard him. "It's awfully lonely up there. I was seeing things, I guess, and they made me run."

"I thought you were training for a marathon."

She smiled. "I'd never make it past the first mile."

The houses loomed. There were children in a snow-battle in a yard up the street. Line was across the road, talking with Still worth. She turned suddenly to Ben, and his eyebrows lifted in wary surprise. Waiting. But she couldn't do it. Here, amid all she'd lived with for the past decade and more, the terror she'd felt had been relegated to something less than physical, though she definitely hadn't forgotten the flight, the pain. But she couldn't ask him to take her back. Something stopped her: the puzzled expression on his face, the quiet crawl of ice along her arms, the idea that going out there would yield her nothing but what Ben had claimed— snow, the quarry … and nothing else at all.

"What?" he asked.

"Nothing," she said. Her hand fumbled at the door latch, pulled it to her, and she stepped out into the street.

"Doc," he said, leaning toward her.

"I'm all right," she said, gesturing him to leave. "I'll see you tomorrow."

She stepped back until her legs pushed into the curbside snow bank, waited until he'd driven off slowly before walking to the open mouth of the driveway. The shadow of the garage was already lapping at the sidewalk, the haze breaking up again to show her dark patches of blue. The children laughed and shrieked. She stood for a moment, watching them, until the cold reminded her of the cold she had felt, and she hurried to the porch, through the door and up the stairs. Her footsteps were loud, and she wished the Evanses would return from Florida so she could sit in their living room, listening to their stereo whispering a favorite opera, drinking tea and nodding while the couple filled an hour or more with trivial details of a trip they'd taken twenty years ago.

But they were gone, and she didn't feel up to the exuberance of Kelly's nonstop talking. She opened the door and shrugged off her coat, letting it fold to the floor. Into the kitchen where she automatically put on the kettle and turned the flame as high as it would go.

"It was, wasn't it," she said to the kettle. "I saw it. I saw it."

She walked dreamlike around the room, pressing a palm to every cool surface, wandering into the living room and switched on the lamp. Stared at the windows until she saw flickering, hurriedly pulled the draperies closed and stepped back to wait.

"It was real."

The bedroom was next.

Coverlet still thrown back, indentation in the pillow where Greg had positioned her head before he'd gone off to make breakfast. She walked around the dresser on the left, paused at the window and glanced down into the drive, saw nothing and continued on into the bathroom. Stared in the mirror. At the tangle the wind had made of her hair, at the suggestions of shadows beneath her eyes, at the raw deep pink at chin and lips and across her high cheeks. She reached for a container of hand lotion and spread it over her palms. Massaged her face gently, feeling the skin loosen, smelling the herbal scent that lingered even after she rinsed her hands.

Workroom. Dust. Clutter. An impotent red sun spiked through the treetops.

The kettle whistled and she ran to it, poured herself a cup and watched the tea from its bag drift into the water.

"It was real."

With an anticipatory wince she sipped the tea, wrinkling her nose at the curling steam. She grinned sourly then when she remembered a fragment of time, an afternoon her mother had told her she had no imagination. Had the woman been with her this afternoon, that much disappointment at least would have been dispelled.

She sat, her palms warming against the cup.

The room darkened.

There was no question but what she had seen at the quarry was not connected with the occult, the supernatural. It was, however, part and parcel complete with stamps connected to the experience in the street and all the rest. A masterful conjuration of illusion. An elaborate attempt to multiply the pressures she'd been under lately. To what end? To break her, she decided. Nothing quite so dramatic as driving her insane, but a shove in the direction which would lead her to believe she wasn't capable of handling the responsibilities of the new department. The pressures she would feel there, too. The leadership she would have to provide after all these years of following. She would believe that she'd bitten off more than she could chew, and she would back out. She would give up the fight. She would pass up the departmental promotion and give it to someone else, someone stronger, someone who wanted it as much as she and would do the job she herself had dreamed of, had planned for, had bucked the odds for over months beyond counting.

Unless it had nothing to do with the job at all.

Unless it was a reaction to something she had done, something she had said; unless it was in itself a reaction to a reaction.

She sputtered a laugh and leaned back in the chair. Her speculations were beginning to wander away from common sense. But she found herself much more relaxed now that distance had been placed between the apartment and the quarry. Now it was a matter of setting up possible villains and beginning the process of logical elimination. And in thinking that she realized she was sounding like Ellery Queen or Sir Henry Merrivale; it was a crime to be solved, with a dozen possible criminals, all with motives as fragile as the illusion.

The tea cooled; she did not notice.

It would be interesting to learn how it was done. It would be fascinating to see how long this calm would last before her temper took charge. She could feel it now, stirring like a disturbed slumbering beast, its limbs jerking in half-sleep, searching for whatever it was that had poked it awake.

Night-red, rising ...

You are a remarkable woman, Patrice, if I do say so myself.

... soaring above the mouth of the quarry, masked in white, bellowing in fury ...

Anyone else would be a prime candidate for a strait-jacket and a padded room. Doctors scuttling all over the place, their glasses sliding down their noses while they stared at you and questioned you and wanted to know how well you got along with your mother, your father, why was it really that you broke up with your husband, and isn't it possible that you've never really gotten over the death of your daughter and so you're lashing back now, striking out at everyone you believe to be your enemy at the college?

Isn't that possible, Dr. Shavers?

Isn't it possible you've finally lost your mind?

... massive forearms stretching toward the clouds, whistling through the air to smash the shed and render it into firewood; less, into dust ...

She felt the cup slip from her hands and shatter on the floor, felt a splash of cold tea land on her ankle. Her boots were off. When, she wondered, had she taken them off? And why, she wondered, is it so damned dark?

She could barely see her hands on the table. But she could feel her fingers twitching, feel the vibrations tingling up her arm to her shoulders, making their serpentine way to her neck and causing her throat to tighten, her lips to draw taut, her eyes to widen until she thought they would explode out of their sockets.

"It … was … real."

Her voice. So small. Mouse-like. Quivering. No confidence there at all. Not at all like the way she had spoken to Ben. Ben, who had just happened to drive out to the quarry because Greg had told him what he had done. Ben, who—if Harriet was to be believed—was ready to agree with Oliver about the state of their career. Non-career. So young. So damned young, so damned inexperienced, and so goddam ready to take on the world.

"Real."

A gasp more than a word.

She closed her eyes tightly, furrowing her brow, pulling up her chin. The bloodwind beast was there. Rising. Climbing. Hidden behind the snow cloud, the snow pillar, the tornado, allowing her only glimpses to fuel the imagination she wasn't supposed to have. It was there. Vividly stalking her, vividly silent, launching her into the forest as it trampled the shed.

Her eyelids fluttered and lifted. There was nothing for it but that she would have to go back. As long as she sat here in the dark she would vacillate between intriguing illusion and horrifying insanity. She had to know, and she had to know now, before she tried to sleep.

And immediately the decision was made there was no hesitation in her movements. She pushed back the chair and heard a leg crunch through the shards of the cup. Carefully, she sidestepped the debris and grabbed a broom from the narrow closet at the back. Swept up as much as she could and dumped it in the trash. Skirted the table so as not to cut her feet on anything she'd missed and walked purposefully into the bedroom. Changed her jeans, slipped on a ski sweater midnight blue and unadorned, found her boots in the bathroom and pulled them on over a fresh pair of wool socks, fished a dry pair of gloves from the top dresser drawer and strode into the living room.

Though it occurred to her that she ought to, she did not feel the least bit silly. This was her sanity she was defending, and nothing she did now would seem any more insane than fleeing what just might be a delusion. She would need luck, of course, in getting out there and back without attracting attention, or without breaking her neck. And luck, she decided with a grin, was exactly what she would have.

Whistling, she hurried into the kitchen to fetch Homer. There was still only the lamp's light from the front room, so she only frowned when she reached around the door and came up with nothing. Frowned more deeply when she half-stepped into the room and saw the shelf was empty.

"Rat," she said. "Where the hell did I put you?"

The bedroom didn't hide him. Neither did the hallway or living room. Despite the fact she'd never brought him in there, she checked the bathroom anyway, checked the closets, checked under all the furniture while she wrestled with the implication that somehow she'd lost him.

Then she snapped her fingers. "Ha!" It was too easy. She'd been working on Greg's present in the workroom. She had used Homer for the model. Therefore, it stood reason's test the grizzly would be there.

But it wasn't.

When she flicked on the overhead light and her eyes adjusted to the glare, the pedestal was empty, as well as the stool.

And it was then she remembered her door had been unlocked.

Chapter 16

On the wall a crescent of light formed by the baseboard and the edge of the lampshade. Within, a shadow, an elongated globe that swelled and shrank as Pat turned her head from side to side. She could hear the water in the pipes trying to warm her, could feel the carpet beneath her soles trying to muffle the sound of a scream that had not yet been born. She pivoted slowly and stared at the door. It was a block of wood with inserted panels, polished and worn and fitting snugly to its frame. She had never seen it before, not now, not since it was evident someone had used it while she'd been away. Once part of her protection, it became alien within the space of a blink, and she backed away from it, half expecting the knob to begin turning, to hear breathing on the landing, to hear footfalls across the threshold.

And it wasn't the first time.

Through all her hysterical outbursts and the accumulation of woes, she'd forgotten the glove. Oliver's glove. And how the statuette had been shifted from the perch to the table.

Twice, then. Twice someone had broken into her apartment; first to retrieve the glove, then to steal the images of the grizzly.

I saw Dr. Billings at the curb, Ben had told her only a few hours ago. But the boy had been here, too.

She took several steps toward the kitchen and halted.

No, she would say to the police if they came; no, nothing else has been taken as far as I know. My watch is still on the dresser, and all the prints—some of them rather valuable, they're signed—are still here. It was only a statuette. Two, actually. Of a grizzly bear. I did them myself and they're not valuable at all. And no, no one has a key to this place but me. The Evanses from across the way are down in Florida, and the two women who live downstairs, well, one's man-hungry and the other is deaf. No, we don't fight. No, I've never had a cross word with Mr. Goldsmith, either. Who am I fighting with? Funny you should ask. It seems like the whole world sometimes. First, there's Greg Billings. He's in love with me, you see, and I think I'm in love with him but sometimes he can be so smothering that I strike out at him. No, not with my fist, with my stupid tongue. We had a fight just this afternoon, as a matter of fact. And then there's the Three Musketeers. One-armed Ben, who saved me from going crazy this afternoon, and Harriet with the freckles who acts more like a puppy dog sometimes than a growing woman, and Cowboy Oliver, whose glove I found outside the other night and then it was gone when I got back from New York and I went over there to demand an explanation, and we, the four of us, we didn't really have a fight but it wasn't the most pleasant experience in the world, either. Do you want to count my parents? I've been fighting with them since the day I was born.

No. No one hates me as far as I know. What an odd question, officer. I thought we were talking about a theft here, not an attempted murder or anything like that.

No, I already told you, no one has my keys but me. I keep them right over here in my purse. Right here on the table by the door. If you'll just wait a minute I'll show you. I keep them right down at the bottom, just like my mother always taught me. Right—

She blinked and pulled away from the purse, suddenly realizing she'd been talking aloud to herself. And realizing, too, her keys weren't where they were supposed to be.

164

"Easy." The word was barked. An order, as she snapped her head around to check the corners, to check the shadows. "Easy. Think." A whisper, now. Calming, demanding calm, while she reviewed the weekend, remembered Abbey asking for the keys for a double date the night before. Saturday night. And unlike Friday, they'd not been taped in an envelope and left on the hall table.

"Easy."

It didn't prove anything. Abbey and Kelly had been up here only a half-dozen times since they'd moved in below, and not at all since the first of the year. Neither one of them had expressed interest in anything they'd seen here, made only socially polite remarks about the furnishings and wasn't it curious how someone could do something so totally different with the same space you have.

It was a simple matter of calling downstairs and finding out. That's all there was to it. But she didn't want to stay here alone anymore. Grabbing her coat from the floor, then, she hurried out to the landing and closed the door behind her. A thought, and she leaned over to the lock, searching for signs of a break-in, the use of a tool to snap back the bolt. But there was nothing. Not even space enough between door and frame to use a credit card, or a stiff cutting of plastic.

Whoever had taken Homer and his image had apparently walked in as if the door weren't there.

The foyer was unlighted. The single bulb in the ceiling had burned out, and there was nothing but the drift of the street glow through the curtained door and the panes to either side. She listened for sounds of activity in Goldsmith's apartment, crossed to Kelly's door and knocked. Waited. Frowned at the lack of response and knocked again, several times, loudly. Her foot tapped impatiently, and a loose fist pressed lightly against her mouth. Kelly, she finally decided, must not be home. She rang the bell, cocking her head to hear it buzzing inside. If Abbey were there, she would see the warning lights flashing. If not—

The door opened inward, the room beyond dark except for a single lamp muffled by a white glass shade. She stepped over the threshold, and the door closed silently behind her. Turning quickly, her left arm caught under the overhanging topcoat, she saw Abbey standing in shadow.

"Abbey? Abbey, are you okay?"

Abbey walked away from her, stumbling once over nothing Pat could see, and sat on the couch. Her hair hadn't been brushed in what looked like days, her face was devoid of makeup, and she was wearing a tattered bathrobe that seemed stiff and uncomfortable.

Pat glanced around the dim apartment, looking for Kelly, then hurried to join the woman so her lips could be seen.

"Abbey, what's wrong?" When there was no response, when Abbey just stared at her blankly, she reached out and took the girl's hand. It was cold, clammy, the feel of someone in deep summer who'd just come out of midnight walking. "Abbey … it's Kelly, isn't it? Your date last night was a flop, but hers was a success, right? She probably made you drive home alone and you're worried about her because she hasn't gotten in touch."

Abbey didn't move, and not for the first time did Pat wish the girl would talk. She could, physically, but someone had told her what the sound of a deaf person was like, sometimes too loud and often toneless. She'd made a decision to use only her hands, which "was limiting only when she felt too weary to lift them. Or when she was depressed.

"You know, dear," she said, pulling up a leg, "Kelly is always telling me how man-crazy you are." She smiled. "I know it's a fib. And I suspect it bothers you when you hear it. But she's done this before, a hundred times since I've known you. Abbey? Abbey are you listening to me?"

Abbey nodded.

"Okay. Well, look, I came down here ... Abbey, did you, have you been here all day?" Waiting. A slow nod. "Have you seen anyone come in or out of the house? Besides me and Linc, that is. Anyone at all? Maybe Professor Billings, the man I work with at Hawksted. Or maybe one of my students."

Abbey's hands fluttered in her lap, a sigh as she gathered strength. A boy. He had one arm.

"That would be Ben. Did you see anyone else? Anyone you didn't know?"

Abbey's eyes widened in suspicion, a slow-growing fear sparking her eyes. *What's wrong?*

"I don't want to frighten you, dear, but I think someone's broken into my apartment. You remember Homer? The grizzly? He's gone, and so is a copy I was making for someone."

The questions came rapidly, and Pat answered them all as best she could, explaining that nothing other than the statuettes had been taken and there had been no one there when she'd returned, and she'd wondered if either she or Kelly had gone upstairs for some reason, perhaps to return the keys and leave them inside. "But if Kelly's not home yet, that's impossible. Damn!"

She threw herself against the back of the couch and folded her arms over her stomach. Shook her head. Smiled quickly when Abbey leaned toward her, searching her face. "No, I didn't say anything. I'm just ... well, I was scared at first, but now I'm furious. I mean, it doesn't make any sense, does it? Someone ignoring all your valuables for a couple of hunks of rock. It doesn't make sense, and if you weren't up there ... hell. Oh, hell, I guess I'd better call the police."

An art lover, Abbey said, grinning.

Pat laughed, not so much at the joke as at the fact that the girl seemed to be coming out of whatever had taken her. She tried futilely to straighten her flaxen hair with her fingers, then blushed and excused herself. Pat had no choice but to nod, and wait, reach over and switch on another light so the room didn't remind her so much of a mausoleum. She also realized that with Kelly unthinkingly keeping the station wagon she had no way of getting back out to the quarry tonight, not unless she called Greg, or one of the trio. And that would be the absolute last resort. It would be bad enough to find nothing there if she were alone, worse if she did it with someone there.

She jumped when Abbey returned, fluttered a hand mockingly over her heart.

I've just read the time. Have you eaten anything?

"No, but please don't go to any trouble, Abbey. I've—" But Abbey was already heading for the kitchen, and Pat had no choice but to follow. Was glad she hadn't protested too strongly when she sat down to a meal of thick Irish stew and homemade bread, a California wine Abbey refused to apologize for, and a chocolate cake heavy with fudge icing.

And it would have been funny if Pat had allowed the thought to take hold. Two women, one deaf and one maybe crazy, both afraid to be alone; one worried about the absence of a friend, the other frightened of the absence of reason. Both of them eating as if it were their last meal, neither of them looking through the doorway to the front room, avoiding glances at the clock, talking as best they could around the food they were eating. About the weather. About school. About Abbey's job in the bank. About the troubles with Kelly's car and how it was barely worth holding on to until spring.

Pat at one point talking so rapidly Abbey had to reach across the table and touch her wrist to slow her down; Abbey at one point so irritated about the car that one hand flicked a chunk of icing off the cake and splattered it against the wall.

It would have been funny, if Pat hadn't kept thinking about someone in her home.

And when they were done and there was nothing more to say, she helped wash the dishes, dry them, followed Abbey back to the couch where they sat at either end, staring at the far wall, at the door, at the floor.

Finally, she slapped at a leg and rose, motioning for Abbey to keep her seat. "It's silly," she said, pulling on her coat. "It's obvious I'm not going to the police, right? In case it turns out to be one of my so-called friends trying to pull a gag on me. So I'd better check with them first, before I make a fool of myself. That, I think, is the best idea."

Abbey looked doubtful. *Maybe it was one of your students. That boy you told me about, Oliver?* She grinned. *Maybe he's a conservationist, and is trying to free the animals.*

"Oh, sure," she said as she opened the door. "Honey, Oliver, for all his talent, thinks of no one but himself." She hesitated. "Are you going to be all right? Alone, I mean, after what I told you."

Abbey stood, her hands buried in the robe's deep pockets. Her attitude was sufficient to tell Pat she'd accidentally stepped on a raw nerve, that she'd probably been fussed over all her life as if her deafness were the same as having her bedridden. It was understandable, and for Pat, after all this time, it was inexcusable, and she left with a fleeting apologetic smile, stood staring at the door a moment before turning and leaving.

Standing on the porch. Listening as St. Mary's down on High Street broke the early-evening cold with a peal of quiet bells. She had no idea what the service might be, but just the sound of the summons made her feel at once lonesome and comforted. It was a curious sensation, one she wasn't at all sure she understood. But it made her grip her upper arms and rub them through the coat as she climbed down to the walk, made her pause at the break in the hedge. Pause because she realized that what she was doing was all backward. In spite of her monologue upstairs, and to Abbey, it was without question necessary to contact the police. To go off like some fictional detective and track down the culprit herself was ridiculous. So what it if was a gag? It was one she certainly didn't appreciate, not now, not ever. And the more she thought about it the more annoyed she grew, especially when she recalled facing the Musketeers at Harriet's house, intending to dress them down for fetching Oliver's glove and finding herself distracted instead over a stupid telephone call to New York.

Planned. It had all been planned to divert her attention.

"How could you?" she muttered, glaring in the direction of Harriet's house. "God damn, how could you?"

It would serve them right to get involved with Abe Stockton, a man definitely not renowned for enjoying a case where the police were called in for nothing more than a spiteful gag. It would serve them right. And it would make more sense. And after a glance to the night sky, she knew it made more sense, too, to examine the quarry in daylight, not now. If she'd been spooked before, she would turn her hair white with a visit by moonlight.

Besides, she thought as she turned around, she didn't see how the illusion could work at night. The first time, when she thought about it objectively, she hadn't seen a thing. There'd only been a sudden wind, and a feeling, nothing more, that something was after her. And it may, in fact, have had no connection at all with what had happened in the hills. That night she'd been drinking; today she'd only been fighting with Greg. And, she admitted sourly, it hadn't really been a fight. More like a sudden dousing with jealous acid.

170

Dumb, she told herself; sometimes, woman, you can be awfully damned dumb.

She pulled at the door, stepped back a pace and pulled again. It was locked. Somehow, in leaving, she had yanked it too hard and the bolt had snapped to. She looked to her left, knowing it would be useless to rap on Abbey's bay window; the girl wouldn't be able to hear her. And there were no other lights in Linc's apartment; he was probably out with his cronies, chewing over the mistakes of whatever war he'd fought in, either military or marital. That left the little-used back entrance, what had once been for the original owners a way to get upstairs without traipsing through the parlor or the kitchen.

Down the steps again, huddling against herself as the cold clawed its way down her neck and up her sleeves, cracking along the sidewalk to the driveway. It seemed long. The house next door was dark, the streetlamp spreading the hedge into a shadow that spilled at her feet. Behind the garage, beyond the houses facing the next street, a hazed bluish glow that made everything on this side seem faced with black.

I don't want to go down there, she thought suddenly. *I don't want to go down there.*

A snort of derision. She'd wavered often enough lately, too often, and what was wrong with using a driveway she'd known for thirteen years? There were no dogs to bite her, no rapists lurking in the yard, no beasts rising from the black hole of the quarry, glimpses of red, bellowing fury—

"Stop it!"

She moved forward, deliberately bringing her heels hard down on the blacktop, listening to the quick echo off the house as the garage grew. Widened. The four narrow windows across its building-wide door catching in brittle ebony shards of branches topped with frozen snow, nursing slowly the ghostly reflection of her face, then her shoulders, as she approached it, saw herself and ducked to one side.

Silly. It was silly.

And as she did every time she came into the yard from this direction, she glanced at the near window, walked a half-dozen paces further on before she stopped. Touched a finger to her jaw and looked over her shoulder. What she had seen—what she had thought she'd seen was a glint of metal. Not a tool hanging on the back wall. Something closer. Something part of something larger. Like an automobile. But that was wrong. Linc didn't own one, and Kelly's was at the mechanic's, and Kelly herself had the station wagon God knew where. But she did see it. She was positive she'd seen it, and she walked back to the door and cupped her hands around her eyes to peer in and check.

And she was right. There was a car in there.

It was hers.

Chapter 17

A minute passed; perhaps more. Pat wasn't sure. All she knew was the cold drilling into her forehead pressed against the small pane. When it began to ache she stirred, stepped back and looked helplessly around her. A laugh bubbled at her lips until she swallowed; a curtain husked closed over her mind until she drove it away with an impatient swipe of her arm. This was no time to retreat, she told herself, though there were plenty of reasons why she would want to, why her equilibrium was disturbed and she staggered back a step.

Her car. Sitting in the garage all the time Abbey was feeding her dinner and worrying about Kelly.

Unless, of course, the girl had known about it all along.

She reached out and gripped the door's handle, strained a moment before flinging it up and back, wincing as it collided with the rear buffer and shot forward a few inches.

The car sat alone, and when she reached out a hand to touch the hood, the metal was cold. Slowly, she moved around to the driver's side and stared in. The keys were not in the ignition, the window had been rolled down, and as far as she could tell in the dark no one was lying in back. It was empty. No sign of Kelly, no indication it had been driven in the last few hours. But she would not reach in, could not touch it again. Glints of highlight from the streetlamp winked at her; the grille glowed when she moved outside; the headlamps and reflectors tricked her for a moment into making her think they were on.

She spun around and raced back to the porch, had her hand on the knob before she remembered it was locked. And gasped when the door swung inward, the hinges creaking, her shadow snapping across the foyer to the foot of the stairs. She blinked several times and shook her head in disbelief, grabbed the knob and pulled the door, opened it, closed it, then jumped inside and stared at it, bewildered. It could have been the frame. It might have been warped and she hadn't shoved it hard enough.

It was possible.

She didn't believe it.

Instead of worrying it, however, she pounded on Abbey's door with the side of her fist. Once. Before it swung inward.

Her first impulse was to turn and run outside, her second to take the stairs two at a time, lock her door behind her and call the police. Neither satisfied her. She called out for Abbey, stretched out a leg and toed the door around to the wall.

The room was empty. The single lamp was still burning, but as she cautiously made her way in she could see nothing in the corners, no one on any of the chairs, no other light in the apartment save for one in the kitchen. She checked there immediately, checked the bath and the two bedrooms and returned to the door, where she buried a hand in her hair and tugged in frustration. It wasn't fair. She didn't know how to react, because there was literally nothing to react to—an empty apartment, no clue to a struggle ... she didn't know if Abbey had left immediately after Pat had gone outside, or if the girl had been dragged out, or if Kelly had been hiding in one of the rooms because she'd done something horrid and was afraid of discovery.

There was nothing to guide her, not even a hint.

"Abbey!"

The name sounded hollow in the deserted apartment. From one of the back rooms a clock ticked loudly.

"Abbey? Abbey, it's Pat!"

The chrome and the glass were as cold as the air swirling about her ankles, lifeless, a display in a store window rather than a place where people actually lived. She thought it again: lifeless. Nothing lived in here, and if she hadn't known the contrary she could easily have believed nothing ever had.

"Abbey!"

She backed into the foyer, confused now, jamming her hands in and out of her coat pocket, turning first to Goldsmith's door, then toward the porch, then back to Abbey's and the light that seemed so brittle under the white round globe. Again she called, but she no longer liked the sound of her voice, how it was beginning to climb the register to panic, how it retreated from the large rooms like something small and frightened.

Her gaze wrenched toward the staircase. The wise thing would be to go up there and call the police. Up there. Familiar Territory, until she remembered that someone had been there, too.

With an anguished cry, then, she bolted from the house, grabbed the hedge to keep her from swerving into the street, and ran down to Chancellor Avenue. Turned left. Ran again. Paying no attention to a car passing in the opposite direction, passing and slowing; to the handful of pedestrians apparently headed for the Inn, who parted quickly when they saw she wasn't about to slow down or try to go around them; to the dog that jumped from a driveway and snapped at her heels, barking, yowling, chasing her for a block before skidding to a halt at the curb and chasing her with its voice; to another car filled with teenagers who leaned out the window and whistled, made suggestions; to St. Mary's and the bells and the peace they tried to promise.

Running until she reached the police station. Slipping on the top step and cracking her knee against the wall. She whimpered and grabbed for it, rubbed it, and pushed in. Stumbling now as a stinging wave rippled up to her thighs. Falling against the railing and holding on with both hands, closing her eyes against the pain and willing someone to appear.

She knew it was less than half a minute, but it seemed like an hour alone there in the high-ceilinged room, hearing odd noises from the cell block, a kettle shrilling, a man singing drunkenly, a radio tuned to a news station rehashing the Super Bowl at virtually full volume.

A shout opened her mouth, but it died the moment one of the back doors opened and Wes Martin stepped out. He was running a brush through his short hair, spinning a toothpick in his mouth, and he was almost at the desk before he noticed Pat waiting. His grin blossomed, held, wavered when he saw her sway. She tried to wave him off, to tell him she was all right and don't bother, but he was at the railing and holding her arms before the words came out, guiding her through the gate to a large club chair alongside the desk. Motioning her to be silent, then, he poured her a glass of water and ordered her with a jerk of his chin to drink it.

She did, gratefully, as she sagged in the chair and allowed her eyes to close. The water was tepid, tasteless, but she didn't care; her lungs were so cold, her face feeling as if it could be peeled like fruit, she wouldn't have cared at all if the water had been boiling and scalded her tongue. And when she opened her eyes again Wes had a pad in hand and a pen, watching her patiently. The dimples in his cheeks were gone; there was only his full face, full lips, the solemn stare of his hazel eyes. A touch of angry red at his right temple, as if he'd been scratching there.

"You okay now?"

She nodded.

"You talk. I'll ask questions later."

She didn't know where to begin, how to phrase it so she wouldn't sound like a stereotypical woman scatterbrained from hysteria. The room ebbed, swelled, as she looked around to buy herself time, but when she saw the white globes hanging from their chains overhead she swallowed hard and cleared her throat.

"All right," Wes said, laying down the pen and swiveling around to face her. He stared for a moment, though she knew he wasn't seeing her, then rose with a slap of his hand to the desk. "Be back in a minute."

It was less than that, but enough time for Pat to wonder if she'd been right in holding back. Her immediate worry was Kelly and Abbey, yet she sensed that all she'd suffered over the past two weeks was somehow connected, up to and including the episode at the quarry. But she hadn't been able to bring herself to talk about it, or about the first occurrence, or about her conviction that for the longest time she was being watched. Mentioning any of that, she'd known before she spoke, would instantly dilute credence of what she had told him. And as it was, it was rather nebulous; someone had broken into her apartment (without really breaking in) and had stolen two pieces of worthless statuary; Kelly had borrowed her car overnight, Pat had found it in the garage, Abbey apparently knew nothing about it, and now the both of them were gone. Missing? She didn't know. But it was awfully damned strange, didn't he think?

Wes returned just as she thought she would have to either burst into insane laughter and break down into tears, if only because either reaction made just as little sense as anything she'd said, much less done, today.

"I've sent a car round to check," he told her as he took his seat and crossed his legs. "With all that snow, there's bound to be prints somewhere. You did say you hadn't actually gone into the backyard, right?"

"Yes," she said.

A silence. She shifted in the chair. Wes picked up the pen and drummed on the blotter.

"You said you were going to ask me questions."

He nodded. "Yeah, I said that. But I would bet I already know most of the answers. For instance," and he looked up to the ceiling, "your friends didn't fight much, no more than ordinary roommates. As far as you know they weren't rivals for the same man. The three of you got along just fine—which is obvious, otherwise you wouldn't have been so free with your car. You have no idea what man Kelly Hanson was staying with, and as far as you know Abbey Wagner wasn't seeing anyone here in town." He lowered his gaze and grinned at her. "Am I right, or am I right?"

"You're ..." She laughed, immediately covered her mouth with a hand, realized she was still wearing her gloves and pulled them off, stuffed them in her pockets. "It sounds so ... so silly, Wes."

"Not so silly, Pat. Just a little less fearsome than you may think."

But you weren't there, she thought. *You didn't see how terrible Abbey looked, and you didn't feel the emptiness in their apartment after she'd left. You weren't there, and you didn't see what I saw out —*

"Pat." Wes leaned closer, resting his forearms on his knee. "Pat, the thing you're not telling me, are you sure it has nothing to do with tonight?"

Startled, she looked away and stared at the glazed double doors, half expecting them to swing abruptly inward and admit Abbey and Kelly in the custody of a patrolman. All of them laughing over what was a stupid misunderstanding.

"Coffee," Wes said then. He stood. "Black, cream, what?"

"Black," she said without thinking, nodded to him distractedly and didn't hear him leave. Didn't hear him return until he pressed the cup into her hand. She sipped, and shuddered at its strength and its underlying bitterness.

Wes craned around to look at the clock on the wall behind him. Nine-fifteen. He was about to speak when a patrolman poked his head into the room and beckoned. With a mumbled sentence Pat didn't understand he left, was back in less than a minute, drumming on the blotter, frowning and rubbing a palm over his face.

"Well?"

"All the doors were open, just like you said. Nobody there. Nobody in back, no footprints except near the garage, and we'll assume for the moment they were yours."

She scowled and leaned back. "The street—"

"A quick tour around the block for a couple of blocks in either direction. She wasn't there, or she was hiding, or she was picked up, or someone took her."

"As simple as that," she said, bitterly impatient without knowing why.

"Yes," he told her, drumming.

"Wes, please," she said then, pointing to the pen.

"Oh. Sorry." Again he swiveled around to face her. "Pat, you said you checked the car?"

"I looked in. I didn't see anyone. It was dark. I didn't turn on the light or anything." She frowned. "Why?"

"You said the driver's side window was rolled down."

"Yes."

"It wasn't, Pat. It had been smashed in. There were pieces of glass all over the floor under the steering wheel, a few on the seat. As far as we can tell, someone tried to get in that way. Probably did."

179

The questions came rapidly, and softly, but she had no answers to satisfy him. She didn't know where Kelly had been the night before, didn't know the name of the man, and certainly hadn't known the car had been returned. The only thing she could tell him with any degree of certainty was that the pieces of marble or stone found on the floorboards had probably been from either her purse or her coat.

"From my workshop," she explained. "I'm always picking things up and sticking them into my pockets or my purse. Then I dig around and they fall out. I'm like a walking gravel pit sometimes."

"Okay," he said. "All right. Let's go back to that first time, when you came back from New York and found"—he leaned over his pad, flipped back a page and scanned it—"Oliver Fallchurch's glove missing. You saw him later and he had both gloves in his pocket. And he didn't tell you how he'd gotten it back."

"No, but ..." She stopped at the expression on his face, put a hand to her eyes and wished she were in bed, that it was two weeks ago and she was starting all over again, waiting for Dean Constable to announce the decision. Or had it only been a week? A couple of days? My god, she thought, how long can a Sunday be?

"Pat."

She looked up quickly, aware of his gaze, aware of the heat that finally forced her to unbutton he coat. "Pat, does this Fallchurch kid live on campus?" She nodded. Then: "Wait! You're not going to—"

"I have to talk to him, Pat, you know that. If he got in your apartment once to get his glove, he might have done it again. You must understand I have to check it out."

"Well ..." She watched as he dialed for an outside line, turned away when he began to speak, to the front doors that shimmered when a wind gust slammed against them. The singing in the cell block began again, was cut off abruptly; the radio was turned off; somewhere in the building a radiator hissed and she could think of nothing more than dry snow blown across a field, whispering over dead grass as if summoning spirits that lay beneath. She hugged herself. Poor Abbey. Poor Kelly. One, the other, the both of them involved in something she wasn't allowed to know, something that … it occurred to her suddenly that perhaps Kelly had lost the keys, that whoever had found them (stolen them?) was the one who'd broken into her apartment. Kelly might have smashed the window to get into the car, and her friend, whoever he was, might have known how to hot-wire the ignition. Embarrassment, then, would have prevented the girls from telling her the truth, at least until the window had been replaced.

And the more she thought about it the more likely it seemed, until she turned to Wes to tell him, jumped when the doors burst open and Greg rushed in, coat flapping, muffler streaming behind him like a speedboat's wake. She looked at Wes, who covered the receiver and smiled sheepishly at her; to Greg, who stood anxiously at the railing.

Finally, it broke. She could no longer hold it, no longer had the strength. She jumped down off the desk's platform and into Greg's arms, the two of them babbling apologies and not hearing each other, kissing once lightly, again hard, leaning back still embracing and watching their eyes.

Greg nodded toward Wes Martin. "He, uh, called me."

"He has a big mouth."

"You have to stay much longer?"

"I don't know. He's checking Oliver now."

Greg's face darkened. "If he's the one who's been—"

A finger to his lips, and he grinned.

"Pat?"

She turned, though she kept a hand linked with Greg's.

"I can't get to him now. I'll try Harriet Trotter, and I'll have a man recheck the house. The car …"

"Oh my god," she said. "Don't tell me."

His laugh was rueful. "Stockton has his procedures, Pat. I'll have to bring it over here for checking." He would have continued, but she interrupted with the scenario she'd developed. When she was done, he was clearly skeptical. "But stranger things have happened around here, so I won't dismiss it now. But Pat … look, I don't want you worrying, okay? I mean, there's no sign of …" He paused, and she knew, and nodded. "I'll let you know when you can pick up the car. And I'll let you know the minute I know something myself."

"You're going to a lot of trouble," Greg said, not unkindly.

Wes grinned. "It's Sunday night, Professor Billings. It beats counting the cracks in the walls."

There was little more to say. A patrolman came into the room with Pat's statement typed and ready to be signed, and once the formality had been taken care of she left with Greg, sat in the VW while he cursed at the recalcitrant engine, then put out a hand to stop him before he pulled away from the curb,

"What?"

She licked at her lips nervously, unsure if she had made the right decision. "You … how adventurous are you?"

"Not at all," he said glumly. "But if it'll get me out of your dog house, I'll do just about anything."

"Even go back to the quarry?"

"What?" He looked at her sharply. "Now? In the middle of the night? For god's sake, why?"

She took a deep breath and held it, exhaled as slowly as she could while her mind raced for a reason not to tell him. And when it failed she pointed up the street.

182

The Bloodwind

"Drive," she said. "I'll tell you on the way."

Chapter 18

"You don't believe me."

The car was stopped at the bottom of the incline that led to the quarry pit. The moon was out, flanked by a carpeting of stars, yet the light that touched the trees, the snow, seemed less an outside source than something that worked from within, something that defined and etched and turned everything grey. All the scene needed now, she thought, was a wedge of geese crossing the moon's face, their cries like souls searching for a graveyard.

She wasn't sorry she'd finally gotten it all off her chest, and she no longer feared what Greg would think about her. But she did wish she knew what he was trying to decide about the story she'd told him. Throughout the drive he'd only looked over to her a couple of times, and she had not been able to fathom his expression, distorted as it had been by the dashboard's own glow. And once he had grunted. Nothing more. Now he was staring at the incline, his hands roaming the steering wheel compulsively, as if he were hunting the best spot to strangle it. His hair was still tangled, a forelock dropping down over one eye until, with a muttered curse, he swiped it back onto a semblance of place.

"Well?"

The trail from the break into the open to the crest of the incline was virtually clear, the only snow left caught in rutted gaps. As if a benevolent, selective wind had wanted to make their trip easier.

"Come on, Greg." Patiently. Not pleading.

He shook his head slowly and dropped his hands into his lap. "I wish to hell I knew," he said. Then he leaned back and stretched his neck.

She had expected something like this—not outright disbelief, but rather an inclination to allow her an opportunity of proof. He would want her to show him, so she could in her own mind understand it was her own mind that had provided the beast that stalked her in the whirlwind. That would be what his plan was, rapidly formed and now working at a way to phrase itself without sounding insulting.

"Do you have a flashlight?"

He reached across her and pulled down the glove compartment. She took the flash from him and thumbed it on, off, on again, and took hold of the door handle.

"Pat."

"I am not now, nor was I ever, in the throes of a nervous breakdown, Greg."

His eyes wrinkled near to closing and she knew with a pang she'd struck home. And why not? Hadn't that been her first and continuing belief, coupled with the drinking and Lauren's memory? Wasn't it perfectly reasonable? Of course it was. And it was perfectly unreasonable that, knowing how reasonable it was, she should feel such a ragged surge of anger.

She stepped outside and pulled her collar close around her throat. She waited. Listening. Feeling nothing of the pressure, of the wind, of the sounds that had preceded the creature's first appearance. They were alone, atop a hill outside Oxrun Station, and the snow had turned to levels of grey and depressions of black. The driver's door slammed, snow crunched; she did not look at him when he came to her side. Instead, she aimed the spear of white light toward the row of sheds. And it was easy to locate the one crushed by what had been hidden in the

185

bloodwind—a spreading mound of rubble tangled with ice and snow, planks poking through the surface and lying scattered about, wind-tossed, it seemed, or vandalized by children.

A moment of telepathy: "You're thinking," she said in a monotone, "that the weight of the snow did it. The walls buckled and it all came down while I was hiding behind it." She handed him the flashlight and nudged him with a soft fist. "Go ahead. Walk over there, Greg, and tell me it just fell down."

He did.

Without apology, without a look, he plowed through the snow to the ruined shed, the beam flicking here, there, once shooting at the bank of trees beyond before turning. He walked slowly, bending over, once reaching down and pushing aside a section of wall. He skirted the main debris until he was standing where she had crouched, glancing once toward the quarry, bending again as though he were attempting to put himself in her position. It was all very methodical, and all very maddening, and the fact of the moonlight bleaching him of all colors but grey did nothing to assuage the unease that gripped her. Yet there were no doubts, no second thoughts; from the moment she'd caught sight of the shed in the car's headlamps she knew. It was as simple as that: she knew. When he returned he said nothing. After giving her the flashlight he jammed his hands into his pockets and began walking the incline. Slowly. Not turning around, not waiting for her to follow. She watched him and shuddered, trying not to yield to the impression that at any minute he was going to scream, and scream loudly. And when he beckoned she moved, just as slowly.

When she reached the top he slipped a hand around her arm and pulled her close.

"I'm trying very hard," he said quietly, and she was startled to hear a catch in his voice.

They started down toward the edge at his gentle urging, and it wasn't until they'd reached the midway point that she realized her stone chair was gone. Or most of it. What remained was a flat section ridged with jagged edges, as if someone had taken a sledgehammer to it and lopped it in half with a single, superhuman blow.

Below she could see the snow glowing, a beautiful jewel-encrusted frame around a gaping black hole. It wasn't ice; it was water.

"There are all kinds of explanations for this," he said then, dropping into a crouch, his hands dangling between his thighs. "A section of the wall gives way, someone throws a rock and it strikes a fault line in the ice, the ice itself is weaker than it looks and sinks under its own weight. The shed was old. Your throne could easily have been cracked by a dozen winters, water trapped inside and expanding to split it apart. A dozen explanations." He picked up a stone and hefted it, tossed it up and caught it, brought it close to his eyes and stared at it. Then he shook his head and threw the stone away. Viciously.

"Is that what you think?" she asked him when he took her arm again and led her back toward the car.

"No," he said. "All of it is possible, but all of it happening in the space of a couple of hours violates the sanctity of my orderly mind."

She hesitated and stared at him, stumbled forward to match his pace again when he looked down at her and grinned.

"Bullshit, huh?"

"Yes," she said; and the word stretched out, hissing as she sagged slightly against him. She smiled, wishing she were a little shorter so she could rest her cheek against his arm or his shoulder. Instead, she pressed her forehead briefly against his hair. Relief, then, and a bewildered fear—she wasn't crazy, and what in God's name was going on?

187

They did not speak for quite a while, not until the automobile had broken out of the trees and was heading back for the village.

"Pat, you understand that I have only your word for that thing you say was in that tornado, or whatever the hell it was."

"But you said—"

"I said—I should have made myself clearer. I believe something weird happened to you out there, no question about it. And I believe something unusual— you should excuse such a miserable word at a time like this—something unusual is going on. But I'm not one of the peasants firing up his torch, Pat. I mean, I've been to college and I've seen the world and Great Jesus Christ, I don't think I can just leap into an acceptance of some kind of creature you can't even describe. Not yet. Good god, not yet."

"I take it you'll want to see it for yourself."

He shrugged. "Pat, please. Understand me, too, okay?"

She did; that was the problem.

"But let's forget about that for a minute," he said, slowing to avoid a patch of ice at the Williamston Pike intersection.

"Easy for you to say."

He grinned. "You sound better."

"I don't feel any better, thank you."

"The thing is, Pat, I also don't believe all of this is happening randomly, either. And neither do you."

His gaze made her nervous, his words solidifying part of that fear.

"I don't think you should go home. Not tonight, anyway."

Her eyes closed slowly, her hand groped for his. "Yes. I was hoping you'd say that."

They were in bed, a loose embrace less sexual than warming. Heads close together on the pillow, ankles entwined. There were two blankets and a sheet, and still she was cold.

In the dark their voices were disembodied, floating.

"You thought it was me, didn't you."

"Yes. For a moment."

"Don't lie, Pat. It was for more than a moment. After all, let's examine the evidence, shall we?" Bitterness, resignation, and a struggle not to tumble into the safety of insanity—she recognized the tone, it had been hers for days and no wonder people had reacted oddly to her. She squeezed his hand reassuringly, but it was a long second before he returned the gesture and cleared his throat.

"We were examining the evidence."

"Sure."

She felt his hand slice through the air.

"First, we have a colleague—that's me—who finds himself hiding in a college—of no small repute, mind— working under, as it were, another colleague who has achieved everything he's dreamt of over the past dozen years. Modest fame, more than just competent skills, a marshaling of a talent he could never hope to have." And sensing an interruption he poked at her hip. "Shut up. This isn't a feeling-sorry-for-Gregory session; this is a facing-the-facts admission ... and one I should have done years ago. I'm a damned good teacher, Pat, but as an artist I'm not in your league."

She said nothing; there was little she could say at the death of a dream.

"So we have jealousy," he continued. "Professional, sexual, and probably something else so deep only a shrink could mine it and have it make sense. Murder has been committed for less compelling motives."

"But I don't think it's you."

"No. Neither do I."

They smiled together, and she snuggled closer.

"Then there's Ford Danvers. Jealousy again, bordering on outright hatred because you're a woman and you've successfully invaded his kingdom, divided it, and left him with all those dingbats who think they're actors."

"He's good, Greg."

"Yeah. The little shit."

She laughed behind a cupped hand.

"But I don't think he's the one, either. Why? Not because he doesn't have the guts, because he probably does. And not because he doesn't think he has cause, because he probably thinks he does. But because Ford would never have smashed up his own car that way, just to get you into trouble with the cops. That car was his kid, always has been. He's an in-fighter, not a Viking. Poison is more his specialty."

A silence that lasted so long she thought he'd fallen asleep.

"Then there's always Ben. And Harriet. And Oliver."

"No," she protested automatically. Weakly.

"You led them on, Pat, and they followed you. You promised them fame and fortune and the key to a world they see only in the movies. Galleries. Cocktail parties. Women and men fawning over them, trying to touch their hems. Museums bidding for their work. Books written about them. Top of the heap before they're thirty." He sighed, long and softly. "I know how they feel, because that was me, Pat. Jesus, that was me before I knew better."

"But I didn't," she said. "Greg, we've been over this before, and you know I didn't promise them any of that."

"No, but you implied the possibility, and for a young ... person like that, there is no difference. And—"

"No," she said. "Please, don't talk for a while, okay?"

He shifted, a hand snaking over her stomach. She laid her own on top of it and pressed it hard into her flesh. She wanted to feel both sides of him simultaneously, palm and knuckles, smooth skin and bone, to feel the reality of him, because what they were talking about, here in the dark, wasn't real at all. It was an intellectual exercise in madness. A college professor did not have enemies who hated her so much they would do anything to drive her out of her mind. To drive her away. To ... kill her. That was the ingredients of a fever dream, of paranoia.

But you've been through all that, she told herself, and by god it is real and someone is trying to ruin (or end) your life.

And suddenly there were glimpses of red in the dark, glimpses of an eye, glimpses of a massive foreign thing rushing at her from a nightmare.

There was nothing else she could do—she screamed.

"Are you all right now?"

"It was like turning on a light when you come home at night. It hit me so hard I couldn't help it."

"But you are all right."

"Yes. Well, maybe."

"You scared the hell out of me, you know."

"You should have been in my place."

"I'm sorry. My fault. I should have kept quiet."

"It's not your fault, Greg. But you just don't come up against something like this every day, you know. It takes a while."

"Yeah, but you've seen it. I haven't. It's easy to believe when you see it right out there."

"Oh god, Greg," she said, "you don't know how wrong that is."

The light came so quickly she thought in disorientation there was someone on the porch roof searching for her, poking a worn flashlight into each of the small windows on the second floor. She wondered as she flung aside the bedclothes how they'd found her here on Raglin Street, how they'd known she'd been picked up by Greg and had gone home with him. Then she stopped, the cold of the bare floor reaching up

191

through her soles to grab at her calves. She rubbed her eyes with her forefingers and sat on the edge of the mattress. Her heart calmed, her breathing grew less shallow; there was no one outside, it was dawn. Somehow, whether by sheer exhaustion or a retreat from fear, she had fallen asleep.

And Greg wasn't in the bed.

She padded out to the hallway and listened, hugging herself, then moved cautiously down the stairs to the front room. Greg was sitting in front of a small fireplace, naked, cross-legged, staring at charred logs with his palms cupping his cheeks, his elbows propped on his knees. She sat beside him and waited, anticipating speech and yet starting when he spoke.

"Question," he said. "A couple, actually. Why didn't that thing chase you into the woods? It could have gotten you easily, and it didn't. Two: what the hell is it? Three: what the hell does whoever it is that's doing this want? Four: why the hell am I sitting naked in the middle of the living room talking about monsters from B movies when I should be in bed, trying to figure out a way to stay home instead of going to work?"

She shook her head.

"Five," he said then. "What do we do about it? Sit around until it shows up again?" He raised a fist, thumped it hard on his knee. "Damn! Damn, I ought to have my head examined."

"Why?" She shifted to face him, a hand on his thigh, searching his stubbled face for signs of retraction.

"Because," he said.

"That's no answer. That's something a kid would say."

"Well, isn't this stuff we've been talking about more suited to kids than to adults? Isn't it? Great hulking beasts rising out of empty fields and quarries, winds that come from nowhere, smashed sheds and stone thrones—my god, Pat, have you really been listening to what we're talking about here?"

"Have you been down here all night thinking about that?"

He nodded. "And unless I get my butt in gear, I'll be here for the next hundred years."

She stood, offered him her hand, and he took it, allowed himself to be pulled to his feet.

"I'm hungry."

"Shower first, food second, school third."

He stepped back, his hands on her shoulders. "You mean—"

"You said it yourself, Greg—what are you going to do, just sit around and wait for something to happen? I don't know about you, but I can't do that. Besides, if we go outside maybe we'll learn something. Anything. Don't ask me what, I don't know." When he headed for the stairs she followed. "Greg, about … about what we were saying last night about all those people— did you decide anything?"

Halfway up the staircase he paused and looked down at her. "No," he said. "As a matter of fact, I was talking off the top of my head. It all sounded good, pro and con, but now … I don't know. It could be anybody." His grin was strained. "Even me, babe, even me."

She didn't echo his laugh, nor did she follow him when he sprinted the rest of the way to the second floor. Her flesh was tight with a chill that had nothing to do with the temperature in the house, and her hands were unable to keep from fluttering mindlessly. So many people, she thought—reluctantly keeping Greg's name at the bottom (very bottom) of the list—and I have to see them all today. No sense. Life made no sense.

And she remained silent through breakfast, through the ride to Hawksted, barely acknowledged her colleagues when they waved to her on the Long Walk.

She didn't like what she was thinking.

She didn't like thinking that Greg might have tried to put her onto someone else just to keep suspicion from himself.

And she didn't like thinking that somewhere out there, waiting with the wind, was a force that had been created by someone who hated.

Chapter 19

At ten o'clock, Danvers summoned her into his office. He was in tweeds, his mustache waxed and gleaming, his thumbs hooked into waistcoat pockets. She thought he looked too damned smug for what he'd just lost in his department, but she said nothing, only nodded when he gestured to the chair cornering his desk. Then he shifted his gaze from her face to the series of theatrical posters framed behind glass on the walls. And it wasn't until then that she noticed for the first time the deep short lines about his eyes, the defiant and melancholy thrust of his chin.

"About the meeting, Doctor," he said, still refusing to look at her. He waited. She said nothing. "The, uh, car business." He swallowed quickly as if trying to hide it. "I've had that car for thirty years, Miss Shavers. I suppose I shouldn't have placed so much value on it. And on top of your ... well, it has been made rather clear to me that I behaved badly. For that I apologize."

She hesitated a moment before saying, "There's no need, really. I understand."

"Well, I do anyway. It's the right thing to do, hardly makes up for the harsh words, but ..." He waved his left hand expansively. "You do understand, of course, that your new position does not mean an abdication of your responsibilities to the department as it now stands. Of course you do. I simply wanted to make that clear so there'd be no misunderstandings in future. Thank you for coming, Doctor. I'm sure you have plenty of work to do."

She rose, nodded to the back of his head, and left. Feeling nothing. Stopping in the corridor to glance back and gnaw on her lower lip thoughtfully. What Greg had said the night before came back to her, dimly, and she tried to imagine Danvers stooping to something as uncivilized, literally, as traffic in the occult. No, she decided; Greg was right, there, but for the wrong reasons—Ford didn't have it in him to do something like that. He was too preoccupied with veneer and pomp to resort to nightmare. He was the kind of man who demanded grandstand performances, an audience for his monologues, and a sweeping exit which would leave her alone on the stage in a fading spotlight.

But there was no relief as a result.

She walked through the next two hours jumping at shadows, staring at faces, examining every word said to her for menacing nuance, every glance leveled at her for lethal connotations. By the time she had finished lunch in the Union she was trembling so hard Janice asked her twice if she wanted a sweater, complaining at the same time of the lack of heat in all the buildings. Apparently, a boiler had broken down during the night, producing an overload which, in turn, collapsed the rest of the ancient system.

In her office at one, she quickly turned on the overhead light and the desk lamp when a cloud sailed across the sun.

She could not concentrate on a letter she felt she had to write to the Trustees because her door was open, and everyone who passed was stared at, scrutinized, as she sought to label them friend or deadly.

She knew what she was doing to herself, but no matter how often and how harshly she scolded herself she was unable to stop. Having accepted the reality of her dream-demon, she suddenly found new focus and uncompromising clarity in everything she saw. A new and unsettling dimension to every sound she heard. She did her utmost to accept the myriad and heartfelt congratulations that swarmed around her, heard herself talking glibly about the triumph and her plans without giving a single thought to the import of her words. Nothing mattered. Nothing but the shadows and the fear and the prayer that Greg would end his seminar early and take her home, lock her in the closet, go out and do battle so she could attend to her life without complication.

At two-thirty it struck her she hadn't seen any of the Musketeers at all that day. Four times, then, she reached for the telephone to call Harriet's home or the dorms, and four times she pulled her hand away and watched it close into a fist. Twice she did call Kelly's apartment; there was no answer. As a last resort she called Goldsmith, got him on the eighth ring.

'"Mr. Goldsmith? This is Pat Shavers."

"Yep."

"Mr. Goldsmith, have you seen Abbey or Kelly around today?"

"Nope."

"Did ... did the police talk to you yet?"

"Yep."

Her grip tightened on the receiver. Laconic was one thing, but playing a New England Gary Cooper was too much for her nerves. She rang off without saying goodbye, grabbed her coat from the rack and walked down to Greg's room. It was empty, his own coat gone. She frowned and went down to the first floor, looked out the side door and released a held breath when she saw the VW still in the parking lot. At the Union, then, she thought, and hurried outside, not wanting to use the tunnel system in spite of the sharp-plunging cold.

He wasn't there.

She walked over to Administration, to the library, checked the main parking lot and all the lounges in the dorms.

He wasn't there.

She returned to Fine Arts and her office, sat at the desk and watched the red slowly fade from her fingers, felt warmth reassert itself with an unpleasant needled tingling. When the telephone rang she grabbed it frantically, nearly dropped the receiver and was panting when she answered. It was Wes Martin, asking too politely if she would mind stopping by the station on her way home. She tried to pry information from him, but he turned officious on her and simply repeated his request.

Kelly, she thought then; my god, he's found Kelly. Or Abbey.

The chair slammed against the wall when she rose suddenly, the door vibrating in its frame when she slammed it behind her. And when another tour of the campus failed to turn Greg up, she accepted a ride offer from a student she knew vaguely, was dropped off on Centre Street across from the station.

She didn't want to go in there. Though the building didn't look at all foreboding, the simple fact of the high, barred windows overlooking the street was enough to make her hesitate. If something had gone wrong, she might be in there in an hour or so, and who would she call? Her parents were less than useless, and Greg had ...

With a hand covering her mouth she crossed to the opposite corner just as Martin climbed out of a patrol car. He smiled and waited for her, held her elbow as he guided her inside, around the raised desk and through the left hand door at the rear of the room. Down a short corridor broken by a door on either side and one at the end; it was through the latter that he took her into an office bare except for a long conference table in its center, chipped and polished and imposingly thick. Eight chairs had been set around it. Martin took the head and motioned her to

198

his left. There were no windows; the only light came from a brass fixture on the wall over her head.

"Do I need a lawyer?" She said lightly as she pulled off her gloves, fluffed her hair.

"No," he said. "Don't be silly."

"Then why all this?" she asked without demanding.

"Because I need to talk to you, Pat, and its too public out front."

"Kelly?"

He leaned back in the chair and folded his hands on the table. She kept silent, because he seemed to need the time to gather his thoughts. He was trying to find the right way to say what was on his mind; she knew that instinctively, and she was grateful he didn't just pounce on her with … whatever it was, whoever it was.

"I just came from King's," he said then, reached into his trouser pocket and pulled out three small plastic bags. When he dropped them on the table she could see they were labeled, though she couldn't read the lettering, and they contained fragments of stone. She pulled away, and questioned him with her eyes.

He touched the one in the middle. "This is from your workshop, the one in your apartment." He lifted a finger to still a protest. "This one here contains what was found on the floorboards of your car."

"I told you how I am," she said nervously. "Damn it, Wes—"

"And this," he persisted, "is from the car that Susan Haslet was driving the night she was killed."

"What?"

"People …" He gathered the bags together, fenced them with his palms. "People have a tendency, Pat, to think that just because we're a small place here we have small operations.

They forget the money behind us. Especially folks who haven't been here a long time."

"Well, that lets me out."

His smile was brief. "Indeed. Right. The reason I'm saying this, though, is so you understand the police don't have to run to a big city to run accurate, thorough tests when we have to."

"So?" She was getting angry now, taking exception to his lecturing tone, to the manner of his posture, to the way he looked around the room without looking at her. He was behaving exactly as Ford Danvers had that morning—hiding from her without actually leaving the room. "Come on, Wes!"

"This is all from the same block. From a block taken from the quarry. Now I know," he said quickly, raising his voice to forestall her, "you have this stuff in your workshop, and I know how it got there, how it got in your car. What I have to know now is, Pat, how did it get in Susan Haslet's car?"

She opened her mouth to tell him she hadn't the faintest idea, snapped it closed when she realized the implications of what he was saying. "Now wait a damned minute, Wesley Martin! Are you trying—"

He shook his head wearily. "I'm not trying to say anything, Pat. Just hold your horses."

"Hold my horses?" She stood and walked to the far end of the table, turned and slipped her hands into her pockets; otherwise, she thought, she might go for his throat. "Hold my horses? That collection of marble you have there is from my workshop. I'll take your word for it. Now you tell me it was in this Haslet girl's car, too, and whether you know it or not, you are definitely implying a connection of some sort. But I didn't know her. To see her, yes, but she wasn't in any of my classes, none of them. And I was never in her car, so I didn't drop that stuff there. Besides, how should I know what a drunk girl will—"

"Who said she was drunk?" he demanded quietly.

"What?" She was confused, passed a hand over her face to gain some time. "But I heard—"

"You heard wrong, Pat. The girl was perfectly sober when she died. We think, but we don't have any proof, that she was forced into that telephone pole. She was hit broadside and slammed sideways into it. Drinking had nothing to do with it."

"Oh." She turned around before she remembered there were no windows to look out, turned back and took hold of the nearest chair. "Oh."

"The car," he said then.

"What?" Distractedly.

"Your car, Pat. We brought it in, remember?"

The room suddenly seemed much smaller, much warmer. What wasn't touched by the light seemed suddenly darker.

"Pat … Pat, we found blood on the door."

She sat, hard.

"The window was broken in, I told you. On some of the glass embedded in the door's weather stripping there we found blood. Minute traces not very old. The idea being kicked around is that Kelly was in the car when the window was smashed, and whoever did it reached in and dragged her out. Cut her face or her hands, probably, or her legs if she was wearing a short coat. We also found threads, green ones. Pat, did Kelly have a green coat?"

She nodded, looked at him down the table's long alley. He was so small, she thought, like from the other end of a telescope.

"Why … why are you telling me all this?"

"It's your car, Pat. She was your friend, sort of."

"But Abbey—"

"Is still missing." His expression told her they held out little hope of finding either of the women still alive.

"I want to go home," she whispered.

Martin parted his hands and spread the plastic bags in front of him again. He did not look up. "Pat, who smashed up Professor Danvers' car? Who broke your car window and dragged Kelly out? How did it get back in the garage without you knowing about it?"

"Please be quiet," she said, putting her hands to her head. She had to think, she had to make sense so he would leave her alone.

"Pat, did you cut yourself when the window broke? Are there any cuts on—"

"Damn you!" she whispered harshly. She rose and rounded the table, stopped at his side and pulled up the sleeves of her coat, the sleeves of her sweater. "Look!" Her arms were pale, lightly veined, completely untouched. "Happy? Bastard." She headed for the door.

"Pat."

"If you're going to ask me any more questions, Wes, I want a lawyer. If you're going to accuse me of something, read me my rights or whatever the hell it is you do and be done with it. Otherwise, I'm going home. Now."

She opened the door, did not hesitate to close it and stride blindly across the floor to the railing. The desk sergeant watched her; she could feel his gaze on the back of her neck, could hear as she pushed through the railing Wes enter the room and stand there silently. It took most of her strength to keep walking, to prevent herself from spinning around and shrieking at him. And once outside she turned right and walked as fast as she dared without breaking into a run. Reached home without remembering seeing anyone at all. Climbed the porch steps and stood in the foyer, one hand patting her chest, the other gripping a fold of her coat and twisting it. She saw nothing but the stairs, and she took them one at a time, watching the landing appear before her, watching her hair, forehead, eyes, nose, mouth, chin appear in the gilded mirror over the table. It was a death's head she saw—skin taut over prominent bones, eyes pouched and sunken, lips without color, chin outthrust, comically pugnacious.

Her door was unlocked.

With an acid, silent thanks to the police she went in and took off her coat, moved to the sofa and stared down at the cushions. Someone had been sitting there, one of the policemen who had searched the apartment. Another had not replaced the cartons and tins in the kitchen cupboard properly. Or had it been all one man? A cop who started working conscientiously and, when it became evident he wasn't going to find anything, ended carelessly.

Homer's shelf was still empty.

She tried the telephone and Greg wasn't home. Neither was Harriet. And no one at the dorms had seen either Oliver or Ben.

She sat at the kitchen table. She stood. She wandered into the workshop and lifted her tools, replaced them, wandered into the bedroom and dropped onto the bed. Crossed her legs. Set her hands behind her head. Stared at the canopy sagging slightly in its frame. Lowered her gaze to the side window overlooking the driveway, shifted it to the back window where she watched bare branches tremble, the flitting shadow of a bird, the red blotch of a sun practically set. She considered all the questions Wes had asked her, all the inferences she had drawn from them, and would not, could not believe she was actually suspect in Kelly's disappearance, Abbey's vanishing. But neither could she dismiss the way he would not look at her, the way he pressed her, the way he assumed it was she who had cut herself on the broken window. Of course, he might only have been doing his job, she told herself as she flopped over to her side; no matter how long they had known each other, he was obligated by his job to make certain she was not directly involved. But she was. Of course she was. As soon as he had described the way Kelly might have been taken from the car, the way Susan Haslet had died, she knew what had happened: the bloodwind's beast has swiped at Susan's car and slammed it into the pole; it had smashed through the window and pulled Kelly out. It had to be. And the only question was—why?

She sat up suddenly, her gasp loud in the dark room.

Oliver; it always came back to Oliver Fallchurch.

Something he had studied, something he had known, something someone had told him led him to believe what he had told Greg months ago—that everything has a life force. Take it another step—if everything has a life force, then it was possible that force might somehow be controlled. Tapped. Released. Directed. And maybe Oliver had learned how. Maybe Oliver, in his disappointment, had tried to frighten her as punishment. And maybe, when she battled that fear in thinking it was something else, something within her, he had grown angry—another disappointment. And this time he had decided to take it all to the extreme.

Susan Haslet's car was the same as hers. Kelly had been driving her car. She had been followed to the Mainland Road corner, and Oliver's glove had been found on the hedge the next morning. She had been followed to the quarry, and ...

"Slow down, slow down."

Slow down, slow down, as she walked back to the kitchen and stood at the rear window, hands on the sill, face close to the pane.

The marble. Fragments of the marble every time she turned around. Until Martin had called her attention to them in Haslet's car she hadn't thought anything about it. She pursed her lips in a soundless whistle and headed for the workroom, switched on the light and stood on the threshold, scanning the benches, the pedestals, the floor for a sign or a signal.

The Bloodwind

A life force.

Homer.

And suddenly she knew what the red-beast was.

Chapter 20

She sat on the high, bare wood stool, the heels of her boots hooked over the middle rung, her hands flat on her thighs. The dark sweater she'd worn for two days now was overly warm, but she felt no discomfort. For nearly half an hour she had examined every particle of stone in the room, run through her mind every sculpture she had created and all those she could remember created by others. She flipped through art books, through magazines, through mental files of classrooms and lectures, museums and parks; and for another half hour she sat perfectly still. Mulling. Discarding. Lifting a finger once as though making a point to her students, lowering it again when she remembered she was alone.

Life force.

It was not the precise term she would have used had she thought of it first, but now that it was lodged there she could not rid herself of it. It wasn't right, and it wasn't wrong; but it was close enough to explain too many things.

Life force.

An artist has craft, and so do many others who hope for recognition. An artist has skills subtle and sometimes daring, and so do many others who study and sweat and sacrifice and slave. But separate the sheep from the wolves, men from boys, wheat from chaff, and it is called talent. Skill, craft, dedication can be taught and can be instilled, but talent cannot. You have it, you don't. If you don't you're competent, and if you do you're an artist.

But suppose talent wasn't something as mysterious as people used to think; suppose talent was for the most part an unconscious acceptance of the existence of a life force, and with that acceptance a learning how to control it, to use it in the creation of what the artist was after. Genius would be the ultimate manipulation, the twisting and the coaxing of that force into a shape visible to the human eye. The force that added depth to a portrait, shades of interpretation to a sculpture, that expanded infinitely the gulf between hackwork and masterpiece.

And suppose further that this unconscious acceptance became fully conscious. Suppose, in its discovery, the discoverer understood that manipulation could extend to something more than mere artwork. Lifework. Literally. Inanimate objects given mobility and purpose.

The red-beast was Homer.

She could see it now, veiled by the snow — the massive paw, the eyes, the snout, the teeth that gleamed. And red. The color immemorial of man's unbridled hatred.

Could everything be animated then?

Obviously not, or it would have been. Therefore, there were forces closer to the surface, more malleable, more accessible. The stone she had fetched from the quarry had broken in half — the one she used for Homer, the other for its mirror image. Homer was nothing more than a quaint statuette; the image, however …

Bits and pieces of it, then, luring its insubstantial form to her, yet not so insubstantial that it could not stave in the side of a car and murder a young woman, could not smash through glass and drag another woman to her death, could not stalk her, could not chase her. She had found in her terror the shards in her pocket and she had tossed them away, which answered Greg's question — it did not follow because it could not follow.

And to a question of her own—it had corporeal existence once the image had been completed.

And the image, and the original, were gone.

Slowly, almost imperceptibly, she lowered her feet to the floor. She stood, one hand back to balance herself, and went into the kitchen. Opened the refrigerator and checked the contents: milk, lettuce, various thin-necked bottles of salad dressing, fruit juice, sandwich meats, fresh vegetables. All of it ordinary. All of it perfectly ordinary. Cheese. Mustard. Olives. An open box of baking soda too long standing on the bottom shelf. Ordinary. Catsup. Jam. Meat in the freezer. Ice-cube trays. Tangible evidence of a living inhabitant, an ordinary human being, a woman who had fought for herself long before fighting became fashionable, became chic, became a rallying cry for women who needed a cause before they would bestir themselves into false safety among numbers.

Ordinary. And thinking of a creature not quite of the supernatural that had grown from a warning to an adversary bent on killing.

There was no doubt about it now; had she not strewn the marble pieces over the snow the red-beast would have left the bloodwind and crushed her screaming into the ground.

The door closed when she released it, shutting off the cold, shutting off the light. There was only the dark copper finish and the gleam of framing chrome.

And the empty shelf behind her.

A blink, and she was in the living room, standing at the French doors, the curtains parted and the streetlamp across the way outlining the porch railing as the moon had done the trees out at the quarry. Her breath fogged the pane closest to her lips. An automobile slipped past behind the drag of its headlamps. A couple walked the opposite pavement, close, arm in arm, heads together and capped. Another car. Old man Stillworth hobbling out of nowhere and up to his porch, fumbling with the lock, stepping in and lighting the inside momentarily before the door closed behind him.

Thirteen years, she thought. *Thirteen years of climbing.*

The alternative was simple and seductive—pack a bag and head for New York. She had done it once already, could do it again. New York was cosmopolitan. It had muggers and mounted policemen and robbers and bag ladies and friendly shopkeepers and surly cabbies and murderers and neighborhood improvement organizations and museums and theaters and crime and filth and excitement and her parents and the real world caught under shadows of buildings too tall. Nothing like the bloodwind could ever exist there. Only here, in Oxrun Station; only here, where she lived.

My god, she thought then, *aren't you tired of running?*

The muffler had been set over her hair and ears like a kerchief, tied under her chin, the ends flung back over her shoulders. The topcoat was buttoned to her throat, gloves yanked on and tugged until the folds in the leather were smooth and her wrists were covered. An extra pair of socks, a sweater over her blouse. Her pockets were empty; she had searched the apartment for a weapon and had found nothing to offer her even a modicum of comfort.

There was only her anger, and a demand for answers.

She had made three telephone calls: neither Harriet nor Greg answered, and the taxi was at her door in less than ten minutes.

Now she stood in the center of the Long Walk, alone, the dark-faced buildings rising in front of her broken only here and there by the lamps in students' rooms. There was no sound. All windows were closed, and nothing escaped. Clouds blocked the moon, and a faint haze had settled around the white-globed lights set every twenty yards along the Walk.

For five minutes, while the cold swirled and the light sharpened.

For five minutes, while she hoped for someone to come along and see her there, watch her enter the building, watch her return.

But no one joined her, and she prodded herself down to the left, up a series of stone steps to a pair of heavy oak doors topped with a flickering light. It expired just as she entered, but the inside was well-lit. On her left, steps heading down to the belowground offices and tunnel extensions; steps to her right she climbed quickly, one hand skating over the banister to the first landing. A door on either side, faint music from one and laughter from the other; directly ahead a wall paneled to the overhanging ceiling. The next landing faced the quad with two narrow windows. The next, two doors again, and a third in the paneled wall that led to a common bathroom.

She stopped on the third floor, slightly out of breath and wondering how the students managed to charge the stairwell every day without suffering ill effects. She clung to the banister for a moment, then faced the left hand door, a rectangular metal insert in its center holding a card with four names typed on if. Montgomery Lions, Hayward Morhouse, Benjamin Williams, Oliver Fallchurch.

Her gloved hand hesitated before it knocked.

And when the door swung open she stepped over the threshold before her courage failed.

The room was large, cluttered with overstuffed used furniture, posters on the walls, beer bottles arranged in tiers on the hearth of the plugged fireplace. In the front right hand corner to one side of the windows was a desk piled with books, illuminated by a lamp with a dark green glass shade. Someone sat just beyond the light's reach, and she moved deeper into the room, aware of the worn carpeting, of a faint locker-room scent that wrinkled her nose.

She gestured vaguely back toward the door. "It was open." Not quite an apology. "Unlatched, I think."

The figure shifted its chair closer to the desk, the legs scraping on the floor.

"Ben?"

"Yes, Doc." He leaned into the light, and even with the shadows cast wavering over his face she could see the sheen of perspiration on his cheeks, the pallid flesh, the pouched eyes. His left sleeve was unpinned, and a sudden movement draped it over a textbook.

It was quiet. No sound from the two bedrooms, nothing from the rooms below and across the landing. When she took another step she could hear her boots creaking, her jeans rustling, the lining of her coat whispering over her sweater.

"Are you alone?"

Ben nodded, then sagged back in his chair, his face gone from the light. "I don't know where he went."

It took her a long moment to assimilate the implication. "You knew I was coming?"

"Sooner or later." She sensed a slow shake of his head. "He's nuts, Doc. This whole thing's got him nuts."

She glanced around her, found a low-backed armchair and took it, hoping she appeared calmer than she felt. Her stomach felt queasy. The room was overly warm, yet she did not remove the muffler nor loosen any buttons; instead, she gathered her hands in her lap and watched them clasp, open, clasp again.

"He plays the role, you know," Ben said quietly, with no apparent attempt to hide the fear that seemed trying to throttle each word. "Cowboy, artist, stuff like that. He does it all the time. I've been with him since we were freshmen and he's always playing the role."

She kept her voice hard. "What's he playing now, Ben?"

It seemed a sigh drawn from torture: "He hates you, Doc. I never saw anybody hate anyone so much."

There should have been relief, she told herself then; she should be feeling an immense satisfaction at having finally been right. But she felt only a shudder that made one leg jump.

"Where is he?"

The figure behind the light shrugged.

"Ben, damnit!"

A whimpering that jerked up her head, made her squint and fail to see the expression on his face.

"Ben?"

"He comes in around dinner on Saturday. He says he's had it, he's not going to be shoved around anymore. He says you even got the police looking for him and he knew all along you couldn't be trusted. He said he was through fooling around."

"Fooling … ?" She almost choked.

The chair creaked, and Ben stood. He walked to the window and looked out at the quad, at the forest beyond. Then he scuttled back into his corner, his hand raking through his hair, rubbing hard down over his face.

"I wanted to stop him, see, but he wouldn't listen to me when I said it wasn't any good. He's so much in love he can't see straight, and he won't listen to anyone else. He just does everything, and the hell with how it turns out. I mean, you should see him, Doc! He's crazy. I really think he's crazy. He's got Monty and Hay out of here most of the day he scares them so much the way he bulls around, and I'm too tired to hold him anymore. God. Oh Jesus!" He rocked on his buttocks, the empty sleeve swaying at his side. "I'm going away, Doc. I got all the forms Friday and I'm transferring the hell out."

"Ben!"

"No!" He stood again and came round the desk to stand in front of her. "No, please, there's nothing you can say, believe me. I've been thinking about this for a long time, and I want the hell out. I can't handle it. I mean, I have enough trouble taking care of myself and this"—he jerked the stump of his arm toward her—"and I just can't handle what Ollie's doing."

She stood slowly, forcing him back a step. Reached out a hand, dropped it when he shied away. "You knew," she said, more in sorrow than disbelief. "You knew all about it and you never said a thing." She ignored the panic fed by his fear that stumbled him back toward the windowsill; she ignored the strangling sound that escaped his throat; she ignored everything but the need to hear the answer she already knew. "You knew, Ben, and you never said a word."

"All right!" he shouted. "Damnit, I knew what he was trying to do right from the start. But I didn't believe him. I didn't! I mean, would you, Doc? Would you believe it if someone came up to you and said he could do what's been going on around here lately? Would you?" He slashed the air. "Shit no. You'd have him locked up. You'd call the funny farm and have him taken away. But he was crazy, man. I mean, the guy had lost every card in the deck. You couldn't talk to him, you couldn't make him see anything but what he was going to do." His hand in a fist, a feint at the window. "Hell. Shit!" His shoulders slumped. Then he turned, suddenly, and Pat thought for a moment he was going to attack her. He pointed at her. "You—" And he stopped, grunted, and brushed past her into the left hand bedroom.

She followed, not knowing what to say and needing to say something in order to learn more. She had to know more, it was the first principle in defending yourself against an enemy set to kill you.

213

Two dressers against the wall, two beds whose footboards were each below a casement window. No rug. Two wardrobes. Ben was at one, yanking out clothes and stuffing them into a suitcase scarred with frequent use. A shirt fell to the floor and he kicked it angrily under the bed; a shoe dropped and he groaned; and when a handful of folded socks tumbled from his hand, he dropped to the other bed and covered his eyes.

"Doc? Doc, I'm scared."

She sat quickly beside him, an arm around his shoulders, thinking this wasn't the way it should be at all. Her fury was still contained, but she should be out on the hunt, not sitting in a dark room comforting a boy trying hard to be a man.

"I am, too," she whispered. "And that's why you have to help me, Ben."

"I can't!" he said, almost wailing. "They said before they'd kill me if I said anything. And I wasn't going to say anything because I didn't believe it. My god, how the hell can you believe something like this, huh? How can you?" He looked up at the wall, eyes blinking furiously.

He'll leave, she thought then; *he'll leave and find a new place to live and in a few weeks, a few months, he'll convince himself it never happened. It was a dream. A nightmare. He'll shunt it aside and live again, and every once in a while he'll wake up screaming and not know what it was.*

"All right," she said calmly, tightening her grip briefly. "All right, Ben. But you at least have to tell me where they went. I have to find them, tonight. You do see that don't you? It's my life we're talking about here, and I'll be damned if I'm going to give it up just because Ollie wants me dead."

Ben laughed.

Pat dropped her arm and stood quickly, backing toward the door as Ben threw himself flat on the bed and laughed hysterically. She lifted an impotent hand, opened her mouth, almost turned to leave so she would not see him finally go insane. But she stood her ground. Listening. Waiting. Watching as he rolled over on the mattress until his legs swept over the side. Until he stood and closed the suitcase, wiped his face with a sleeve and shoved her to one side.

"Ben!"

He opened the door.

"Ben!" She ran after him.

He stopped.

"Please," she said. "Just tell me where Ollie and Harriet are and I'll leave you alone."

"It's funny," he said. He was grinning with no mirth at all reflected in his eyes. "It's really funny."

Confused, she glanced to the desk, the windows, back again to him. "What? For Christ's sake, Ben, what the hell's so damned funny?"

"You," he said. "I thought you knew."

"Knew what?" A fist was at her throat to stifle a scream.

"Ollie," he said. "Weren't you listening to me, Doc? Didn't you hear what I said?"

"Benjamin," she said, lowering her voice as the last shred of her patience died and became dust.

He leaned casually against the jamb, the suitcase between his legs. A slow look around the room before he met her gaze and sighed. "Doc, sometimes you can be really dense, you know? Do you really think Ollie has the brains to think up all this crap? Ollie? Our Ollie?" His expression darkened to scorn. "He hasn't got the imagination of a flea, and you know it. If it wasn't for her, he'd just be spouting garbage like everyone else on this godforsaken campus. He'd be a freak like all the other freaks, only this one wears a cowboy hat. Christ, a cowboy hat in Connecticut." The scorn began to slip. "When he met her for the first time we all thought it was great, you know? Ollie

215

finally finds someone who likes his act and lets him know she knows it's an act. But in a nice way. I honest to god, Doc, thought she was good for him."

Freckle-head, they called her. Pat couldn't believe Ben was talking about the same woman.

"Then it turned out she only needed him because there has to be two. I'm not sure why. Maybe it has to do with however it is they get things to work. More power, something like that. And Ollie—he was getting frustrated because the show wasn't coming off and it was just what she needed. She used him, only I didn't see it until it was too late and I couldn't stop him then."

The scorn was gone, and Pat saw him pale again, saw him tremble. And what had she once called Harriet? A redhead trying to be an all-American blonde? God almighty, how wrong she'd been.

"That's when they said they'd kill me if I told."

Harriet weeping in the living room. Please, she'd said, don't be angry with them.

"See, it was her. She wanted Doc Billings—"

"What?" She blinked, unsure she'd heard the name right.

"Well, who the hell else, Doc?"

"No." She put a hand to her forehead, to her lips. "That's—"

"Doc, you don't know, you really don't know."

"But she's just a girl, for god's sake," Pat protested softly, suddenly aware the door was open to the landing. But when she looked at him he would not close it. "Just a girl. What does she know about men? About life? God, she's been locked up in this damned town all her life, how can she—"

"Hey, Doc," Ben said, his head tilted, one eye almost closed. "Hey, are we talking about the same thing?"

It was an effort not to stutter. "Yes," she said. "Yes, we are. We are talking about Harriet Trotter and what she's done to Ollie. That, Ben, is what we're talking about."

Suddenly the desk lamp sputtered out, the bulb over the landing sputtered. A wind battered at the panes, a draught fluttering papers greyly to the floor. Ben snatched up his suitcase, ran out and down the stairs. Pat followed, calling to him, shrieking while she held onto the banister. He paused for a moment on the next landing down, behind him the campus lights wavering through the narrow slit windows.

"Ben, please!"

"Doc, you're great, but I ain't sticking around, not now."

"But Harriet—"

"Jesus Christ, Doc!" he yelled. "Jesus Christ, will you please wake up? It isn't Harriet that's doing it, it's that bitch Abbey Wagner!"

Chapter 21

A nd the lights went out.

The afterimage of Ben's face floated in the black, a distorted grimace of anguish and fear that faded each time she blinked until she was alone on the landing, listening to the rising groans of protests, the opening and slamming of doors, the receding slap of footsteps. Her mouth had opened to call Ben's name, but she made no sound. It was futile, and she knew it. He had driven himself into a nightmare which would cling to him like a second skin, and no amount of screaming would ever wake him again. As much as she was determined to end it, he was determined to flee in its shadow. It was a choice she had almost made herself, and only the dark prevented her from collapsing on the top step and giving way again.

Slowly, then, she moved downward, her right hand clutching the worn and smooth banister while her left was outstretched, searching for the wall, or for obstacles that had no business being there in the dark. Every few seconds a light would flare outside, from candle or flash, but it would fade before shadows had an opportunity to form and accentuate the black that settled over the campus.

It was out there.

She had the front door handle in her grip.

Out there.

She had braced herself for the swarming cold.

Out there. Waiting.

She stepped back as if slapped and listened to the wind soughing through the bare trees, smothering the voices of students passing along the Long Walk. The doors trembled slightly, and she needed no further prodding. She turned and headed down, belowground, fingers trailing along the wainscoting until she swerved left into the tunnel that would, if she didn't get herself lost, release her at the front parking lot. It would have been easier, much easier, if she could locate a flashlight, but all the doors she passed were locked, and none of the students had come down with her.

There was laughter. She could hear it faintly, filtering through the building's thick walls. A pane of frosted glass glared and darkened. A door slammed, echoing after her as she forced herself not to break into a run.

Out there.

Her foot kicked against something that skidded away ahead of her, and she ground her teeth to keep the scream from escaping. It was no time to panic. She had to keep moving, had to keep hoping that she would be able to find a way off the campus without the red-beast discovering exactly where she was. Without anyone else being killed before it found her.

Abbey. Abbey Wagner.

A splinter in the paneling thrust into her thumb and she whimpered, jammed it into her mouth and sucked. And with the movement the wall fell away, she was in the middle of the floor and she was falling. She knew it. She could feel the darkness giving on all sides, could feel her weight shifting until there was no weight at all, nothing left to anchor, and she threw out an arm, her fist crashing against the wall, opening so her palm could diffuse some of the pain. A moment for a deep breath, another for a choked sobbing, and she was walking again, almost trotting. Her ears aching with the strain of listening, her throat so dry it felt coated with sand. She stopped several times to allow the sounds of her own footfalls a chance to fade—but there was nothing behind her, nothing ahead, the roaring she was hearing swelling somewhere inside.

She swallowed hard and pulled back her hand to claw lightly at her neck.

She stumbled forward, her stride shortening as she estimated the turn that would take her to the left. She did not want to enter the wrong tunnel now, to find herself caught beneath the English building or Science. At least here, despite the dark, there were people overhead; there, if she screamed, no one would hear her.

The turn.

Abbey Wagner. How many times did they have a drink together and laugh over Kelly's escapades and commiserate whenever poor Kelly came home crushed. How many times had Abbey been thinking that Pat had to die? How many months had it been before the woman had discovered the way to drive off a rival?

She stopped and sagged against the wall.

In all the literature she'd read, all the novels, all the stories, the seeking of some manifestation of supernatural power was done not for the gold or for the silver or for the assurance of immortality—it was, underlying all, for the power. The power to achieve all those things and more. It seemed almost comical then that Abbey should have discovered the workings of stone simply because she was different, was different and in love.

No, she thought; there has to be more. Life means more; my life means more. How in this day and age can something so precious be threatened by something so … so … She shook her head and pushed back into a shambling walk.

Hand along the wall.

Feet flat on the ground.

Sounds fading, sounds dying.

"Oh!"

Her toe stubbed against the bottom step of the tunnel's end. Immediately she fumbled in the dark for the railing, hauled herself up and fell against the door, the brass bar snapping down under her weight and the door flying open. She wasn't prepared, and she tripped over the threshold, was able to negotiate the first two steps before balance failed her and she fell on her buttocks, sliding to the bottom where the ice took her into a snow bank.

A moan she couldn't stifle; her back stung, and her elbow where it had cracked against one of the stairs. She rolled onto her side, unwanted tears burning to her cheeks until she swiped them away angrily and scrambled to her knees. To her feet. Swayed as she looked around for orientation, for a sign.

The parking lot lay below her, the buildings of the quad lifeless in spite of the candles she could see, the voices she could hear already preparing for a nightlong party. She was tempted to join them. It would be such a simple thing to lose herself in the crowds now filling some of the rooms, to have a drink, to be cajoled into laughing, to wait safely inside while the red-beast waited. A simple thing, and too simple. One girl was dead (and Kelly, where was Kelly?), and herself nearly dead. If Abbey was truly that filled with hate, it would be easy enough to talk herself into sacrificing a handful for the one.

The tails of her muffler were pushed to her chest. Her nose ran. Her ears burned. The back of her neck felt as though a razor had been drawn over it by the flat of its blade. She glanced at the dark rows of cars in the lot, made darker by the glow of the snow as the clouds shredded and the moon came out. There would be no keys there, and she had no idea how to hot-wire an ignition.

Walk. She would have to walk. Once on Chancellor Avenue she would be able to hitch a ride into town. To see Wes and tell him and not care if he thought her crazy as long as he didn't send her home for a rest. He would apologize, of course, for nearly accusing her earlier, would feel guilty and perhaps want to accompany her to the door. But the last thing she wanted was to be anywhere near the apartment tonight. There were shards of that marble lying in the workshop, and as long as she stayed away she knew she was safe.

Her hands, then, unbidden, dove into her pockets. Searching. Her heart stopping a beat when her fingers closed on a lump, starting again when it proved to be lint.

Safe. For the moment she was safe.

And she walked around the lot and down the road to the trees. Where the moon was sliced in ribbons and the branches clawed for the stars, where patches of ice glittered too much like water, where the wind sighed down to a breeze and toyed with her hair, the hem of her coat. She kept to the right side, every few yards glancing over her shoulder in case a car should come along. But it did not take much time before even the few faint glimmerings of window-based candles were screened by the firs and she was left alone with the remnants of the moon. Teeth chattering. Chin quivering. Her only accompaniment the crack of her heels and the whisper of the breeze.

Briskly. Spine rigid. Eyes straight ahead. Refusing to think that perhaps she'd been wrong, that perhaps the red-beast no longer needed the spore of the marble. She assumed it was drawn to the pieces by order, that in whatever state it existed its guidance was limited to that and nothing more. Which explained Susan's death, and her own narrow escape. But what it did not explain—

A branch split, and she spun around wildly, hands to her chest.

And when she turned back toward the avenue there was someone in the road.

A stumbling step forward before she stopped. Her mouth open, breathing deeply, raspingly; the figure standing quite still just fifty yards away. The face was hidden, the outline hazed, its head oversized and grotesque until she realized it was wearing a wide-brimmed hat.

It was Oliver.

Waiting. While over his shoulder plumed streams of cold white.

"Doc," he said, his voice carrying though he did not speak loudly. He shook his head once. "You should have stayed up there, you know."

There were too many things to say to him, too many conflicts from pleading to rage; she lifted a hand toward him, pulled it back and turned to run.

And stopped when she saw Abbey step out of the forest.

"No." A whisper, a denial.

"Doc," Oliver said, several quiet steps closer, "you never should have left the quarry, you know. You were supposed to be up there looking for more stupid rocks. You were supposed to fall. You weren't supposed to run."

Abbey was standing in a wavering patch of moonlight. Her blond hair touched with grey, her eyes turned to shadow. She kept her hands in her pockets, but Pat could see her smiling.

"You're something, you know that, Doc?" Closer. Still soft. "I mean, you didn't take off and you didn't fall in the quarry and you should have been dumped for that car thing. 'Course, that was pretty stupid, I know that. Don't blame that on Abbey. It was my idea, and I put the stone in the wrong car. It was dark in the parking lot. Stupid, right?" Closer. Softer. A smile that carried the dark humor of execution. "It's like you always told me, Doc—you got to think it all out before you start to work. I should've listened to you, I guess. All these dumb mistakes just because I was too stupid to listen."

She turned her back on Abbey, startling Oliver into halting.

"Dumb mistakes?" she said, almost ending in a scream. "A poor girl's dead, and that's a dumb mistake?" When Oliver didn't answer, she advanced a stride, was grimly pleased to see him fall back. "And what about Kelly?" she demanded. "Where is she? Damnit, Ollie, where is she?"

"She found out," Oliver said, and needed to say no more.

"Bastard," she said quietly, suddenly too weary to be angry. Then she jerked a thumb over her shoulder. "What does she do, Ollie? What's so special about her that you'd do such a thing?"

She could see his face now—hard-set and old.

"She isn't doing it for you, you know. She wants me away so she can have Greg. I don't get it. What's in it for you?"

"I got so I like it," he said with a shrug.

So calmly, so matter-of-fact. She would have preferred a shouting match, or a voice laced with consummate evil—any emotional tirade just to prove he was human. But he only stood there, watching her, talking to her as if they were discussing the results of a test or the prospects of the upcoming baseball season. *I got so I like it;* no apology, just speech.

The breeze grew somewhat stronger.

"Are you going to kill me?" So reasonable, she thought; *I sound so goddamned reasonable.*

Oliver shook his head. "Not me, Doc. I'm what you might call the spaniel in this. I hung out the game, if you know what I mean." He reached into his jacket and pulled out the statuette. "Then I set the trap."

It took her a moment to hear Abbey moving, but the girl was too fast around her, was standing next to Oliver before she could react. Abbey was smiling, softly, and pulled her hands from her pockets.

I was so sad about Kelly, she signed in the near darkness, *but she couldn't understand me. Oliver does, though. And I was so upset*

224

until you came in and started talking about Greg. You were the one, Pat, who made me see I was right.

"My god, you're crazy."

I know things, Pat, and that's not the same. You have your brains to get what you want. I know things. And I use them.

"I don't kill."

The breeze, stronger still.

Lauren is dead.

Pat's lips drew taut, her hands clenched into fists, "I didn't kill her and you know it."

You didn't keep her out of the boat.

She was stunned, gaping, could not marshal the imprecations that swarmed round her tongue. And when Oliver raised his hand she could only stare at him stupidly, suddenly throwing up her own when he tossed the statuette at her. She caught it, and held it, a finger tracing its snout before she realized the others had turned around to run. Her scream, then, was ragged with the taste of blood in her mouth, but she hadn't taken two steps before the breeze became a wind that turned the air red and coated the stone grizzly in shimmering blood.

She ran.

Thought was denied her when fear clawed onto her back and gripped hard; thought was denied her when she saw over her shoulder the snow spill from the banks, from the branches, from the forest. Saw the whirling, the spinning, felt the pressure and the cold, saw the glimpses of fangs, of claws, of an eye that was searching.

Taller now, than she was, coasting effortlessly along the road, gathering snow no longer white while branches crashed into splinters.

And the bellowing, the challenge, that almost stopped her in her tracks.

She wasn't sure; she might have screamed.

She ran, that's all she knew, her eyes on the two figures racing past the twin pillars and cutting sharply to the left.

Bellowing. Screaming. A shadow growing in front, swallowing her own as the snow lifted to blind her. It stung, it drew welts, it cascaded down her throat until she finally closed her mouth. Refusing to look around. Arms pumping, legs reaching, the blood wind and her own wind freezing the tears on her eyelids, on her cheeks, on her lips.

She tripped.

Just as she reached the campus entrance what she thought was a shadow was a fallen branch on the road. It snagged her ankles, and she fell forward, rolling slightly to land on her shoulder so she could get to her feet again without losing much momentum. Turning and looking at last at the red-beast. Striding down the road in the midst of its white dervish, a paw thrashing out of the whirling, a snapping at the air, and eyes that were golden in spite of all the red.

An engine snapped her head around.

Abbey was behind the wheel of Oliver's pickup, and Oliver was yanking at the passenger door handle.

Thought returned, and Pat ran. Instinct more than planning, as the small truck pulled away slowly and she realized she was still carrying the statuette. With one sweep of her arm she brought it down on Oliver's nape, heard him shriek, heard the statuette land beside him, heard herself grunt as she flung herself at the vehicle and grabbed hold of the tailgate.

She was dragged for several yards before she was able to pull herself to the bed, sprawled and rolled over just as the red-beast cleared the pillars.

Don't look, she pleaded, but her head would not turn.

It broke onto Chancellor Avenue in a white-and-red maelstrom that whipped branches and twigs and stones from its center. An arm reached out, a paw opened with black claws, and Oliver was lifted fifteen feet into the air. Screaming. She could hear him screaming over the roar of the engine, over the bellowing of the beast. And her eyes would not close when the red jaws exposed teeth, when the teeth caught the moonlight. Screaming. She heard him screaming when the jaws clamped down.

And the red-beast was gone.

The bloodwind was gone.

A cowboy hat in the road, spinning on its crown.

Chapter 22

Screaming. She could hear him screaming.

Screaming. She could hear herself screaming as Lauren was taken from the water and placed gently on the quay.

She cowered beneath the cab's window, knees drawn to her chest, eyes still open, the wind taking the muffler from her hair and looping it down over her chest. Her hands were fists pressed hard under her chin, her elbows squeezing tightly against her ribs.

And the cold in two assaults: from the air that sucked the breath from her lungs; from within, where a sheath of dark ice had settled around her heart.

Silly thoughts: Ford Danvers twirling his mustache like a vintage Edison villain; Greg stomping around his classroom studio searching for the paintbrush lodged behind one ear; Harriet and Ben appearing one day at her office door, arm in arm, dressed (as Ben put it) to the nines for a night at a college dance; her station wagon in need of a wash and a waxing; the canopy over her bed sagging in its frame; the workroom wanting dusting; Kelly swooning and laughing over a man she'd just met; Linc arguing with Stephen over the value of chianti, while Janice stood to one side and raped the pianist with her eyes.

Silly thoughts that swamped her while her tears turned to ice; silly thoughts that prevented her from remembering what she'd seen until the pickup began to slow, the jarring of the small truck subsiding and bringing back the world.

And once the images had faded, thought linked again with coherence, she knew how she would die if the red-beast came again.

She slid, then, toward the low sidewall as the pickup swerved as close to the verge as the plow-born snow banks would permit and maneuvered clumsily into a wide U-turn. Pat crouched even lower, her chin on her knees, watching the trees swing until Abbey was headed back toward the college.

The statuette. Pat knew it had to be retrieved, though she didn't know if Abbey had seen what had happened to Oliver. There was no time to decide, however; Abbey streaked to the entrance and braked so hard, Pat was thrown against the cab's rear wall before she could grab hold. The door swung open, and Abbey stepped cautiously to the road.

Pat leapt.

She had gathered her legs under her as she crept toward the side, and just as Abbey passed her she flung herself over and grabbed the woman's neck. They went down silently, shoulders and hips thudding hard on the blacktop, legs kicking and free arms thrashing. A grunt, a curse, and an elbow rammed into Pat's stomach. The topcoat absorbed most of the blow, but her grip loosened nevertheless and she found herself flung to one side viciously, a knee slamming into a hubcap and sending lingering streamers of sparkling fire up toward her spine. She reached out desperately and took hold of Abbey's ankle, slowing her until Pat could scramble to her knees and yank. Abbey fell, hands taking the spill while her foot slipped from Pat's fingers, lashed back toward her face.

They stood, Pat leaning against the wheel well and gulping for air, Abbey swaying by the tailgate, her hair dark with perspiration and plastered like fissures across her forehead.

229

"Abbey." A gasp. "It's no good."

Abbey smiled. Slowly.

"You're alone. Oliver's dead."

Abbey laughed. Silently. And pulled from her coat pocket the marble red-beast grizzly.

Pat's mouth worked mutely, her throat constricted and her head shaking disbelief. Then she turned toward the school entrance and saw the other image on the blacktop, caught just at the reach of the pickup's headlamps. When she looked back, Abbey was caressing the grizzly's cocked head, her face in the glow of the taillights a demonic, dreamlike red.

And Pat understood. An intuitive leap based on half-formed impressions that suddenly, here on the road at a time long past midnight, coalesced like a kaleidoscope finally making sense.

Oliver was wrong in part of his assumption: not all that was inanimate had the life force he'd assumed. And she'd been wrong, too, in thinking the same—the two blocks she'd found in the quarry were not identical save in texture and color, so what Oliver had been carrying was not the red-beast at all. Abbey had kept it, and Abbey had been the one to slip into the apartment to gather up the pieces chipped off the statuette. Oliver had been a dupe, and Pat had almost fallen into a similar trap.

Abbey moved, then. Had been moving so slowly while Pat was thinking that she hadn't noticed it, until the woman had already passed her and was running for the image lying on the road. Pat broke into a sprint and threw herself on Abbey's back, spilling them both out of the reach of the headlamps' thrust.

Almost unheard: the sound of stone rolling across the blacktop.

Heard all too well: the sound of Abbey's forehead slamming hard against the road.

But Pat would not relent even though she felt the woman slump into a temporary daze. She struck out with her fists, struggled to find an effective way to use her boots, finally rolled out of the way and lunged frantically for the grizzly. Had it and rose, passing a bruised and bleeding hand wearily over her eyes, then holding the statuette suddenly over her head when Abbey pushed herself to her haunches.

No! was a command and a plea, hands held out, fingers spread, face contorted into something feral and defeated.

Pat hesitated, but only because the sight was so repellent. Then she spun around and slammed the grizzly against the road, once, twice, grunting satisfaction when the arms split off, the teeth shattered, the pedestal cracked as she pounded it mercilessly, furiously, until all she held in her hand was the grizzly's midsection. A moment for a breath, and she stamped on every piece she could find, crushing some into dust, kicking others into the snow bank. Panting, blinking perspiration from her eyes, licking at her lips like, she knew, an animal savaging its prey.

Turning. Glaring. Reaching down and picking up Homer and holding it to her chest.

Abbey had sagged, all fight drained and all resemblance to the woman Pat had once known lost in the strain that produced acid lines about her eyes and skull-like shadows to her cheeks. She lifted her head after several seconds' dry weeping, searching the branches and cloudy night sky for something Pat knew with a warm rush could no longer be conjured.

She laughed once and shortly, and the sound startled her into a realization that from the moment Oliver had stopped his screaming the next few minutes had been spent in silence. She had spoken, but she hadn't heard herself; the pickup's engine still idled, but its rumbling passed unnoticed.

And unnoticed until now were the headlamps jouncing in the distance, growing and flaring brighter, pinning Abbey to the road and draining life from her eyes.

Pat staggered but kept her place. She felt no joy when the vehicle slowed and pulled up behind the truck, felt no elation when a sudden whirling red broke over the patrol car's roof. She only watched as Wes jumped out with handgun drawn, watched as Greg joined him to stare at Abbey, kneeling.

And then there was Ben, abruptly at her side with his hand deep in his pocket and his face ashamedly averted.

"I couldn't do it," he muttered. "I ran all the way into town."

Greg was before her as Ben shambled away, holding her arms and searching her face intently with a gaze that finally forced her to look up.

Empty. She knew her eyes were empty when Greg gnawed on his lower lip and turned back to Wes. But the policeman was handcuffing Abbey and pulling her gently to her feet. Greg told him he would bring Pat in with the truck, said nothing as Ben passed them, Oliver's hat dangling from his hand. Wes did not protest; he only nodded curtly.

And once they were alone he slipped his arm around her waist and led her to the truck. Opened the door. Helped her in. Engaged the gears and gripped the wheel.

"Ben found me home," he said, glancing sideways, looking front. "I left early." He raced the engine. "I wanted to make sure it was … I had to think, Pat. In spite of everything you showed me, I had to think."

"Yes," she said, looking down to Homer and stroking absently his head.

"We thought you'd be at her place. You weren't. We went upstairs and looked around, and Ben found … he found Kelly there, Pat."

She closed her eyes tightly.

"Abbey was apparently going to try to pin a murder on you, as well. Kelly was—hell!"

Pat knew. The bed's canopy had been sagging.

Then Greg shifted and stared at the statuette in her arms. "Are you sure that's the right one?"

It took a long time, a great effort, before Pat could say, "No." A longer time before Greg wrenched the truck around and they drove back to the village. In silence. Each alone. Greg worrying at a knuckle between his teeth while Pat remembered the afternoon she had seen Homer in the flesh, the care she'd used to bring him to her home, the mornings she'd grinned at him, the evenings she'd made wishes. And it was less the horrors she had faced that finally brought quiet tears than it was the death of her talisman, the snatching away of her crutch.

A hand on her knee, and she was quick to cover it with her own.

"You'll be all right, Pat."

She wondered, though she supposed she would. But in all of those dumb movies they never showed her the after—like how she would face each rising of the wind, how she would drive Oliver's screams from her sleep, how she would explain to Greg that she didn't want him to touch her.

She would be all right, but she would be different. And with half a lifetime to go, she wondered if she could stand it.

Then the thought formed, only a vague impression while she'd been watching Wes take the woman away. "Greg," she said.

"Hey, you feel up to it?" He took his eyes from the road and watched her, slowed then when a car turned out of Centre Street and gave him the benefit of a horn. He parked in front of the police station and put a hand to the back of her neck. "We can always tell him—you should go to the hospital, you know, for a checkup or something."

233

"No," she said, bringing Homer's head to her cheek. "I'm okay. I'm not hurt." She stared at the double doors, at the blocks of marble on the facade. "It's Abbey."

"You're really not going to tell him about—what did you call it, the bloodwind?"

"No," she said. "I just … Greg, if she can do it once, she can do it again."

"She'll be in prison for murder, Pat. For the rest of her life."

She turned to him suddenly, Homer slipping from her grasp and sliding to the floorboard between her feet. "She'll have a lawyer, Greg, a good one. She's not stupid; she knows. She'll be jailed, I know that, but sooner or later she's going to get out. One way or another she's going to get out."

Greg could not meet her stare. Instead, he waved off her fears with an insincere half-smile and opened the door, and as he passed in front of the hood, now in the light, now in the dark, she knew what she'd be doing for the rest of her life—

Working at the college, perhaps loving Greg again, making amends with her parents and trying to keep Harriet on course; fighting with Danvers, watching Stephen and Janice marry, doing her own work better and perhaps achieving another level of success; fixing her car, repainting the apartment, adopting a child to prove she hadn't really lost Lauren.

More than she could handle; enough to bring her ease.

Until the sun set.

Then she would turn out the lights and stand at the window, stand at the window and listen for the wind.

Every night, every year. Standing. And listening. While Abbey was in prison, perfecting her hate.

About the Author

Photo by Jeff Schalles

Charles L. Grant taught English and history at the high school level before becoming a full-time writer in the '70s. He served for many years as an officer in the Horror Writers Association and in Science Fiction Writers of America.

He was known for his "quiet horror" and for editing the award-winning Shadows anthologies. He received the British Fantasy Society's Special Award in 1987 for life achievement; in 2000, he was the recipient of the Lifetime Achievement Award from HWA. Other awards include two Nebula Awards and three World Fantasy Awards for writing and editing.

Charlie died from a lengthy illness on September 15, 2006, just three days after his birthday. He lived in Newton, NJ, and was married to writer/editor Kathryn Ptacek for nearly twenty-five years.

Book List

Horror
Novels
Black Oak: Genesis
Black Oak: The Hush of Dark Wings
Black Oak: Winter Knight
Black Oak: Hunting Ground
Black Oak: When the Cold Wind Blows
Fire Mask
For Fear of the Night
In A Dark Dream
Jackals
Millennium Quartet #1: Symphony
Millennium Quartet #2: In the Mood
Millennium Quartet #3: Chariot
Millennium Quartet #4: Riders in the Sky
Night Songs
Raven
Something Stirs
Stunts
The Bloodwind
The Curse
The Grave
The Hour of the Oxrun Dead
The Last Call of Mourning
The Nestling
The Pet
The Sound Of Midnight
The Tea Party

The Universe of Horror Trilogy
The Soft Whisper of the Dead
The Dark Cry of the Moon
The Long Night of the Grave

Collections
Dialing the Wind
Nightmare Seasons
The Black Carousel
The Orchard

Science Fiction
A Quiet Night of Fear
Ascension
Legion
Ravens of the Moon
The Shadow of Alpha

As "Geoffrey Marsh"
The Fangs of the Hooded Demon
The King of Satan's Eyes
The Patch of the Odin Soldier
The Tail of the Arabian, Knight

As "Lionel Fenn"
The Quest for the White Duck Trilogy
Blood River Down
Web of Defeat
Agnes Day

The Kent Montana Series
The Really Ugly Thing From Mars
The Reasonably Invisible Man
The Once and Future Thing
The Mark of the Moderately Vicious Vampire

668, the Neighbor of the Beast

The Diego Series
Once Upon a Time in the East
By The Time I Get To Nashville
Time, the Semi-Final Frontier

The Seven Spears of the W'dch'ck

As "Simon Lake"
The Midnight Place Series
Daughter of Darkness
Death Cycle
He Told Me To
Something's Watching

As "Felicia Andrews"
Moonwitch
Mountainwitch
Riverrun
Riverwitch
Seacliffe
Silver Huntress
The Velvet Hart

As "Deborah Lewis"
Eve of the Hound
Kirkwood Fires
The Wind at Winter's End
Voices Out of Time

Curious about other Crossroad Press books? Stop by our
website: http://crossroadpress.com
We offer quality writing
in digital, audio, and print formats.

Subscribe to our newsletter on the website homepage and
receive a free eBook.